The Baby
Left
Behind

BOOKS BY JEN CRAVEN

Best Years of Your Life
All That Shines and Whispers

The Baby Left Behind

Jen Craven

Bookouture

Published by Bookouture in 2023

An imprint of Storyfire Ltd.
Carmelite House
50 Victoria Embankment
London EC4Y 0DZ

www.bookouture.com

ISBN: 978-1-83790-730-4
eBook ISBN: 978-1-83790-729-8

To all the mothers, the want-to-be-mothers, and the mothers who are doing the best they know how.

"Look at the sparrows; they do not know what they will do in the next moment. Let us literally live from moment to moment."

—Mahatma Gandhi

PROLOGUE
CATE

One year before

WHAT THEY SAY IS TRUE: IT REALLY IS LIKE SQUEEZING A watermelon through a straw. I stand back from the foot of the bed, doing my best to peer over the doctor's shoulder. When he leans one way, I go the other. I don't want to miss it. The tiny hole I noticed in my shirt this morning, a single missed stitch, is now an inch wide thanks to my nervous fingers. It's been a decade of waiting—no way I can feel completely collected.

Hadley lets out a guttural scream.

"You're almost there," the nurse says. "Another push or two. You can do it."

How can she be so calm?

"I can't!" Hadley cries. She flings her head back against the double-stacked pillows, utter exhaustion contorting her pretty face.

"You can." The nurse flips over the wet washcloth on the girl's forehead. Hadley's so young, too young to have a baby, and even though my heart breaks for what this experience will be like for her, I'm selfishly thankful for her teenage pregnancy because it's finally bringing me a child I can call my own. One person's loss, another person's gift.

"Here comes the next one," the nurse says. "Push. You've got this." She shoves an arm under the pillow and uses it for leverage.

Hadley holds her breath, drops her chin to her chest, and bears down. A vein pulses at her forehead. I catch myself holding my breath too but release it—no one needs a bystander passing out in the delivery room.

"Head's coming down," the doctor says. These are practically the first words he's spoken since he sauntered in here at the last second, leaving the nurses to provide all the care over the past ten hours of labor. This whole experience is so different to how I expected it to be. I always thought I'd be the one in the bed, pushing in agony for a prize that was so worth it all.

I stand on my tiptoes and involuntarily bring a hand to my mouth. Oh my god! It's absolutely incredible. My daughter is being born, and I get to watch. How many moms get to say that? Emotion catches in my throat, and I bite my lip and smile. How long I've been waiting for this moment. And after everything that's brought me to this point. It wasn't my first choice, but sometimes life decides you don't get a say in the matter. Now, in this moment, the past washes away. All I care about is that I'm finally fulfilling the dream I've had for as long as I can remember.

"Another push, Hadley," the nurse says, yanking back on one of the girl's feet. "Here we go. And one... two..."

I count along with them. C'mon, Hadley, c'mon, Hadley.

The doctor pulls like he's in a tug-of-war match. My eyes go wide. *Easy!* I want to say.

"Here are the shoulders. Little push now." Then a second later, "And here's the rest of her!"

The baby comes out in a swoosh, followed by blood and fluid that soaks into the thick pad under Hadley's bottom. The doctor lays the baby on Hadley's chest, while the nurse wipes away the mess to reveal perfect pink skin underneath. We agreed to this—Hadley being the first to hold the baby. Still, I have to squeeze my hands together to stop from reaching out.

"Oh my god," Hadley says as tears roll down her cheeks. She brushes a shaky thumb across the newborn's little eyebrows. Color returns to her face, and I'm amazed at how quickly pain can seemingly cease, how quickly a person can forget.

I don't realize I'm crying too until I taste salt. I step toward the side of the bed. Hadley looks to me, back to the baby, then to me again. An undefinable sentiment passes between us.

"Ready?" the nurse says.

Hadley barely nods.

The nurse swaddles the baby and places her in my arms. "Congratulations, Cate. She's beautiful."

I stare down at the chubby cheeks popping up from the tight bundle of blue-and-pink-striped blanket. Little white dots scatter her nose. They'll disappear, along with the swelling and any other traumas of birth, so the parenting books tell me. Within days, her color will even, and she'll settle in as a little cherub. Even now, she's perfect. This sweet girl may not look like me, may not carry my genes, but I already feel our hearts connecting. I can't wait to bring her home.

We sway and I hum a little lullaby. The one Dad used to sing to me about birds in flight and coming home to nest. My little bird.

The room disappears. It's just her and me—mother and daughter. My utopia finally realized. So much waiting, so much heartbreak to get us to this moment.

A sob pulls me from my trance, and I startle. What did I do? Did I squeeze too tight? I'm so new at this, I don't want to hurt her. But the sound's not coming from the baby. It's coming from the bed—from Hadley.

Our eyes meet. For a second, I think she's happy for me, for us. The ultimate sacrifice of love. Tears of joy for doing what she knows is right, what we'd agreed upon and signed paperwork for. Her decision must be so hard. I can only imagine the roller coaster of emotions she's feeling. But then I look closer and realize it's not a happy cry. Or even a bittersweet cry. There's something else behind her frown, something primal. Something rooted in a feeling I'll never understand. My stomach and smile take a sudden drop.

No.

"I'm sorry," Hadley says through cries. "I just can't."

PART 1

ONE

CATE

I was six when I first stuffed a balloon under my shirt and pranced around pretending to be pregnant. I was sixteen when I found out that would never be possible. The burn has followed me ever since.

I thumb through my Instagram feed, soaking in dozens of posts filled with baby boys in red suspenders, little girls in plaid taffeta. The algorithm knows me well. An Oreo ad featuring a chubby infant next to an empty plate where only a few crumbs remain, and a caption that reads, "Oops, looks like someone ate all Santa's cookies!" It has over four thousand likes. I tap the heart to add mine and keep scrolling. Acquaintances blast their family holiday pictures out into the world with hashtags like #blessed and #alliwantforchristmas and #theonlygiftineed.

I want to scream through my phone. You already have it! I'm the one who wants it. Look up the definition of longing in the dictionary and you'll see my face. But turns out wanting something desperately isn't enough. Just ask my ovaries.

"What on earth," Mom's voice assaults my ear from where she's snuck up and peered over my shoulder at the phone. "Whose post is that? They could get arrested for child pornography. Heavens." Her breath is minty-fresh, because of course it is.

"It's just a baby butt," I say, considering the picture. My friend's daughter, no older than one, stands in front of a Christmas tree, extending an arm to touch a glittery ornament. Her chunky thighs have more rolls than Mom's dinner table. Seriously, is there anything cuter? My chest constricts with the weight of hunger—not the food kind, the purpose-filling kind.

Mom circles around and perches on the edge of a chair opposite me, ankles crossed, hands in her lap, exactly as one would picture a woman named Marcia to do. She embodied Marcia Brady long before the TV show: The girl who can do no wrong morphed into the woman with impossibly high standards.

"There are predators out there," Mom says, still fixated on the innocent picture on my phone. She cocks her head in the way that makes my body temperature rise.

I keep my head down, not wanting to start a debate. If it were my baby, I'd do the same damn thing. I'd have a whole camera roll full of pictures just because I could.

"If Becky ever posted the boys naked, I'd have a fit." Mom's head shakes a bit when she talks, making her bell earrings jingle. We might have convinced her to lose the embroidered snowman vest, but she put her foot down at the costume jewelry.

I bite my tongue to keep from saying what wants to come out: Becky would never do that, because Becky is perfect. Perfect daughter, perfect mother, perfect everything. Marcia 2.0.

"Speaking of," I say, swiping out of Instagram to check the time on my lock screen. "Where are they?" Like I'm champing at the bit to see her. Like I don't have anywhere else to be besides alone at my house.

"Oh, they should be here any minute." Mom peers out the large bay window that overlooks the front yard and driveway where I used to regularly lose at neighborhood flashlight tag. Fabric ties hold back the sheer curtains Mom takes down to wash and iron twice a year. Outside, old colonial houses line the cul-de-sac at the end of Oakridge Lane, all symmetrical and stately with their gable roofs. My childhood home hasn't been updated much in the twenty years since I've lived here. Then again, neither have my parents—the Connallys, the most quintessentially white, middle-class Americans ever. Meals at seven, twelve and five. Mercedes SUV in the driveway. Candy in beveled dishes on end tables.

I recline in the patterned wingback chair, telling myself to relax my jaw. It won't be long. A couple hours of playing happy family and I can go home. Being here puts me on edge. The wholeness of it all, whereas I feel more like Swiss cheese, missing some parts.

I cross my legs. The extra pounds around my midsection dig into the waistband of my pants—a roll of skin that came into my life like an unwanted birthday present when I turned forty.

A crunch of tires over gravel makes Mom spring from her seat like a jack-in-the-box. Does she get as excited when I arrive? Doubt it. It's only me—the disappointing one. I don't bring along with me a movie-star-handsome husband and two perfect grandchildren.

I crack my knuckles. Uncross then recross my legs. "Is it B—?"

"Becky's here!" she squeals. "Oh, and there're my little princes!" Mom's leaning so far to see out the very fringe of the window, her cardigan nearly slips from her shoulders. She claps and runs to the front door, opening it just in time for my nephews to barrel into her legs.

"My little heir and spare," she coos, running a hand across each of their tow-colored heads. I cringe every time she uses that phrase—how awful it will eventually make Owen feel to be considered second-best. But whenever I bring it up, I'm quickly poo-pooed as a bore for not going along with Mom's obsession with the British monarchy. She thinks having a daughter with the same name as Kate Middleton and a lapdog named Lady Di means we're just like the royal family.

"I'm Cate with a C," I used to tell her. "And 'Rebecca' is nowhere near 'Pippa.'" Not to mention the brother, which we don't have.

"Close enough," she'd say with a dismissive wave. Dad would roll his eyes: Let her have her fun.

Once the boys were born, Mom's fixation deepened, and it became clear: If Landon and Owen were the princes, then Becky was the future queen.

Naturally. Skip right over me, the first in line.

Only no family is perfect, royal or not. Mom just chooses to see what she wants to see.

"Aunt Cate!" High-pitched voices break me from my thoughts, and I shift to my feet as two little boys run toward me.

I pretend to struggle picking up Owen. "Ugh, what a lug," I say, making him giggle. It's wistful, and my heart pinches. Being a perfect auntie only fills so much of the hole.

"Look!" He opens his mouth an inch from my face and uses two fingers to see-saw a bottom tooth.

"Whoaaaa," I say in dramatic fashion, because that's what favorite aunts do. "That your first one?"

He nods.

"I've lost five already," says Landon, not to be outdone. "See?"

What I would do to play Tooth Fairy myself.

While I thoroughly inspect the inner crevices of my nephews' mouths like a newly minted dental hygienist, their parents come through the door. Becky, all thin and shiny—even the beauty mark above her lip taunts me—and Shane, dad and partner extraordinaire.

"Merry Christmas!" Becky calls, louder than necessary, as though she needs to make her presence known. "Hey, Catie."

My baby sister comes at me with a wide smile and goddamnit if it isn't genuine. When we hug, I catch a whiff of her thick blonde hair. It smells like orange blossoms, the same as Mom's. A couple years ago, my bestie Ryan and I nicknamed her "Becky with the Good Hair," to which Mom replied, "It's those prenatal vitamins, Cate. You'd know if you'd ever settle down."

My gaze dropped. "I'm sorry," she said quickly. "I shouldn't have... You know I..." But the apology trailed off.

Comments like those slip from Mom's lips without a thought—good-intentioned, albeit a sting to my core. I swallow them down with all my other inadequacies: Bs that could have been As, my non-existent cooking skills (looking up how to boil water), a gym membership that goes unused. And then there's the big one. The one that keeps me awake at night and prevents me from taking the quicker route home because it passes a play-ground. It's a hidden curse, but one that's very present in my daily life: That I can never have my own children.

Christmas dinner is supposed to be a happy time, but all it does is remind me that a new year is right around the corner. A new year that brings so many possibilities. Will it finally be the year I become a mother? Or will it be another three hundred and sixty-five days of heartbreak? There are thousands of babies put up for adoption—surely one has to be my match.

"I want another roll," Owen says from the far end of the table. He sits on his knees, and even then is just tall enough so the walnut lip hits him mid-chest.

"May I have another roll please," Dad corrects him. Henry Connally is a stickler for proper manners.

"May I have another roll please," Owen repeats then takes

the basket from his grandpa's outstretched hand. Dad gives him a loving wink.

I could go for another roll too but don't want to deal with Mom's silent judgment. The look that says, *Do you really need that?* I'm an average size twelve but somehow didn't get the lean Connally gene, and I can't help but imagine Mom blames my unmarried status on that fact. There's not a single carb on Becky's plate. Must be why she fit back into her size-four jeans only months after giving birth—twice.

I glance around the table. Everyone's here. Our perfect family all together, putting my deficiencies on full display. I love them but despise them. It's thus far proven to be an incurable disease.

"So," Mom starts, setting her elbows on the table and resting her hands under her chin. "Mary Littleton's granddaughter told her there's a new math teacher at the high school. Said he's, oh I don't know, mid to late forties? But still good-looking. Muscly. I think she said he does that CrossFit or whatever it is." She cuts a green bean neatly in half before bringing one piece to her mouth.

My gut clenches, knowing where this conversation is going. Seriously, Mom? Can't I get a break on Christmas? It takes everything in my power to stay at the table and not leave before she gets the rest of her story out.

"He's single," she continues, eyebrows arched with possibility. "Mary's granddaughter said he doesn't wear a ring. Not even an indentation from where a ring once was. You can always tell by that indentation. So, you know, never married— even better."

"Mom," I say dryly.

Becky and Shane snicker at each other across the table. It's easy to take Mom's meddling with a grain of salt, to see it as a good-intentioned deed from a loving mother. But it's another thing when you're on the receiving end over and over again. My insides smolder, but Mom keeps going, as though she doesn't hear me.

"... and so what I was thinking was that I could arrange for you to meet him, Cate."

"Mom."

"Sounds like a very nice man."

"Mom."

"Maybe you two would hit it off. He might even be open to" —she lowers her voice—"adoption. That is, I'm assuming you're going to try again."

"Mom!" All faces whip to me. "Enough! Can't you take a break for one day?" I snatch the damask napkin from my lap and fling it onto the table with such force the wine glasses clatter. She acts like I've never dated a single soul, like I'm some barren spinster. There've been guys over the years, just no one who's stuck. So sue me.

"Leave her alone, Marcia." Dad to the rescue again. I don't know what I'd do without him.

"What? I'm not allowed to help my daughter find happiness?"

"What if she's perfectly happy as she is?" he rebuts, despite knowing the truth: I'll never be fully happy. Not with the one thing I've always wanted in life being taken from me. "You'll find someone when the time's right, won't you, Birdie."

I soften at his use of my childhood nickname. They said I'd had the tiniest little mouth they'd ever seen—a baby bird's mouth. Cute on a little girl, not so cute on a grown woman with full cheeks and a long chin. Alas, another insecurity.

"Marriage isn't the be-all and end-all," I mutter. That archaic nursery rhyme pops into my head. You know the one I'm talking about: First comes love, then comes marriage, then comes a baby in a carriage. Pisses me off. It's the twenty-first century—you don't need to follow that order. Those first two ships have sailed for me.

Everyone's quiet. The room has suddenly become very small. I twist in my seat. The wallpaper's creeping in, inch by inch, ready to smother me. Even Landon and Owen stare, as though they can see all my flaws, all my efforts to prove my parents wrong. Leave it to me to ruin a perfectly nice holiday dinner with an outburst. *She started it*, I want to say but instead change the subject in hopes of turning this all around.

"I saw Mr. Godfrey died. Remember how he gave Becky her first detention for talking so damn much?"

Mom shakes her head. "You and your obituaries."

"They're interesting. Little snapshots into someone's life." I'm trying to lighten the mood and it's failing miserably.

Becky playfully slaps my arm and says, "Such a funny little hobby."

Could have been worse, I think. My "funny little hobby" might be odd, but it's harmless. Just like everything else about me—I've been a straight-laced, follow-the-rules kind of girl my whole life. Cried after drinking a Smirnoff Ice at eighteen because I was worried my parents would find out. I was the kid who didn't need to be yelled at—the words "I'm so disappointed in you" were punishment enough.

Mom and Becky exchange a giggle. There's a pressure in my ears, a boiler steaming, loud and long. Maybe I'll just erupt, right here and now. Nothing I do is good enough for them.

I stab a bean and shove the whole thing in my mouth. Manners be gone. It's Christmas and I should want to be here with my family, but all I can think about is getting home to my own space where I'm not scrutinized or the object of unwanted matchmaking.

"So," Mom starts again, "I was reading in *Woman's Day* about a new chicken recipe. They call it the Love Potion because it's supposedly so good, a man will want to marry you if you cook it for him. Isn't that wild? A chicken...!"

I drown out her words in the rest of my Cabernet. If only it were that easy. Cooking a chicken to get a man, to then have babies. No chicken recipe is going to work on a broken body. I was a perfectly healthy baby—at least on the outside—and it wasn't until my period never arrived that my doctor became concerned. A couple tests later and boom: Mayer-Rokitansky-Küster-Hauser Syndrome, a fancy way to say I was one in five thousand girls born without a uterus. So there I was, sixteen years old and smacked with a new twist on the life I thought I'd have. But sixteen is all parties and friends and crushes, not serious adult things. The idea of babies was a distant thought, a problem I stuffed down deep to deal with later. Only life has a way of bringing "later" around quicker than you think. And now my maternal clock doesn't just tick, it throbs.

Every time I go to see Dr. Handrian, I'm met with pity. My empty hollow where normal parts should be. The young nurse with the round face eyes me like I'm the saddest person on the planet. How *awful* my life must be. One time I actually caught her blinking away tears. They've heard me mourn, crying buckets right there on the paper-covered table, breasts naked under a thin gown, never to be filled with maternal milk.

If longing and tears were enough, I'd have a herd of babies by now. I've made deals with higher powers, scratched the idea of a herd down to the bare minimum. God, if you're up there, just bring me one. I'd do anything for just one.

TWO

My Cape Cod is smashed between a row of other modest yet quaint houses no more than a ten-minute drive across town. At twelve hundred square feet, it's practically one of those tiny houses compared to my parents'. But there's only one of me—as Mom loves to point out whenever possible—so it works. Small and cozy with a computer nook where I hang mood boards for current art campaigns and a gas fireplace unit that doesn't quite do the job like a wood-burning one. The second bedroom would make a nice nursery.

Even before I knew how babies were made, that had always been the plan: Meet a great guy in college, date for 2.5 years, get married, have babies. It was a no-brainer, my future laid out before me because that's what well-bred girls in nice Ohio suburbs did. That's what Henry and Marcia did, so that's what was expected of their children. Ridiculous now, but as a child, I'd been thrilled! Who wouldn't want to have a big white wedding and a gaggle of angelic offspring? Being a mom was part of my DNA—at least figuratively. If babysitting at age ten didn't solidify it, then playing with dolls well into middle school surely did. Would it have made a difference if we'd been aware about my condition since birth? It's hard to say. I suppose maternal instinct knows things before your head can figure it out.

I fling myself onto the couch, having gratefully peeled the black pants from my body and hung them in the closet, never to be touched until next Christmas. Leggings hug my curves with much more grace. On TV, Tim Allen begrudgingly dons a Santa suit much to the amazement of his wide-eyed son. The animation is terrible, but nearly three decades later, I still love this movie. Every year it brings back memories of Becky and me snuggled under a blanket with a bowl of popcorn. I was always the one to finish it. Those were some of the best times of my life. Before adulthood kicked in.

My phone vibrates with an incoming text.

Still at the crystal palace?

I smile. Ryan's referred to my parents' house in this way ever since we became glued at the hip in sixth grade. I didn't get it then—our house was brick after all—but the first time I visited his house in a different part of town, it all made sense. My privilege was obvious. To Ryan, our life was one to strive for. The thing about crystal, though, is that it's easy to break.

No, I'm home. Enough tension to last a while.

Beckster?

Marcia. She tried to set me up on a date in the middle of dinner.

Oh, Marcia... but hey, if you're not gonna go, can I?

I let out a laugh. Only Ryan. What would I do without his perfectly timed humor?

Be my guest. He's a math teacher. Mom says he's hot.

Hot math teacher? Um, yes please.

Ryan Stadler, my best friend, my third limb—we're different in so many ways but ultimately want the same things: love, family, and acceptance.

There's a pause, and then three little dots appear again.

Want some company?

My heart gives a little pang. It's like he can tell even through text when I'm feeling down. I thought I'd had enough of people for the day. But Ryan's not "people"—he's my person.

Door's open. Santa Clause on TV.

Bernard the chief elf? Say no more. I'll bring drinks.

Thirty minutes later, Ryan comes through the door, liquor and limes in hand.

"I feel sort of like the three wise men," he says, helping himself to the kitchen. "Only I don't think Cosmos were one of their gifts."

"Make mine stiff," I call. Stiff enough to drown my sorrows. I don't like being whiny, and I usually go about my life as positive as possible, but holidays have a way of bringing out the feels. Tomorrow will be back to normal. Now, I'm happy to let a martini glass numb the pain.

He whips us up two pink cocktails, not bothering with measurements. Gays are excellent mixologists, he once told me, though he's never tended bar in his life. He joins me on the couch, hands me a drink. I take a sip and breathe out a response. "Fucking fantastic."

"I seriously missed my calling."

He's in joggers and a hoodie, his hair ten times thicker than mine and coiffed neatly. We're such a stereotype I can't help but laugh: the chubby, single forty-something and her gay best friend. What can I say? We've had more fun in the twenty-seven years we've known each other, and he's the one person I've never felt judged by.

"Christmas on a Sunday sucks," he says. "Not even the next day off."

"Yeah, but at least I can work in my pajamas." Ah, the blessing of remote jobs. When else but now would it have been possible to work for an advertising agency based in a whole other state? I get to create campaigns and design graphics, all from the comfort of my home, while Ryan, who works in insurance, wears khakis and a button-down every day. I'll take mine as a small win.

"At least tell me the royals got you a nice gift," he says.

"Does a monogrammed rolling pin count as nice?"

Ryan chokes on his drink, a splash flying from his lips and dribbling down his chin. "Stop."

"Right?" My idea of cooking is takeout. "Oh, and Becky got me a self-help book."

"You Connallys."

"Is my failure at life that obvious?"

We laugh.

The movie goes to commercial, abruptly switching gears from a whimsical toy workshop to a weepy-eyed little girl holding a sign that reads, "Looking for my forever family," accompanied by depressing instrumental music. A woman fills the screen, talking passionately about the power of adoption, and opening your heart and your home to children in need.

"Seriously?" I say, pointing an accusatory hand at the TV. "Even the media wants to rub it in my face."

"Maybe it's a sign. Have you been manifesting? There's definitely an energy around you lately. I feel it. Something good is coming. That call—it's coming."

"You know what happened the last time I got the call."

He drops his head. Of course Ryan knows what happened —he was the first person I called sobbing that afternoon almost exactly one year ago. How can a person go back on an agreement? We'd had everything planned. I'd gone to all the prenatal appointments. I was present. I was ready. This was supposed to be my chance, my turn to be a mom. But then the baby was born, all seven pounds and three ounces of her, and everything fell apart.

I heard they named her Melanie. She'd be turning one now.

Ryan scoots closer to me, wraps his arm around my shoulder. "It'll happen. I know it will. And when it does, you're going to be the best damn mom there ever was. Me too. Parent rockstars."

I try to blink away the water that's pooled in my eyes, but a stray tear slips out, the Cosmo loosening my inhibitions already. Fuck it, Ryan knows everything about me—there's no point hiding.

He wipes away the tear with his thumb, then holds up his martini class and we clink.

"But really though," he says with a smirk, "about that date."

I can't help it—I laugh instead of cry. I'll save the tears for later.

THREE

The Red Hen is Akron's nicest restaurant despite its name, which makes it sound like a diner along a dusty, rural road. I've been here once or twice. Another date in another life. Let's hope this one's not as disastrous.

I park at quarter to seven—exactly on time—but sit in my car for another couple minutes, alternating between reading today's obits and eyeing the people coming and going. It's a toss-up, what I'd like to do more: read about dead people or get a glimpse of this muscly math teacher. There's just something beautiful about typing up the whole of someone's life into a skinny black-and-white column. Most are inspiring, listing all the highs, the achievements, a long life well lived. But others are tragic, and it's those ones, the ones with lives cut short, that serve as a reminder.

What would mine say if my life were to come to an end today? What—who—am I leaving behind?

Ultimately, I set my phone down. I want to see my date before I go inside. Not that I'll judge a book by its cover—I know all too well what it feels like to be on the receiving end of that—but still, it's not like much has changed in the world. Women have to be careful.

I prop an elbow against the window. I can't believe I'm giving my mother the satisfaction of following through on this blind date. But she just wouldn't let up. "C'mon, Cate, it's just dinner. And who knows, maybe he'll end up being Prince Charming!" I'll give her one thing—Mom's persistent. She's as incessant as I am desperate for her approval, so there you have it.

"I got a super-cute dress the other day—you can borrow if you want," Becky added, to which I'd given her a look. "What? It's stretchy!"

You know what else is stretchy? Jeans. And they'll do just fine.

I swipe on some tinted lip gloss to make myself feel like I've at least tried. It's just a dinner. But I've been here before—been on enough Tinder dates to write a tell-all book. Nothing sticks. The few men I'd actually been interested in all ghosted me when they learned of my defective body. The rest just didn't meet the mark—too *this or that* to fit my equation. Ryan says I'm the pickiest woman on the planet.

"There's nothing wrong with you," Dad had said after a junior architect broke my heart, leaving me sobbing into the chest of the only man who'd ever loved me for me. "You're perfect just the way you are. Be patient. Someone will come along. You'll see."

Oh, Dad. There's clearly something wrong with me, which is why I'm giving up dating altogether—after this one last shot.

Five more minutes and I head to the door. My wait was pointless. I wouldn't be able to pick Mr. Math Teacher—okay, fine, his name is John—out of a lineup anyway. Mom's definition of very handsome could be completely opposite mine. Oh, please don't disappoint me.

The sprightly hostess greets me, and I pull the chunky scarf from my neck, give my hair a fluff.

"Just one tonight?" she says, seemingly taking pleasure in my aloneness.

"I'm meeting someone."

"Ah." She scans a list. "John? He's at the bar." She points to a large, U-shaped bar dotted with backless bar stools and tiers of sparkling bottles like a crowning glory.

My heeled boots click against the floor with each step. Like the black dress pants from Christmas, they don't get worn often, and I groan internally at my effort to impress someone who could very well turn out to be just another dud. My pinkie toe throbs.

Mom's voice again, lifting up at the end: *You never know.*

Okay, Marcia. One more try. I suck in my gut, cursing the shapewear underneath this outfit.

The man I assume to be John sits at one of the curves, a tall draft beer on the bar top in front of him. He's remarkably average, which is fine because so am I. It's not like I ever saw myself snagging some Brad Pitt type. Just give me a guy who's open to alternative routes to parenthood and I'm good to go. Looks are secondary to everything else.

"John?" I say, cocking my head.

"You must be Cate," he replies and extends his hand, which I take awkwardly. "Would you like a drink?"

There's a kindness to his dark eyes, a gentle, everyman-ness to his body language that instantly puts me at ease. His front teeth overlap ever so slightly, but instead of being a turnoff, the imperfection is charming. We're on the same level, John and me. Damnit if Marcia isn't right: Maybe this could be the one.

John was not the one.

"I've never heard someone chew so loud," I relay to Ryan on my drive home. I've kicked the boots off my feet and press a socked foot to the gas pedal. "Even with the music and the people talking—it's a Friday night, the place was packed—I could still hear the food sloshing around inside his mouth."

"Loud chewers. The worst."

"And then he started talking about his nieces and nephews, and it wasn't all *I'm enamored with these little people.* It was more like *kids annoy me.*"

"So you obviously didn't—"

"What? No, of course I brought up adoption. Why shouldn't I? It's hopefully part of my near future. Anyone I'm going to be serious about has to be on board."

"Yeah, but on a first date? And when you already got the I-don't-like-kids vibe?"

"What do you want me to do, pretend it's not high on my priority list?"

Ryan's quiet for a second. "It's just a big ask, Cate."

My stomach compresses. The comment hits hard. It is a big ask—*Hi, want to date me? I'm trying to adopt a baby.* Not many guys want to be an insta-dad.

"I'm not sacrificing motherhood for marriage," I say with the full weight of conviction that burns in my soul. Take me or leave me. "I don't need a husband to do it. And besides, men are basically full-sized toddlers, so I'm told. I don't need two."

"Hey now."

We laugh. I'm a little buzzed from an extra glass of wine, but it was necessary to make it through the meal. Jokes aside, my point is valid. There was a time in the not so distant past when I came to a crossroads, a full-stop, hit-you-in-the-gut moment when I questioned my true desire. Which did I want more: The husband or the baby? The answer was easy. Convincing everyone else was another story.

My mother's face flashes in my head and, in a cruel twist of timing, my phone beeps with another incoming call. The word "Mom," accompanied by a photo from one of the happiest days of her life: Becky's wedding.

"Marcia's beeping in," I say to Ryan.

"Ready to start planning the wedding, no doubt."

I'm not in the mood for her clamoring. But if I don't answer she'll keep calling. The corner of my mouth perks up into a smirk. Let's fuck with her.

"Talk tomorrow," I say, then a second later, "Hey, Mom."

My answer catches her off guard. "Oh, I was hoping you wouldn't answer and that would mean you were still at dinner, engaged in deep, connecting conversation. So tell me, how did it go? I've been sitting here all evening waiting to hear—your father's already gone to bed."

I can picture her, still in her button-down and slacks, sitting neatly on the couch with a Nora Roberts book, anticipating a call I had no intention of making.

"You want all the deets?"

"Of course!"

"Well, he's a bit hairier than I expected."

"Hairier?"

"Chest, back... even his ass."

"Wait, what? Cate—"

But I'm on a roll now, a pleased smile on my face. "He had a weird grunt, sort of like when tennis players hit the ball, and then right before he climaxed, he—"

"Cate! Stop! I don't want to hear this!"

I laugh so hard tears come to my eyes. I imagine her holding the phone away from her ear like it's a disgusting, smelly rodent.

"You didn't honestly sleep with a man you just met, did you?" she whispers, as though—God forbid—Lady Di might hear.

"No, Mom. Jesus. I didn't have a one-night stand and call

you to talk about it. Christ. But even if I did, that's my preroga-
tive. I'm forty-one years old, not sixteen. Plus, adults hook up all
the time." I wipe the wetness from under my eyes, probably
smudging my mascara in the process, but who the hell cares?
I'm going home to an empty house.

"Oh, Cate." Her tone's disapproving even through the
phone. I hear the rest of her thought even though she doesn't say
it out loud: Why can't you be like your sister?

"We never would have gotten to the bedroom anyways," I
say with a shrug. "The minute I said the word adoption—"

"You've got to stop blurting that out on first dates!"

"Why? It's going to happen."

"I know it is." She's trying to soften now, trying to pretend
that she views adoption on the same pedestal as biological
Connally children. "But wouldn't it be nice to find a partner
first? Someone who can help you bear the burden?"

"A child's not a burden, Mom."

"That's not what I meant. Don't twist my words."

"I'm a fully capable adult with a good job, my own house. I
can do this by myself." My job's better than good—I'm looking
at a promotion to director of digital content any day now. My
boss and closest work friend, Darci, has mentioned it more than
once in not so many words. A salary bump and major cred in
the company.

None of that matters to Mom though. She's quiet. We've
had this conversation before, many times to be exact, over the
last few years.

"You blame me," she says quietly, and the words hit me like
a sucker punch.

I let out a deep sigh. "I don't blame you."

"You do. You blame me for doing something wrong during
my pregnancy. Like a drink once or twice caused you not to
form correctly. Or that I played too much tennis, or slept on the
wrong side. Both my pregnancies were exactly the same, and—"

She doesn't bring Becky's name into the conversation because she knows that would just be adding fuel to the fire. Becky, the one who didn't get fucked up in utero. The one who went on to have two perfectly healthy children without any worries, and would probably have more just because she can.

"I don't blame you, Mom," I say again, and it's true. It's not her fault. Her sip of champagne on New Year's Eve is not the reason my uterus decided not to form. No amount of back-swings at the country club could have impacted my development. It's nature, and it sucks, but it's life. I've come to grips with my condition—there's nothing I can do about it. But that doesn't mean I'm going to just sit back and not explore very feasible alternatives.

"Listen, I didn't call to get in an argument," she says after a pause.

"K." My energy is zapped, sarcasm gone. All the hurdles of testing and diagnoses from childhood still follow me around like a wrecking ball, swooping in and knocking me out just when I think I'm on solid ground. "I'm gonna go."

We mutter short goodbyes and I hang up just in time to let out a massive scream that shakes the beads dangling from my rear-view mirror. In the next car over at the red light, a woman eyes me in shocked concern. I'm fine, lady. Everything's fine.

The light turns green. I press a heavy foot to the gas.

FOUR

"Sandra, you're on mute. Sa—Sandra, you're muted. It's the button at the—there you go. Yes, we can hear you now."

Technology is a blessing and a curse.

I'm on a Zoom call with the rest of the ad team, discussing promos for the upcoming line. Remote work has wildly shifted the way companies do business, which hasn't been a problem for millennials, but poor Sandra is nearing sixty-five and Zoom is not her friend. I text Darci a meme about boomers and technology. She responds with *LOL* and we both smirk at each other on screen.

While my gray-haired teammate drones on about advertising budgets and marquee placements, my mind drifts—as it often does. It's been three weeks since my fateful date with Mr. Math Teacher and the night I deleted every dating app from my phone. I went home that night and shut the bedroom door at the top of the stairs, sealing in all the hopes and dreams and powder-scented baby products. The crib, the changing table, the closet full of miniature clothes—everything for the-baby-that-was-supposed-to-be-mine. Thinking of dating and marriage automatically makes me think of the child I want so badly—like the two are inextricably linked, even though I know they're not. Despite how much I've worked to mentally separate the two, when the sadness about one creeps in, the other soon follows. The room is just too painful to walk past every day. If I keep the door shut, I can try to pretend like what's behind it isn't really there.

I'm about to text Darci another funny meme—this one with Leonardo DiCaprio holding a tiny glass of wine and laughing—but instead my phone rings. My heart leaps at the number flashed across the screen. I know this number. I've saved it in my contacts and waited for it, day in and day out. It hasn't called—until now. *Ringgggggg...* The phone's on silent. It's my ears that are ringing. I blink again to be sure. The contact is still there:

Heartfull Adoption Connection.

At once, my palms turn clammy and the air sucks from my lungs. Is this The Call? Is there another child waiting for me? My eyes bounce from screen to screen, laptop to phone. It won't ring much longer before my voicemail picks up.

"Cate?" It's Sandra again, her camera mis-angled so that it looks as though she's talking to someone just off the edge of the screen. "Thoughts?"

What? I have no idea what she's been saying. All I know is I need to answer this call. I can't miss it. I feel my blood pressure spiking. Work can take a brief intermission.

"I'm sorry, guys, I have to go." And in one quick click, I leave the Zoom meeting at the same time I bring the phone to my ear.

"Hello?" I touch my hairline. It's damp. Hope sits high in my chest, ready to burst out.

"Hi, is this Cate?"

"This is she." Proper, just like Marcia Connally taught me.

"Cate, hi. This is Kathleen calling from Heartfull Adoption

Connection. Wow, it's been a while! Feels like forever ago when —never mind, I have great news! Are you sitting down?"

Great news. Oh my god.

"Yes," I manage, and I'm glad I am sitting because I've suddenly gone lightheaded.

"We have a baby. A little boy, just born today. You've been matched."

"Born today? And she... she just decided..."

"Yes. I know, it's a little sudden, I'm sure. Many adoptions are planned, but some... some are last-minute decisions."

She's busy explaining the details, but I drift away. A baby. A baby boy. My... son? I can barely breathe, the air in the room somehow devoid of oxygen. Is this really happening? It's all I've thought about for the last year. My fingers tingle as I fan myself. Stay present, Cate. Do not pass out.

"Cate?"

"I'm here. I—"

"It's a lot, I know. Take a second."

"Are you sure? I mean, after last time..."

"Yes. The birth mother's planning to sign the papers shortly. They're monitoring her now—a bit of excess blood loss. But we have everything ready. Should be all official later today."

I try to conjure an image of a woman in a hospital bed, but I have no information with which to form the picture. I know nothing about this person—not her age, her hair color, her build. I can't help but remember Hadley, the teen mom whose delivery I watched. How relieved she was when it was all over, the way she looked at the newborn—and then the way she took her back.

No, this is not Hadley. This is a whole other birth. I wipe last year's ordeal from my mind and try to set a more positive scene. The woman's image is blurry, nothing more than a silhouette. But the baby—the baby I can see perfectly, wrapped in the classic newborn hospital blanket, a stretchy hat pulled over his little head.

"Cate?"

A small laugh-cry escapes my lips. "I can't believe it."

"It's been a journey," Kathleen says in sincerity. "I'm so happy for you."

My eyes glass over. I place a hand on my heart to steady its beat. This is really happening. "So now what?"

"Can you be there tomorrow morning?"

Wait, where is "there"? The agency is in Cleveland, but its reach extends to the greater Ohio area, and even into Pennsylvania and New York. I'll need to notify work. I wasn't exactly prepared for a spontaneous road trip. But it doesn't matter—I'd travel to California if that's what it takes.

"Of course," I say. "Where?"

"Cleveland."

Less than an hour. My baby is so close. It feels at once like I can reach out and touch him, and also that he's light years away. Less than an hour's drive to pick up my child. The idea is settling in my brain, wiggling in to find a cozy spot of permanence. I'm going to be a mom. Any reservations I've held melt away, replaced instead with pure elation. I bolt off the office chair and cross the small hallway, coming face to face with the closed door of my would-be nursery. Flinging it open, everything becomes crystal clear. This is it, this is my time. The room goes from black and white to Technicolor, the fruits of all my longing finally coming true.

"Yes," I say again. "I'll be there." I hold the phone with my shoulder as I drop to my knees and rummage through the closet for the car seat that's been waiting for this moment. It still has its brand-new smell. Round two, only this time, coming home with a baby.

Kathleen gives me all the details—where to go, what to bring—and I scribble it all onto a Post-it for fear I'll forget the minute we hang up. The whole time I'm breathing fast, alter-nating between laughing and biting back tears. It's wildly surreal.

When we end the call, I stand frozen in the middle of the nursery. Tomorrow there will be a baby here. He'll sleep in this crib, I'll dress him on that changing table. If my heart could explode, it surely would have by now.

I manage to move to the glider in the corner of the room and drop myself to its smooth, cream seat. Then I rock, imagining a tiny bundle in my arms. I'll hold you forever, little one.

"*What?* You're kidding. Are you kidding?"

Ryan just about jumps through the phone, and his flurry of excitement only adds to my own.

"Would I really be kidding about this?" I say, and then we both scream, and I jump up and down in the nursery where I've started going through baby clothes. Last time was supposed to be a girl. Now I'm getting a boy. Good thing I'd collected a lot of gender-neutral options.

"Have you called your parents?"

"Not yet. You were first."

"Oh my god, Uncle Ryan is going to spoil this little dude so bad! Can I be your welcoming committee when you get home? You know I'll be there with bells and whistles. Shit, I better order balloons. Okay, gotta go. Ahh!"

The phone clicks, and I chuckle. What would I do without Ryan? But his uncle reference reminds me I should call my family. Another grandbaby coming your way! I dial my parents' home phone, which has to be one of the only remaining land-lines in town. The number is burned into my brain, along with all the memories of racing to be the first to answer, of Becky listening in on my calls as a snoopy preteen. What did we ever do without cell phones and caller ID?

It rings twice before Dad picks up. "Hello?"

"Dad," I say, suddenly choked with emotion. "Hey. I have something to tell you guys. Is Mom there?"

"Who is it?" I hear my mother say, followed by the clinking of dishes. It's five-thirty on the dot, which means she's cleaning up dinner.

"It's Cate," Dad says. "Hang on. I'm putting you on speaker. Is everything all right, Birdie?"

"Yes, yes. Am I on? Can Mom hear me too?" I can't hold it much longer—I just want to shout from the rooftops.

"I'm here," Mom says. "What is it?"

I can picture them leaning over the phone together, Mom's wire-framed glasses perched on the bridge of her nose, Dad's thinning hair combed to the side. They probably think it's something bad; I've probably panicked them. Time to cut the suspense.

"I got the call!" I all but shout.

"The call? Oh, the call! Oh my goodness! Oh, Catie!" Mom's enthusiasm sends warmth through my chest all the way to my toes.

"I know!"

"Oh, that's so wonderful. But wait. Are you sure?"

"Yes. Don't worry, I thought the same thing. I mean, who wouldn't after last time? But they said it's for sure. Birth mom's signing the papers. I'm going to go get him tomorrow!"

"Him? It's a boy?"

"Yes! A perfect little boy." I'm a boy mom. It feels so right.

Dad lets out a chuckle of amusement. "We're going to be halfway to a basketball team around here pretty soon with all these grandsons."

I get his quip, though none of us have to say what we're thinking: There's no Connally DNA in this new one. Will he be treated as an equal? Or will there always be a stain on his image? Will he always be the odd one out? Right now, I can't think of the shitty misfortune that stole my chance at biological children, nor the complexities that befall adopted children's identities. It doesn't matter anymore—none of it. My baby is here, and tomorrow we'll be together. He's part of this family already.

"I better go shopping," Mom chirps. "Diapers and clothes and—"

"I have everything, Mom." I look around. This nursery is packed with every piece of gear and supplies I need, all the way down to the pale pink bottle of baby lotion. This isn't my first rodeo.

"Yes, but—"

"There'll be plenty of time for shopping."

"Oh, fine. I'll hardly be able to sleep! Okay, I'm going to go call Sharon and Marilou. They'll be absolutely tickled! My friends have all been praying for you, you know."

"No, Mom, don't. Not yet," I say, my eagerness coming to a quick halt. "Let's just wait until he gets here, okay?"

"Oh, honey. It's not going to happen again. That much bad luck can't befall one person."

"She's right, Birdie," Dad says. "Enjoy this moment."

"Do you want us to come with you tomorrow?" Mom says.

I shake my head. "I think I want to do it alone. Meet him for the first time, you know?"

"Okay, well, we'll come right over as soon as you get home. Now, you better give your sister a call to tell her the good news. Tell the boys they're getting a little cousin!"

Mom's joy radiates through the phone and swells my heart. She hasn't mentioned anything about a husband, nothing about a father for the baby. Maybe this is good enough for her after all.

It is for me.

We hang up, and I call Becky, who promptly screeches into my ear.

"I'm so happy, I'm crying!" she says, and I hear her sniffle.

Why does she have to be so goddamn nice? She wants to know every detail, so I go through it all a third time. Yes, this time's for sure. No, she can't meet me at the hospital. Yes, I have everything I need.

Welcoming a new baby is a family affair.

The retelling, the questions, have completely drained me, and when I disconnect with Becky, I flop to the ivory shag rug in the center of the nursery. I lie on my back and let the dancing lamb crib mobile lull me into a happy daydream. My hands rest on my lower belly. There'll never be a baby in there; I'll never get to feel those kicks Becky always oohed and aahed about. I won't get to look at a small human and recognize my face in theirs.

But that's okay. I've come to terms with it. That storyline wasn't meant for me. This—tomorrow—is my destiny. I close my eyes, wishing I could fast-forward the hours until he's safely in my arms, forms signed, sealed, delivered.

A pang of doubt—so small I can almost reason it away—settles in my tummy, a dark cloud over one of the happiest moments of my life. No, I tell myself. It's not going to happen again. It won't. It can't.

FIVE

TOAST IS EVEN DRIER WHEN YOU'RE NOT IN THE MOOD TO eat it. I nibble small bites—maybe peanut butter wasn't the best choice—not because I'm hungry, but because Marcia Connally says breakfast is the most important meal of the day, and since this is the most important day of my life, I figure I better not skip the most important meal.

I've been awake for hours, the idea of sleeping laughable. I'm showered, packed, and ready to go, and now killing time by forcing dry bread down my throat. I take a sip of coffee, scroll through social media for so long my phone battery nearly drains completely. I'll charge it in the car on the way.

A picture message flashes. I open it.

HOW CUTE ARE THEEEEEEESE?

Ryan's sent a screenshot of Gucci baby booties. Oh, come off it. I roll my eyes. Three hundred for footwear he'll outgrow in a month? I don't think so. Adorable, yes. Practical, no. We'll be an Old Navy family, I'm sure.

Save it for his college fund.

I reply with a heart-eye emoji.

Is it time to go yet? Still so early. It's either wait here or wait there—which would be less excruciating? Another sip of coffee.

Over the next half hour, a handful of texts come in.

From BWTGH (Becky with the Good Hair): *Happy adoption day!!! Can't wait to meet my new nephew!*

From Marcia: *Are you sure you don't want us to come with you?*

From ♡Dad♡: *Don't get out of your car downtown. Not safe.*

I've washed and folded the clothes. I've swept and dusted the nursery. I've pulled the bouncer into the living room. What else is there to do? The minutes crawl by. I close my eyes and imagine a hospital not far from here, overlooking Lake Erie. In a room on one of the dozen floors, a baby waits for me.

My phone rings. I shake my head and answer.

"Ry, I can't talk now. I'm about to walk out the door."

He ignores me. "Are you just dying? I'd be dying if I were you. How much longer? Let me stay on the phone with you, huh? I'll just tag along for the drive. It's like I'm there but I'm not there."

"Seriously, Ryan. Not now. I'm either going to throw up or completely combust from nerves." I laugh before I hang up so he knows I'm only partially serious. I have to focus. I don't want to be late meeting my son for the first time. Impressions matter.

I grab my coat and give myself one final inspection in the mirror. Do I look like a mom? Yesterday I was just me, but today I take on a new identity.

I'm pondering all this when the phone rings again.

"Ryannnnn," I groan. I'm going to kill him. I peek down at

the caller ID. But it's not Ryan. My stomach flips—it's the adoption agency's number. But why would they be calling?

Ring... ring...

It's fine. Kathleen's probably just confirming my departure, making sure I'm still on time. I swallow past a thick tongue, give my hand a shake, and pick up.

"Hello?"

"Cate. It's Kathleen."

As soon as she speaks, I know this conversation isn't about where to park and which door to enter. I instinctively peer at the empty car seat on the floor. No, no, no.

"Where are you? Have you left yet?" Kathleen says, and I do my best to hold out hope. She's checking to see how soon I'll be here because my baby can't wait to see me. She's telling me she'll meet me at the door with flowers.

"No... I, uh... I'm just about to leave." I try to keep my voice upbeat, even though something is pulling down—hard.

"Cate, I need you to sit."

"Sit?" What? Why?

"I'm so sorry, Cate."

Razorblade tears are already blurring my vision. I think I really might vomit. I'm not hearing her correctly. This is a misunderstanding, right?

"She—"

"No, Kathleen. No. Don't say it."

"—changed her mind. Minutes ago. She refused to sign over her rights. I'm so sorry, Cate. There's nothing we can do."

A hole opens in my core, burning at the edges with a fire so hot I feel like I'm about to explode. This can't be happening—not again. I pinch the skin on my thigh. Wake up, Cate! This is a goddamned nightmare!

"Cate?"

"But—but—" The dam bursts, and now I'm heaving giant sobs.

"I know, I know. It's unimaginable. Is there someone there with you? Someone you can call to come over? I don't think it's best to be alone with this news."

I topple to the couch and drop onto it, my legs mush. "Why me?" I cry. "Why? It's so unfair."

"I'm so sorry," she says again and again, like it's her only form of consolation. "The odds—they're unheard of."

Yes, the odds are unheard of for this to happen to the same person twice. But I am that person, and it's happening. These are odds I never wanted to be in favor of. There is nothing worse than longing for something that is just out of reach.

I drop the phone to my lap, too tired to even hold it to my ear a second longer. All I can do is cry. Why does the universe want to punish me? I'm a good person. A stable, loving woman, ready to devote my life to the care and nurture of a child. Is it too much to ask?

As though from the other end of a long tunnel, I hear my name. Kathleen's still on the line. I pick up the phone again. My sniffles must tell her I'm back.

"Cate," she says. "Don't give up. We'll try again. There are thousands of children waiting to be adopted."

I don't want to hear her wishful thinking, her annoying optimism. Right now, I want to wallow in the cruel fate I've been handed. So I hang up. And then I howl—long and low, knowing I'm alone but not caring if I were in the middle of a crowded arena. It's an ache even stronger than before, a fresh wound on top of one not yet healed.

I cry until the well runs empty. I should have a baby in my arms right now. Instead, I'm here, in a house big enough for two —baby-less. Alone.

A thought pops to the surface: My family.

What am I going to tell them? Yet another thing Cate can't quite seem to get right. It's not my fault, but somehow I can't help but feel certain they'll find a way to make it feel as such.

Mom's faint smile. Becky's head tilt. The sad eyes. Everything that screams poor Catie. I don't need them to feel sorry for me.

A car rolls down the street, bumping to a jacked-up bass. The music thumps in my ears, momentarily tuning out my hammering pulse. Life moving on outside my window. How? How can the world keep turning when mine has stopped? Another failed adoption. More dashed dreams. Time to shut the nursery door yet again. Maybe it's time to lock it for good. This obviously isn't my path. The thought crushes me.

I swivel to look at the car seat that sits empty near the door. The tiny straps should be holding in a fragile body right now. But they hang there, limp, empty. Like me. My womb. My life.

SIX

I DON'T KNOW HOW LONG I LIE THERE ON MY GRAY
Wayfair couch, only that it's possible to cry yourself to sleep
more than once. Each time my eyes open, it takes a second to
remember: the call, the letdown, the emptiness. And then the
tears come again. When I finally glance at the clock, I'm
shocked to discover hours have passed. It's now mid-afternoon
and half the day is gone. My phone is face down on the coffee
table, undoubtedly with a string of texts from my family. Do I
have him yet? Are we home? I slide the phone further away.
The last thing I feel like doing is talking to anyone.

I roll onto my back and stare up at the mud-swirl ceiling. It's
painfully ugly, and I've wanted to redo it for years, but now the
repetitive curls send me into a hypnotic distraction. I follow the
individual lines with my eye, pretending they're a path, and that
at the end is a prize. Only the swirls go on forever in one long,
continuous stroke, never reaching an end. And then my eyes
prickle once more, at the symbolic parallel to my life. I'll never
reach that pot of gold at the end of the rainbow.

I sniff, wipe my nose with my sleeve, and let the heaviness
of my eyes pull my lids shut. There, in the darkness, I hear a

sound that makes my eyes flash open. It starts as a whimper, a disgruntled squawk, then becomes more insistent and high-pitched. It's a cry—there's no mistaking it. But as soon as my brain recognizes this fact, I dismiss it. So now I'm going to hear phantom baby cries? The cruelty of it.

But the sound continues, now a wail, angry and repetitive. I slam my hands over my ears. Stop! This isn't fair! Haven't I been tortured enough? I sit up and drop one hand, then the other, praying the imaginary crying has stopped.

It hasn't. And that's when something clicks. Something that says this isn't a figment of my imagination at all.

I rise from my paralysis and glance around, as though the sound were coming from inside the house, pulling a prank on me. But it's not as clear as that—there's something muffling the cry, a barrier between it and my ear. Almost as if it were just on the other side of a—

I lunge for the front door, whip it open, and gasp. The shrieking hits me in the face with resounding clarity. I stare down, trying to process how such a noise could come from something so small.

A baby. No, an infant. A very new infant. Bundled into a car seat on my front stoop. A blue hat crouches down to his eyebrows, and a dinosaur-print blanket is tucked across his legs. Next to the carrier sits a navy blue diaper bag, zipped up like he's off to an overnight stay.

My mouth gapes, and I momentarily recall the scene in *Mary Poppins* when Michael is scolded for looking like a codfish. But I can't help it—this is so shocking, so confusing. I look left and right to the neighbors' houses, to their driveways, down the street. The road is empty, the houses are shut up. There's not a soul in sight.

"What in the world...?" I breathe.

A gust of wind makes me jump, sending my arm hairs even further on end. It's frigid out here, and if I'm cold, then surely an infant is even colder. This doesn't make any sense—why there's an unattended baby on my doorstep. But the whipping cold has frozen all logic, and my first thought—my only thought —is to get this tiny being inside where it's warm.

I reach down and lift the carrier from the ground. The motion makes the baby's head jiggle back and forth and, for a split second, his cries stop, only to resume at an even higher decibel. A sliver of white pokes out from where it's wedged next to the blanket, near the baby's legs. I pull it out. It's a single sheet of white paper, heavy like cardstock, and about the size of an index card. On it are five words, scrawled in a small, spidery script:

Take him. Please forgive me.

And there, at the bottom, in lieu of a signature, a hand-drawn bird in flight, with a round body and feathered wings. A black sparrow. I flip the card over, searching for more, but am left without explanation.

As I step back through the door, car seat in tow, it feels like I'm gliding through a dream. Is this real? Is my imagination playing tricks on me? The baby wails again, confirming it all. This is not make-believe.

A million thoughts flood my mind. Where are this child's parents? How long has the poor thing been outside my door? And more importantly, why was he left there in the first place?

SEVEN

THE BABY'S CRY IS RELENTING, LOUD AND HIGH-PITCHED. He's angry with a capital A. I brace either side of my head with my hands. I need to call someone—the police? Child services? Someone out there is missing a child—whether intentionally or not. The logical thing would be to drop everything and make a call. Where's my phone?

A shrill scream, and I wince.

That cry. Must stop the cry if I want to think straight.

"Okay. It's okay," I say—to both him and myself. My fingers fumble with the buckles at his chest and between his legs, and his little face turns crimson in fury. He's so tiny—he can't be more than a week old—the car seat swallows his entire body. I worry I'm breaking him as I get his arms free from the straps. He squirms with the roughness of my hands and lets out an unhappy wail.

"I'm trying, little guy."

The buckles release. I lower the handle and lift him from the seat. His legs instinctively curl up like they would have in the womb. I bring him to my shoulder.

"Shhh," I say, bouncing lightly. But he's shrieking now, wide-mouthed and gummy, eyes squeezed shut.

"Okay, what do you need? Diaper? Yes, you're probably wet. Let's change you." My eyes dart around the room as though a diaper will magically appear. I stumble on the bag at my feet and squat to rummage inside with one hand. "Of course. The diaper bag. Relax, Cate. Focus. You're prepared for this."

I suck in a gulp of air and hold it, slowly let it out. Like magic, a calm washes over me. I *am* prepared for this. I've been prepared for this forever. Maybe not this exact scenario, these exact circumstances, but a crying baby? I can handle this. Get him changed, then call the police.

The baby's legs kick in protest as I lay him on his back right there on the couch—no time to climb the stairs to the nursery where there's a perfectly padded changing table. This kid is not happy.

I unzip his striped sleeper and gently pull out his legs. They're scrawny, not yet filled out with cute baby fat, and I'm reminded of the first time I saw my nephews in the hospital after their births. The area around his belly button is red and healing from where an umbilical cord stump recently fell off. When I release the Velcro tabs on the diaper, his arms fling open to the sides, fingers extended. I remember reading about the Moro reflex. He wails again.

I've never changed a diaper so fast in my life. Then again, it's been a while since Becky's boys were in diapers. Even then, I wasn't in a panicked rush. If the boys were crying, I could laugh it off and hand them back to their mom. *Here you go, Mama, they're your problem!*

Now, there's no one else here. Just me and a baby that's not even mine.

I zip him back up, hoping that will do the trick.

It doesn't. He starts to fuss again, protesting something I can't determine. *Neh. Neh. Neh.* The cry is whiny and nasally, and I wish I knew how to speak baby. But now's not the time to worry about that.

No amount of rocking or bouncing soothes his cries. His back arches, head flailing around to the point of astonishment— I had no idea newborns could move so much. I can't possibly call the police until I get him—and myself—calmed down.

My chest is tight. I pace the living room with him in my arms. What do I do? The bag is upturned from my aggressive diaper search, its contents spilled out onto the hardwood floor. Something jumps out at me like a flashing neon sign. A bottle.

You idiot, of course he's hungry. Who knows how long he was outside before I found him. Newborns eat with voracious frequency—I remember Becky cluster feeding around the clock, Shane bringing her endless cups of tea that were supposed to help with lactation.

I snatch the bottle and spin the top off with one thumb, before it hits me: formula. I didn't buy any formula. After the call came in late yesterday afternoon, I'd spent the evening prepping everything—washing the crib linens, sorting clothing, installing the car seat, even sterilizing pacifiers. But the one thing I hadn't considered was to have formula on hand.

"The hospital sends you home with a ton of samples," Becky reminded me last night. "You should wait to find out what kind the baby responds best to before buying more, it's so damn expensive."

Damn you and your advice, Becky. What soon-to-be-mother doesn't have a plan for feeding her baby? I'm already horrible at this.

As soon as the thought comes, I chide myself. Of course I can't keep this child. Still, the last thing I want to do is strap him back into the car seat for an emergency store run. And even if the authorities got here ASAP, it still wouldn't bring comfort fast enough for the poor thing.

"Please, please, please," I beg as I tear apart the small navy bag. And then, like a blessing, out fall two skinny packets of formula. "Oh, thank God."

I shuffle to the kitchen, flip on the faucet, and run my finger under the water until it reaches a lukewarm temperature. I fill the bottle to the four-ounce mark, dump in the powder, replace the lid and give it a shake. There's something the baby blogs say about preparing bottles—the right way and the wrong way, something about hot pockets of water—but right now, all I know is that it isn't nearly hot enough to scald him, and I just need him to eat.

I adjust the baby in a cradle hold and offer the bottle to his lips. "Here, here!"

He takes it immediately, alternating between sucking and jagged breaths, his body calming after discomfort.

I'm breathing hard too. That was intense and my pulse is through the roof. But it's okay. It's all good now. He's eating, he's happy. Breathe, Cate.

I go to the window and use my chin to hold the bottle in the baby's mouth while I pull aside the curtain. There has to be someone around. A stranger watching from a parked car, an absent mother peeking from behind a tree. Who would just leave a baby on a random doorstep? I recall the Dateline about postpartum women up to their eyeballs in anxiety who do something drastic. Or the teen mom who gives her baby away in a last-ditch attempt at saving him. No, I think, it can't be anything like that. That's on-screen drama. Those are ripped-from-the-headline stories. I'm just a normal, largely boring individual. There must be an explanation. I strain my eyes.

Again, my assumptions are dashed—the only things I see are snow-covered yards and a trail of salt down the sidewalk. Not even footprints left behind as a clue. I draw my brows together in utter bewilderment.

We move back to the living room, and I sit at the side of the couch, elbow propped on the armrest supporting the baby's head. His eyes are open, and I stare at them for the first time. They're dark, almost black, like his warm-hued skin but even darker. His body pumps heat, so I remove his hat to cool him down.

"There, that's better," I say. "You sure know how to get worked up, don't you?" I stroke his head full of midnight hair. There's a slight curl to it around his ears—it's not poker straight and airy like my nephews' was at birth. I run a finger down his nose. His lips are full. We're opposites in so many ways.

My mind hums with confusion, an odd sense of disorientation. Am I dreaming? Wasn't I just weeping for a lost baby only minutes ago? If my hands weren't full, I'd slap my own cheek. This can't be real.

Oh, but it is. I can count the hours I've been awake today on one hand, yet somehow in the span of time some people spend getting ready in the morning, I've lost and gained a child.

I reach for my phone. A string of texts pop up, but I only see the first. It's from Kathleen, and I'm not sure if she sent it the minute we hung up or just now. Either way, the message sends a jolt through my core.

I completely understand your devastation and wish there were something I could do to change this situation. Have faith, your baby is out there. I'll check back in with you soon. Until then, sending big hugs.

Your baby is out there.

I look back to the little boy in my arms. Everything's calm now. I can think straight. I should call to report this baby I'm now caring for. But something stops me. This moment, it's so perfect. He's so content. His eyes locked on mine, saying thank you, thank you for knowing what I needed. It's like we're communicating through silence and touch. Can't I just enjoy it for a few minutes? The call can wait a bit longer, can't it?

I put the phone down, and a thought makes its way into my conscience. Someone will report a missing baby. This boy's family will eventually be looking for him. I'm just keeping him safe while it all gets sorted out. I'll call—I will. But why the rush?

He chugs the first half of the bottle, slowing down as the remaining ounces drain from view. I'm mesmerized, can't peel my eyes from him. By the end, he's milk drunk—limp in my arms. I pull the empty bottle from his mouth and he continues to suckle. I smile.

On my shoulder, he lets out a burp—to which I exclaim "Whoa!"—then rests his head against my collarbone. I give his back gentle pats. His spine is bony under my fingers. How incredible that we all start out this small. It passes in a blink, but once upon a time we were all innocent and defenseless and at the mercy of someone to care for us. Did Marcia hold me this way? My insides glow at the thought.

We nestle into the couch, finding comfort together. I lay my head back. His body rests on my chest, a little bundle of love. Our breath syncs.

This is it. This is heaven. This is what I was supposed to be doing for the next eight weeks of parental leave. What I envisioned when I submitted my paperwork less than an hour after getting Kathleen's first call. My belly churns. It's so unfair. I'd give anything for him to be mine. But he's not. This is a fantasy. And it's wrong.

Your baby is out there.

Is he? Or is he right here?

It would be immoral to keep this child.

Just a few more minutes. Then I'll call. Just a few more minutes.

Before I know it, exhaustion wins, and I join him in blissful dreamland.

EIGHT

I'M BEING ATTACKED BY BIRDS. HUNDREDS OF SPARROWS, their black beaks pecking at me, my legs, my face, my back. They rise from the notecard, taking shape, wings flapping. They fly into my chest, bumping against my ribs. Another, then another. What do you want from me? I was only trying to help! I haven't done anything wrong!

My eyes blink open, surroundings coming into clarity. I'm in the living room. It was just a dream—there are no angry sparrows. Since when do I fall asleep on the couch in the middle of the day? I can't remember the last time I took a nap.

Another bump against my side. I jump—the birds are back! No, can't be. It's something hard, almost like a kick. But it couldn't be a kick—a kick would be much harder, unless it were a tiny kick from a tiny—

"Oh my god," I say, reaching to my side where the baby has fallen and wedged himself between me and the arm of the couch. I pull him out, butt first. So it really was his little legs trying to get my attention. He whimpers twice, then stops.

"I'm so sorry." I turn him over, relieved his kicking means

he's still alive, yet still mortified I managed to nearly smother him.

He writhes, his jerky reflexes making his limbs do funny things. They're so alien, these little beings. He scrunches his nose, like he's disgusted at me for my negligence, then lets out the perfect little sneeze.

"Oh my goodness," I say dramatically, as though it almost blew me over. I'm lost in the moment, gazing at him, daydreaming about stroller walks to the park, when it hits me again at full force.

This child is not mine. This child showed up on my doorstep. This child should be reported to the police.

I check my phone. How much time has passed? How long were we asleep? Nearly two hours! My skin itches. I open the rest of the texts from Mom, Becky, and Ryan. Have we made it home? Can they come over yet?

Enter full panic mode. They can't come over now! There's a baby here, but not the right baby. This one doesn't belong to me. Yet he's here, lying on my lap, hands clenched into fists up to his chin. I should have seen this coming. They knew I'd be home by now—who's to say they're not on their way already? If there's one thing I know about Ryan, it's that he has serious FOMO.

What am I supposed to do? What would Becky do? I hover over the dial pad. Call now, Cate. Call the police. Don't take this any further. Stop this while there's still time.

My finger is suspended. I bite my lip. Something's tugging at my heart—hard. I stare at the boy nestled on my thighs. The weight of him has settled my runaway despair. His very presence mended my broken soul. Can't I just pretend a little longer? I blink in succession. It's the most bizarre experience. No baby, then a supposed-to-be-baby, then no baby again, and now a different baby altogether.

A vision flashes through my head. I imagine a woman, hood pulled tight around her head, sunglasses disguising her eyes, sneaking up my steps to deposit her baby at my door. The anger comes, swift and hot. My muscles quiver from my feet to my neck. Who knows what would have happened if I hadn't been home to hear his cries and bring him in? He could have frozen to death. What kind of mother does such a thing? How unfair that someone like her got a baby and I didn't. Then another possibility: What if it wasn't the mother at all? Is this a kidnapped baby that someone else has handed me? Either way, a child was left alone and with nothing.

The thought of such negligence makes me fume, until I consider there are probably family members. Grandparents, maybe aunts or uncles. Maybe this baby's short time on earth hasn't been all bad. Even if his mother doesn't want him, someone else in the family will. I hope they'll provide him a better future. That alone comforts me, and my heart rate quells. He won't be alone. He'll have his family.

But not now. Not yet. I'm not ready to give him back. I flex my fingers and reply to the texts.

No company today, okay? Really want to soak it all in first. Everything is good. Will call tomorrow.

Tomorrow. I'll go to the police station in the morning and explain everything. Then deal with my family—the devastating news that everything fell apart once again. They'll try to put me back together, but sometimes shards of a soul are just too cracked to mend. Tomorrow I'll shatter into a million little pieces. But for now, I'm whole. At least for one night.

A text comes in from Ryan.

What? I'm obv an exception, right?

Sorry, Ry. Just give me till tomorrow.

I know how much this must crush them, how eager they were to be my welcoming committee. But this is nothing. They'll be even more crushed tomorrow when they find out the truth. Lying is not part of my character. I've been the good girl my whole life, so this all feels immoral. A wave of nausea threatens. The guilt could destroy everything.

If I let it.

When I return my gaze to the baby, his eyes are wide open, staring back up at me. He's not scared. He's not cold. He's not hurt. He's as content as could be. My fears melt away.

"Well, hello! Aren't you bright-eyed after that nap?" I take his little hands in mine and move them around as I speak. He's too young to smile, but he doesn't cry, and that alone makes me happy.

We sit, then we walk, then we sit again. I draw the curtains and flip my phone to silent. Nothing exists except the here and now. The two of us in this house, going about normal newborn life. Only there's nothing normal about it—that I know. I should have called the authorities the moment I found him, screaming baby or not. There's a right and a wrong in this situation, and I know which side I'm on, but that doesn't stop me. Because it's only one night.

Whether or not I'll get in trouble for this is a distant thought. It lingers on the edge of my conscience, but I don't want to go there. Somehow it doesn't matter. How could someone be punished for helping? I saved him. And besides, it will all be over in the morning—just like a pinprick to a balloon, this fantasy will burst.

But for now, I hold the baby on my shoulder and we sway through the living room. It's a slow dance filled with tenderness, desperate wishes, and sadness that it can't last forever. Long into the evening we cuddle, and not until the stars sprinkle the clear sky do I lay him in the crib and fall asleep on the chair inches away.

Just one night.

NINE

I'M WOKEN WITH A START—BANGING ON THE FRONT DOOR.
Three consecutive pounds. I spring up, half awake, half delusional, blinking myself coherent. Wait, where am I? Why am I
in the nurs—

The crib—it's not empty. There's a baby in it. The baby
from yesterday. It all comes flooding back.

Unexpected discovery, mysterious sparrow, hysterical baby,
a bottle that soothed him, lulled to sleep, endless cuddles. But
he's not supposed to be here. I was supposed to call, and now—

Bang, bang, bang.

Who is here and pounding so incessantly? Then my mind
skips to a radical place. Shit. The cops are here. They've found
out—somehow they've found out. What exactly? Have I done
something wrong? It's not like I kidnapped him from the
grocery store. Still, why is there a lead block in my stomach? My
conscience knows this scenario isn't right. This baby shouldn't
be sleeping in my crib. I bring a hand to my belly, which
suddenly feels uneasy. But how did they find him? No one saw
us. I checked for people multiple times. There's no way.

I fumble off the chair, heart rate spiked, sleep still stuck to the corner of my eyes after two middle-of-the-night feedings. What do I do, what do I do? I look at the baby. He's still sleeping despite the noise, lying on his back in a gray sleep sack.

Bang, bang, bang.

I jump, and then tears immediately flood my eyes. I'm not ready. I didn't want it to be like this. I was going to wake up and call, on my own terms. And now there's police about to knock my door down like I'm some sort of criminal.

Am I criminal?

The shrill doorbell does it—the baby's eyes flutter open. He rolls his head from side to side, waking up. What an innocent little thing, perfectly content after a stretch of sleep. Maybe I could leave him here, go to the door and feign ignorance. He'd stay quiet, right? *No, officer, there's no baby here. You must be at the wrong house.*

I consider it for a split second then give myself an internal slap. Don't be a dummy, Cate. They'd surely search the house. The police aren't going to just leave because I pretend I don't know what they're talking about.

I look to the baby. I'll take him with me, both as a confession and a comfort. I imagine giving him one last squeeze before handing him over. If only the circumstances were different.

I unzip the sleep sack, wiggle his little arms out, and pick him up. "Good morning, sweet boy." There's a lump in my throat I can't wash down. Too hard, like guilt and sorrow tangled up together.

I descend the stairs on light feet, holding on to every second I have left. This was all just a fantasy, Cate. It was never real. It's time. Do the right thing.

I square my shoulders and tuck my hair behind my ear with my free hand. Reach for the doorknob and open.

"Congratulations!" The chorus blasts me in the face, and I squint to fully understand what's happening. It's not the police. Instead, my parents stand on the stoop, Dad holding balloons,

Mom a pan covered in aluminum foil. I know right away it's lasagna—what she brings to everyone who's either celebrating or grieving.

She thinks I'm celebrating. I thought I was grieving. Now, I'm too shocked to tell which is true.

I look past them, into the driveway, still expecting to see a cruiser with flashing lights.

"We just couldn't wait," Mom says. "Your father's been up since the crack of dawn. We just had to come straight over. Oh Cate, let me see him!"

She crosses the entryway, and I instinctively draw back, letting them in.

Mom sets the lasagna down then throws her hands in the air. "Oh my goodness, he's so tiny! Oh, Henry, look how sweet."

She grabs Dad's forearm right behind her. He's beaming with pride. The two of them look like the grandparents from a commercial: Every hair in place, eyes filled with delight. I haven't said a word. Too paralyzed in the moment to even process their appearance and what it means for this very sudden situation. Mom wipes a stray tear from the corner of her eye. "This is all just so perfect."

I retreat even further. "I... wait... it's not—" But I can't get my words out. Everything's happening too fast, and I'm still half asleep, tired from being up through the night feeding a newborn. This wasn't the plan. I told them I'd let them know when I was ready. I should have known Mom wouldn't respect my wishes.

She's right on top of me now, and there's nowhere for me to retreat.

As Mom leans in closer, her smile drops flat quicker than a skydiver in free fall. She brings a hand to her mouth. "Oh my! He's... he's Black?" She whispers it, as though not wanting to offend the infant.

"Yes. I mean, I don't know, I—"

"You don't know?"

"Well, I mean..." I'm fumbling, and now would be the perfect opportunity to come clean, but her comment pisses me off and I feel the need to defend this child. Who cares what his skin color is? "Yes, he's Black. Well, mixed race I think actually."

His exact genetic makeup, I can't be certain, but the baby's coloring is beautiful. Like warm terra-cotta, made only richer by his deep brown eyes and rosebud lips. A stark contrast to the fair-skinned, oatmeal-haired Connallys, who require the highest SPF to survive the summer months. We're of the ghostly variety, Nordic ancestors mixed in there somewhere, although Becky always manages to have a healthy glow, because of course she does.

Mom catches a look on my face and backtracks. "Oh! Well, I—that's just not what I was expecting is all."

"It doesn't matter," Dad says, leaning in, placing a massive hand on the baby's head. A gentle giant, that one.

Mom balks. "Of course not! That's not what I meant. You know I have friends of all colors."

The Asian nail tech doesn't count, I want to say but don't. I keep my eyes down, not wanting to let Mom's words sting, even though they do a little. Racist is not a word I'd use to describe her, and she would never intentionally hurt someone. But implicit racial bias is part of all of us. She's a product of her generation and the very privileged white community she's inhabited for most of her life. I can't fault her for that. A conversation maybe—but now's not the time.

"Listen, you guys," I say. "There's something I need to tell you." My throat is closing in on my words, threatening to cage them in. They're going to be so disappointed in me. No, forget disappointed—more like embarrassed, shocked. Shamed. *How could you not call right away?* That's what it'll be. I can hear the reactions in my head: *This is not how we raised you. How could you do such a thing? Cate, who are you?*

But it's like they don't hear me. I'm speaking to the wall. They've got a one-track focus, and it's currently wrapped snugly in the bend of my arm. I could blurt it all out right this second and it wouldn't process. They're lovestruck.

Mom turns to Dad. "Let's wash our hands, Henry. I need to hold that baby!"

They go to the kitchen and I'm left standing like someone who just had the rug pulled out from under them. I was supposed to wake up and call the police, to end this charade, despite the heartbreak that would accompany it. It was going to be hard, but it was right. Then I'd face the music of my actions. Instead, my parents derailed that plan. They're here. They think this child is mine. And every minute that passes makes it harder and harder to go back.

"Okay, me first," Mom says, returning to the living room.

She's like a giddy kid and, despite my anxiety, I can't help but grow at how happy this is making her. She's proud of me. Proud of this new milestone in my life. I'm now successful by this metric.

I hand the baby over on autopilot, then step back and watch the whole scene unfold like a movie. Only it's not a movie—this is real life. Dad wraps his arm around Mom's waist, the two of them staring into the face of what they think to be their newest grandchild. The pure elation is palpable, and I'm entranced.

"A new little prince," Mom purrs.

"Wait," Dad says. "We don't even know his name."

I see spots. His name? Of course he has one, and I'd wondered it myself. The note didn't say. Was he a Daniel or a Dillon? A Lucas or a Leo? Did he have a family name or something new and creative? It didn't matter—to me, he was perfect, and the last twenty-four hours have been nothing short of magical.

Temporary magic.

Mom and Dad eye me, and I realize it's now or never. Do it, Cate. Tell them the truth. But instead of thinking how to explain everything, my mind travels back to yesterday as I rocked the little bundle in the nursery and brainstormed names I'd choose if he were really mine. Not too trendy, not too unique. Something classic.

Only one felt right.

I lock eyes with Dad as a warm rush floods my body. "It's Henry. I named him after you."

Dad's neck goes red and his eyes well. He bites his bottom lip, the same way I do.

"Oh, Cate," Mom says, hand to her heart.

Dad steps close and pulls me into a side hug. We both look down into baby Henry's face. "Thank you, Birdie," he says softly. "This is one of the greatest honors of my life."

I swallow hard. The lie paints my tongue red. There is no going back.

TEN

It doesn't take long for Ryan to show up. "You guys must have had the same thought as me," he says excitedly, giving my parents a hug. "Leave it to Cate to keep us on our toes! I just couldn't wait for her to call." Then to me, "Sorry. You know I can't help it."

These people have no boundaries.

Another person to lie to. If my parents weren't bad enough, somehow Ryan feels worse. I'm sinking.

Mom's still holding Henry. I can't believe how easily his name has slipped into my vernacular. It's like he's always been here—was always meant to be here. Only he wasn't.

I'm in the corner chair, knees pulled up, practically biting away my cuticles but somehow managing to smile. I can't possibly look calm. They must think it's all just overwhelming. They're right—but in a different way.

"Did you hear? She named him Henry," Mom gushes.

"Oh my god, he's the perfect little Henry!" Ryan bounces in place like a rubber ball. "So respectable and cultured. It's like he's a little old man already." He turns to my dad. "What a fitting honor. You must be so proud."

Dad nods. "Another Henry Connally, who would have thunk it?"

Ryan rocks on his heels. He crosses his arms in that way one does when they're trying desperately to restrain from doing something—in this case, snatching a baby into an embrace and soaking up all that newborn goodness.

"You can hold him," Mom says with a laugh. "Here."

"Oh, but he looks so—"

She flaps her hand. "I've had him for almost two hours. It's fine."

She doesn't have to tell Ryan twice. He's as baby crazy as me, only he's still holding out for a partner first, whereas I missed the boat on that one. We'd always talked of being new parents at the same time, raising our kids as best friends, miniature versions of ourselves. There was even a time when as pimply teenagers my parents thought we'd end up together. Ryan and Cate, always joined at the hip. We'd have made the perfect couple, according to Mom. But that was before he came out to everyone. Mom dropped the idea pretty quickly after that, along with the majority of people who assume gay men will never have kids. Ryan doesn't talk about parenthood as openly as me, but I know his number-one goal in life is to be a dad. It's something that's bonded us over the years. He's got all the websites bookmarked on his laptop.

Ryan cradles Henry in his arms and sways naturally in place. "I can't believe he's finally here," he says, and I notice his chin quivering.

I stand up and slap his bicep. "Stop, you're going to make me cry." The dam is close to rupture. I'm holding on by a thread. If I cry, it'll all come out—everything, even the ugly.

"I'm just so happy for you."

His face is so genuine, filled with such pure happiness, just like my parents', I can't help but bask in it. Knowing the people you love are smiling because of you—it's the best feeling in the world. I never want to lose this. And it's all because of Henry. The power this itty-bitty person has to fill a room—I've never seen something so small prompt such emotion. It's like he's a little pop of dopamine, swaddled in Pima cotton.

We stand there, the three of us: Ryan, Henry, and me. Mom and Dad watch adoringly from across the room. An outsider would have thought we were one happy family unit, just like Mom predicted all those years ago. What seemed laughably impossible then feels different now.

Ryan runs a hand through Henry's dark hair, and I anticipate the question before it rolls from his lips. "So he's—"

"Mmm-hmm. Half, I think. Actually, maybe Hispanic."

"Think? Don't they tell you the birth parents' race?"

My nerves zap. I have got to stop saying "think." Adoptive parents are given all the details of the baby's history. I should clearly know this child's makeup.

"Well, yeah—" I stumble. "I mean, they do. I just haven't really gone through all the specifics in the paperwork." Warmth rushes to my face, and I hope the lie hasn't made me blush.

Ryan doesn't seem to pick up on my oversight. For someone who knows me better than anyone in the world, I'm surprised any of this is getting past him. There it is again: The ability of an eight-pound human to suspend all reason.

"Troy from work—his daughter's skin tone is just like this." He strokes Henry's cheek. "I'd kill for this natural tan."

"Gorgeous, isn't he?" The truth is, my guess is only a guess, based on miniature features.

The two of us coo over him for another few minutes until the doorbell rings. My knees buckle. Not again—I can't take any more surprises. It must be the police this time. There'd be no one else to expect except—

"That'll be Becky," Mom says, sashaying to the door.

I give her a look. I was supposed to be the one inviting people over.

"Oh, don't be mad, Cate. We're all just excited. You can't leave out your sister!"

Another person. I'm plunging deeper.

Becky flies through the door like an off-duty supermodel on her way to Starbucks. Even with her hair up on her head, ripped jeans covering her toned legs, and sneakers on her feet, she still looks incredible. When I dress like that, I look like I rolled out of bed and didn't even try. To be fair, I did roll out of bed pretty abruptly this morning. I'm still in my oversized T-shirt and sweatpants. And to think this is how I would have met my fate with the police. Talk about a perp walk.

"Where is he?" Becky squeals and then sets eyes on Henry, whom Ryan passed back to me, not wanting to be trampled by an overeager new aunt.

"Oh my goodness!" she says, and I wince. It occurs to me this is about the hundredth time I've heard this expression—or thought it myself—in the last twenty-four hours. It's the first thing people think, the first thing that escapes their lips, upon seeing a baby. The adorable deliciousness of a sweet-smelling bundle just wipes out any semblance of normal speech.

Becky drops her designer bag on the floor and comes up beside me.

"He's Black," Mom says bluntly, as though it were a badge she's proud to show off: *Look how cultured and modern I am with a Black grandson.* "Or maybe Latino," she adds.

The rest of us exchange glances. Ryan stifles a laugh.

"Yes, I can see that, Mom. But thank you for pointing it out."

"Isn't he perfect?" Ryan says. "They look like they were always supposed to be together." He squeezes my arm, a reminder not to let Mom get to me. He's been squeezing my arm like this for over half my life.

Becky presses her hands together in prayer. "Can I hold him?"

I don't want to let Henry go, don't want to let another person fall in love with him. I still need to go to the police. None of this should be happening. If another person holds him, they're dragged into this mess. But Becky's eyeing me impatiently.

"Sure."

I hand him over. Becky brings Henry to her shoulder, cradling his head with one hand and patting his bum with the other. She's such a natural. Mother incarnate. I'll never match her in the mothering department. I'm already starting out on the unethical side of things.

"Oh my goodness."

There it is again.

"Careful, Beck," Dad says. "You'll get baby fever."

"Too late," she says, and we all chuckle.

Henry starts to squirm. Too much passing around. I should have known better. Despite all Becky's most expert baby-soothing moves ("This always works—I can't believe he doesn't like the football hold"), his cries escalate. It makes me even more anxious to see him upset.

"Maybe he needs a new diaper," Becky says, and she goes to lay him on the couch, but I swoop in, remembering the healing belly button. A baby supposedly born twenty-four hours ago would still have a slimy stump where the umbilical cord was cut. There may not be many differences between a two-day-old and a two-week-old, but something like this is a dead giveaway. What else will I have to hide?

"Here, let me." I take him back and bounce him in place, giving little shushes in his ear. Within seconds, he calms.

I calmed him. It was me he wanted. He knows me. I feel weightless. What parent wouldn't want this feeling? I think of the note with the black sparrow. *Please take him.* I don't understand how anyone could write those three little words—it seems so incomprehensible.

"He's probably hungry again," I say, followed quickly with, "Damn." I used the last packet of formula from the diaper bag at six this morning. Shit, I'm not prepared for this. Once again, it wasn't supposed to be a problem. There was enough formula to get through the night, and then the baby would be in police custody.

"They didn't send you home with some from the hospital?" Becky says.

Oh no. Think fast. "Um... They were out." Another lie. Do labor and delivery hospitals run out of infant formula? I doubt it. Enough with the questions!

She gives me a curious look but just as quickly rushes to the door. "Don't worry," she says, with a dismissive wave, "I brought some. And diapers. And wipes. It never hurts to have lots of backup! I made a Target run while Shane has the boys at basketball practice." She flashes that megawatt smile, and our parents bloom. Becky to the rescue again. Becky, the dependable one.

"Thanks," I mumble.

She comes back in with two huge boxes of newborn diapers and wipes—the expensive kind, not the grocery-store brand I'd probably have bought—and a canister of formula.

"How many ounces is he drinking?" Becky says, passing me to go to the kitchen. I follow like an incompetent child. She tears the lid off the canister and starts to scoop the white powder into a bottle.

"I can do it," I say.

"Don't worry—I've made thousands of bottles; I can practically do it in my sleep." She adds another scoop.

"No really, I got it." This time it's more forceful, with a step forward to boot. I grab the bottle from her.

She raises both hands, palms out—"Just trying to help"—before returning to the living room with everyone else, and leaving Henry and me alone in the kitchen. He's upset again, and I work as fast as I can to fill his bottle with one hand. This was too long of a stretch without eating. Mom-guilt flares hard. "It's coming, buddy," I say.

What is happening? Why am I still pretending this is real? Because it feels real, that's why. If I block out that disappointing phone call, the second failed adoption, and then my surprise visitor, it's surprisingly easy to create a storyline in my head. I left to pick up a baby and came home with a baby. No one cares about the murky middle. Once there's a baby in the picture, all those details melt away.

I pop the lid back on the formula. Shake, test, insert, breathe. The crying stops. Jesus, babies really get *hangry*. I lean down and kiss his forehead. "Better?"

Bottle happily in his mouth, we rejoin the group. I toss around an idea in my head: What if Henry really was mine? What if I kept him—not just for one night but forever?

ELEVEN

The four of them stick around all day. I'm burned out from lack of sleep and the mental gymnastics of my current existence. Never have I felt so torn over what to do. The internal debate has zapped me. I can barely keep my eyes open. But something about this feels safe, here in my house with my closest people. Like nothing can touch us if we stay just like this. I can close my eyes and not worry that I'll wake up and Henry will be gone.

While I doze on the couch, they play pass-the-baby. No one can get enough of him, and I'm struck by how incomprehensibly normal it all feels. This is what families do when a new baby comes home. Sit around, stare and talk, high on the most potent drug I've ever tasted: baby love. Feed, diaper, sleep, repeat. It's easy and predictable in the most natural of ways, and before you know it, an entire day has passed.

The sun sets by five, dropping down into the frosty horizon and blanketing the street in silhouette. Mom and Becky set my small four-person table for dinner. The placemats I've had for years but never use touch at the corners. Dad rolls my computer chair in for the fifth spot, insisting on taking it even though it's lower than the rest. We pass the lasagna right to left, followed by a tossed salad and perfectly crisp asparagus spears. Cooking is another thing Mom can check off her list of perfections. I grew up with meals from Julia Child's cookbooks, sauces made from scratch, and seasonings I couldn't pronounce. There weren't leftovers because we'd devour it all. It never occurred to me that other families didn't eat like this—didn't have the means to.

I serve myself enough to appease Mom but not enough to warrant criticism, doubtful I'll even be able to take a bite. Guilt has a funny way about that. I continually glance at Henry in the bouncer chair a few feet from the table. He doesn't make a peep the entire meal. An angel baby.

"Unreal how much they sleep," Ryan says, to which Becky responds with a mini dissertation of newborn development and nap schedules—because, you know, she is an expert.

"Enjoy it while it lasts," she says. "Those first few days are golden. But just wait. They start to wake up. And then shit hits the fan."

"Becky, don't say 'shit,'" Mom inserts without a beat, like Becky is seventeen instead of thirty-seven. It's a quiet joy on the rare occasion Becky gets scolded.

"It's like their internal clocks are completely backwards. Sleep all day, up all night. Out of nowhere—boom. If you want help with sleep training, Cate, just ask. I've got a great book, all the important parts highlighted. I make sure to dog-ear my favorite pages."

I nod.

"The boys are amazing sleepers," Mom says, like I've never heard of Becky's magic touch to get babies to sleep through the night by six weeks. "I'd take her advice if I were you, Catie."

"Got it," I say, shoving a bite in my mouth to block the real response that wants to come out: *I can parent just as well as*

Becky, thankyouverymuch. Lack of sleep is to be expected, but how hard can it really be?

Becky is going on about the four-month sleep regression. How awful it is, how out-of-the-blue, how she and Shane spent a week getting no more than four hours a night. But I'm not thinking about sleep—or lack thereof. I'm wrapping my head around the idea of having a four-month-old at all. Henry's a newborn now, but soon he'll be a month, and then four, and then a whole year. I've set this train on its course, and it's a lie I'll have to navigate the rest of my life.

Is a lie worth it when it gets you what you've always wanted? There are kinks I'm going to have to work out, a story I will have to make sure is iron-clad.

Ryan leans back in his chair, hands to his belly. "Delicious as always, Marcia."

We all echo the sentiment. Yes, delicious, you've outdone yourself again.

"It was nothing," Mom says, words of affirmation her love language.

We sit for a while, stuffed to the brim—them with lasagna, me with turmoil—until Dad excuses himself from the table. "Be right back," he says, and there's a glint in his eye like he's up to something. He returns a minute later with a bottle of champagne, holds it up like he's presenting it to the table.

My mouth drops open. "Is that—"

"The '98 Dom Perignon, yes." He stands tall, a soft smile on his face. "I've been saving it for just the right moment. I didn't know what exactly but was certain the universe would tell me. Now I know—today's the day."

I sit up straight and feel my eyes tingle at the corners. He's picked me. My baby's arrival. Not the boys, his princes, not even Becky. This moment, his eldest daughter finally realizing her life-long dream of motherhood. What should feel like an honor leaves a sourness in my mouth. I take a sip of water to wash it away.

Dad pops the cork, making everyone but Henry jump. Becky giggles. He pours the bubbly into the random assortment of glasses Mom's found in my kitchen. Mismatched wine glasses, one engraved with "It's five o'clock somewhere," a pair of plastic champagne flutes.

As the leader of our family, Dad raises his first. We all follow suit, arms outstretched to the center of the table. I'm ready for him to make a sweet toast to Henry, the newest member of our family, his youngest grandson, the boy who shares his name. How special this moment will be.

Instead, he takes a different turn.

"To Cate, my beautiful firstborn. The one who made me a father and who now is a mother herself. I couldn't be more proud of my little Birdie."

Nothing about Henry. This toast is just for me. He chose this moment to focus on his daughter instead, somehow knowing I needed the outward adoration far more than a newborn who couldn't understand.

It makes me shrink instead of grow.

There are tears in his eyes and he doesn't even try to blink them away. Everyone looks to me with smiles, like I was just awarded the medal of honor. But I stare right at the first man I ever loved and wish this feeling would last forever.

"Thank you," I mouth, because no sound will come out.

"Cheers!"

We all take a sip. The bubbles dance on my lips, the velvety liquid at first sweet, followed by a yeasty aftertaste—a metaphoric parallel to the last two days, only in reverse. It all went from sweet to bitter to sweet again, and now with my family surrounding me, and this baby at my side, that awful morning feels a million miles away—an eon that's passed from dark to light.

I look to Henry again and a flood of fervor lifts my soul. I push away any lingering conscience. The note told me to take him, so I did. Whoever it was needed help, and they chose me. This is where I'm supposed to be. This is my child. I am his mother now.

I did the right thing.

Believe it, believe it, believe it.

I do.

Radiant faces stare at me from around the table. They're proud of me. Mom's proud of me. And I have a baby—finally, a baby. It's all I've ever wanted. If this is what soaring is like, I never want to come down.

I take another sip of champagne, let it sparkle against my tongue. This time, there are only fruity notes, nothing sharp.

TWELVE

MY ANGEL BABY HAS A DEMON INSIDE HIM.

Henry screamed from nine to midnight, passed out for two hours, then did it again from two to four. I thought I was going mad. All those baby-shakers in jail? I get it. Of course I'd never do it, I'd never actually shake a baby... but there's a fine line between sane and insane.

We paced the house. We bounced. We swaddled. We ate. We shit our pants and got cleaned up again. It was like he was crying for no good reason. "What do you want?" I moaned at one point. My phone has fifteen browser tabs open to various baby sites I hope will give me the answers to all my questions.

"Babies cry—that's what they do," I remember hearing Mom tell Becky when Landon was born.

Becky had a normal case of the baby blues, but after a couple weeks, the clouds parted and he'd started sleeping for longer stretches at night. I didn't get it then—of course I didn't; how could I? How could anyone who's never been through it? I sure do now. This middle-of-the-night madness—it's no joke.

Stay calm, I told myself on repeat, as the little lamb clock inched along. Tick, tick, tick. Minute by minute, second by second. Stay calm, that's the mantra here. Because if I don't say it over and over, then the other thoughts will come. The ones that say "This is karma" and "You're going to regret this." And I don't want to let those thoughts in.

It was trying and it was taxing, but it was temporary.

As the sun rose, so did my spirits. Darkness only intensifies anxiety. Things are always worse in the night. But in those early hours when Henry finally dozed back off again and I crashed into bed, it felt as though the light would take away the stress of nighttime and bring with it another chance to do things again. I didn't know what I'd do differently, but the mere chance to try alleviated the worry. Like childbirth—so I'd heard —the minute the pain is over, you say you'd do it all again. It was all worth it.

You can do this, you can do this.

Now, with Henry in his bouncer at my feet, I swipe concealer under my eyes. Can bags be darker after only two nights of new motherhood? Impossible. But also—I lean closer to the mirror—quite possible. Oof.

Henry gives a little grunt, his mouth curling in what I now know is his pre-cry face. It's incredible how well we've gotten to know each other in such a short amount of time.

"No you don't, sir," I say, and stretch my leg to rock his seat with my foot. His frown melts away, happily distracted with the motion. Look at me—multitasking mama. I've so got this.

It's day three as a mom. Today's agenda is simple: Hit up the grocery store. Formula for Henry. Chocolate in all its forms for me. Saviors in the form of nourishment.

A text appears on my phone from Jill Hughes, my neighbor two houses down.

Congratulations, mama! Neighborhood meal train coming your way!

My gut clenches. How does she know about Henry already?

Another text, this time from the new couple across the street: *Congrats, Cate!*

What? They barely know me. We haven't even been outside. Something's up—and it's not good. Perhaps I thought I could keep Henry in a private little bubble forever but not with the neighbors starting to find out about him. Baby news is like a wildfire—it spreads before you have a chance to tame it. This is a narrative I need to control.

I lift Henry and head downstairs. I peer through the window on one side of the front door, expecting what? A caravan of neighbors? There are no people—but the yard isn't empty.

"She didn't," I say.

Oh, but yes she did. Sometime in the span of when she left here last night and the pink hours of the morning, Mom planted a massive sign in my front yard. I can read it from behind: "Welcome Baby." There's a bushel of balloons tied to my front banister, featuring a giant mylar rattle surrounded by an ombre of blues. I know it was Mom. She's the type to decorate your office for your birthday (me, when I turned thirty) or write on your car with window markers (Becky's for her wedding). The woman can't help herself. She calls it pride; we call it embarrassing.

I'm filled with contradicting emotion, both grateful for her happiness but also hesitant about this invasion of privacy. Maybe I don't want my whole street to know I now have a baby. At least not yet—not until I've got a foolproof story cemented in my brain. That's also on today's agenda. Something shifted after our family dinner and Dad's toast. No more should-haves or would-haves. This is it. Henry's here, and I need to start reframing my mindset.

Now, Mom's lawn announcement kicks it into high gear. The neighborhood knows.

Thanks so much! I reply to both. An acknowledgment without giving away too much.

"Well," I say to Henry, who's peeking over my shoulder. "A meal train. I guess I don't need to cook for the next week." I give the air a little fist pump, as though it would make him laugh. This new-mom thing isn't so bad! Well, except for the sleep deprivation and the persistent checking of the news. I'm constantly on the lookout for missing-baby alerts, for someone to show up at my door wanting him back. But I'll get used to it. I have to get used to it. If only my parental leave lasted longer than eight weeks. If only we could stay here like this forever.

I load Henry into the car and we head to the supermarket a few miles from my house because despite dinners coming my way from neighbors, I still need the basics. The sun is out, a rare treat for January in Ohio. I try to soak in its positive energy, bask in its confidence. That is, until I get a glimpse of Henry in the mirror attached to the headrest and see his head completely folded to one side, ear practically lying on his shoulder. I pull over and circle the car, then take two gentle hands and readjust his little head so it's straight. "There," I say. But within seconds, it's flopped down again, and I'm left with worry that I've done something wrong in the process of buckling him in.

A quick text to Becky—begrudgingly but knowing she's my greatest resource—alleviates my fear.

It's like their necks have no bones, she writes back. *Don't worry. Totally fine.*

It's our first time leaving the house, and while it feels incredible to get some fresh air and see different surroundings outside my four walls, nerves are eating my stomach. Maybe I'm not as confident as I thought. What's more, we're not protected out here. There are people—people we don't know who might know something we don't. People who might stare and ask questions expecting answers. I blast the air conditioning and aim it directly at my face.

You got this, Cate.

The story is simple really. I've practiced it a dozen times this morning until it felt solid. I got the call, drove to the hospital, picked up Henry, and have spent the last three days in new-mommy bliss. Yes, he's biracial. No, there's no father in the picture. Yes, we're all thrilled. The end. Who's going to fact-check something that sounds so logical?

Believe it, believe it, believe it.

But what would be even better would be if I had proof—even fake proof. A birth certificate. I make a mental note to address this later.

I turn up the music, let the familiar rhythm set a sense of ease. Here we are, mother and son, making a shopping trip. Women have done this very thing for hundreds, if not thousands, of years before me. And now it's my turn. I look into the back seat and catch a quick glimpse of his reflection. I smile and let out a long exhale. Something so simple as a run to the store feels utterly new and exciting with a small person in tow. My little sidekick.

At the store, I put his car seat in the buggy of the cart, not on top by the handle—mommy bloggers say that's a no-no. Very unsafe. The motion of the cart keeps him asleep, so I meander the aisles, tossing in a mixture of healthy and junk food. Brown rice balanced out with Cheez-Its, bag of leafy romaine paired with full-fat ice cream. It's all about moderation.

"Cate?"

A woman's voice snaps me out of my trance of deciding which chips would go best with a tub of sour-cream-and-onion dip. I turn. It's Aimee, former high-school-friend-turned-acquaintance. We'd once been so close we compared blow-job stories. Now, I couldn't even say what she does for a living.

"Aimee, hi!" I give a closed-mouth smile, trying to

remember if I brushed my teeth this morning. I don't think I did.

"I had no idea you had a baby!"

The storyline runs through my head. I'm ready to recite it at a moment's notice but instead simply say, "Yep."

She takes another two steps closer and leans to see Henry. "He's adorable."

Heart on fire. My child is adorable.

She does a quick glance at my ring finger but isn't smooth enough for me not to notice. Nope, not married, I feel like saying. She doesn't ask, and I don't offer. I'd like to think my generation is much more open than my parents' to alternative family paths. Marcia probably still thinks I'm destined for eternal damnation, but is my life really that sinful compared to the people out there who have kids and treat them like shit? Doesn't one good parent outweigh two bad ones?

"What's his name?" Aimee says.

"Henry. After my dad."

"So sweet! They must be so happy."

I nod. This is such a new feeling, this goodwill from others —all because I have entered a new club: Motherhood. I'm one of them. I'm included now. I stand a little taller, my feet feeling like they're lifting off the floor.

If only they knew the struggle it's been to get here.

So, now, Aimee either thinks I got knocked up or Henry is adopted. She's considerate enough not to ask.

"We're all thrilled," I say.

She takes another look at Henry—people just love staring at babies. How good it feels to be met not with sympathy but adoration. I imagine how happy everyone will feel for me. How thrilled my OB-GYN Dr. Handrian will be. His nurse, the young woman who'd listened to so many devastating conversations about my condition—she can rest easy, knowing one more patient's problems are solved.

Aimee is still talking, and I snap out of my joyful daydream. "We have a local mommy group that meets twice a month. You should totally come! My kids are a little bit older now, but there are a few new moms with babies. I think Maddy's only twenty-six, but she's sweet, and anyways, all we do is talk about mom stuff so it doesn't matter."

"That would be... fun," I say, though I have no intention of attending. The thought of all those gawking faces makes my hands sweat. Too many people with too many questions. The basics of my story are good; I don't want to think on my feet any further than that. What if I mess up and call my own bluff? No, home is where we're safe. Just the two of us. Maybe things will die down once the baby phase passes, once time has moved farther away from birth. No one cares about birth stories once a child is in preschool. There are too many other life experiences to talk about—friends and playdates and T-ball. For now, there's nothing else a newborn brings to the table except how he got here.

"Well, see ya around," Aimee says, turning and taking her bouncing brown ponytail with her. We've reached the extent of our acquaintanceship.

The further she gets, the more I can breathe again. Maybe coming out in public wasn't such a great idea after all. I give my hands a shake and re-grip the cart. This is real life, and we need to do real-life things.

Henry and I finish shopping, his car seat surrounded by all our essentials. The gray-haired woman behind the cash register makes eyes at Henry as we file through the line. Her eyes bounce back and forth between us, and I imagine what must be going through her aging baby-boomer brain.

Yes, Ruth, he's mine.

A high-school-aged boy bags the groceries into my reusable totes. "Your son's really cute," he says.

Gray lady gives him a disapproving look, like me and my

biracial baby are somehow tainting this teenager's wholesome life experience. Welcome to the twenty-first century, Ruth. Families come in all shapes and sizes.

"Thank you," I say to him. I sound like a broken record, accepting all these compliments. It hasn't gotten old.

By the time we get home, unload the car, and put everything away, I'm drenched in sweat and Henry's ready for a bottle. I feed him in the living-room recliner and we rock in silence.

Aimee's words ring in my ears. *I had no idea you had a baby.*

I can't keep him a secret forever. This whole paranoia about living in a bubble isn't sustainable. Maybe I should introduce Henry to the world. Show everyone I've joined the mom club. Hiding him seems even more suspicious. Who would publicize a baby they'd kept unethically? That makes zero sense. I reason it all into justification. Letting people know about him actually takes the target further off my back.

Henry's so peaceful in my arms. I grab my phone and snap a picture, then crop it close so it's only his little hand resting against the soft cotton of his pale yellow sleeper. No face, no identity. Let's not go too far too soon. Just enough to share my joy. I post it to social media with the caption, "Introducing my little Henry. Sometimes the best gifts are worth waiting for."

Within minutes the image is flooded with likes and comments. Turns out birth announcements are one of the biggest highs on earth.

That evening I type the most unimaginable Google search into a private browser: How to get a birth certificate. The first results are government sites for ordering legitimate replacements or making corrections to existing records. That's not what I need. I tweak my search: How to buy a birth certificate.

Bingo.

The top result hits the nail on the head, its big blue text screaming at me from the screen:

Realistic Fake Birth Certificates starting at only $49 each! Comes with Raised Seal and Printed on Premium Paper. Free Shipping!

I click and order with a foul taste in my mouth, all the while convincing myself it's for Henry's sake.

THIRTEEN

I HAVEN'T SHOWERED SINCE FRIDAY. OR WAS IT THURSDAY? Wait, what is today? I tick off the days of the week on my fingers. Tuesday, today's Tuesday. Henry's been here for four days—er, is it five? My brain is complete mush. Simple math is now a foreign language.

I knew the newborn phase would shake up my sleep routine, but holy hell, I didn't realize it would be quite so extreme. It's like the child is a vampire—he comes awake when the sun goes down. C'mon, kid, you're killing me.

I'd be lying if I said there weren't one or two moments when I wanted to scream, to drop to my knees, and beg him: Please just go to sleep! But those moments have been fleeting. Mostly, I'm a mix between almost calm and borderline freakout. A walking zombie but a functioning one. I remind myself that this is exactly what I wanted, exactly what I'd been praying for. Well—almost.

In these short few days (and nights), I've learned what Henry likes. Swaddled with arms in, not out. A bottle the minute he decides he's hungry. Doesn't mind a wet diaper, but poop—that's a hard no. He likes to be held up on my shoulder, looking back, not cradled in a traditional baby pose. For this reason, I see more of the side and back of his head than I do his face. But when he naps, I wrap him in a light blanket and stare at the whole of him, watch his expressions go from happy to sad to happy again all while in dreamland. He likes the baby swing but loves his mama's arms more.

I take a massive yawn and press my fingers to my eye sockets. Sleep when the baby sleeps—that's the classic advice. I heard it endless times when Becky's boys were born, and now it's my turn. Only, it's not that easy. There's still stuff to do—laundry, last night's dishes—and I've even ticked off a few boxes on my to-do list at work. Mom thinks I'm crazy, but if I truly take off the full eight weeks, I'll be too far behind to ever catch up. Corporate America doesn't stop just because a baby enters the chat. Plus, after nearly twenty years of full-time work, it's hard for me to just drop everything, as much as I'd love to. I'd always pictured myself as a working mom, part by choice, part by need.

Which is how I end up here most days: Sitting on the couch in my pajamas while Henry naps. I scroll Facebook, catching the occasional status update but really doing brand digging. Even though Facebook's not nearly as hot as other platforms, most companies still have a presence, and this is where I get some of my best ideas for new graphics and ad campaigns.

The phone rings—I swear Ryan is the only person my age who still likes having phone conversations.

"Hey," I say. "What's up?"

"How's my favorite little nugget doing?"

"My pits stink, and I'm pretty sure I could mold a flamingo with my hair, but otherwise okay, thanks for asking."

"Very funny."

I laugh. "He's fine. Sleeping. Then he'll eat, then he'll poop, then he'll sleep again. It's all very exciting."

"Want company? I'll bring the rosé."

Company means more façade. It means I have to be on. No slip-ups. But I can't stay in this cocoon forever. I have to act like my normal self or else my family will start to wonder, which is why I respond, "Say no more."

"Good. Be there in ten."

We hang up, and I stare at the phone. There's a certain nasty feeling that comes with deceiving your best friend. This lie is growing, layering. Will they ever forgive me? I shake the question from my head. There's nothing to forgive if they never find out in the first place.

Again, the image of the hooded woman comes to me, but this time she's not careless but desperate. Hopeless and out of options. Who could this person be? I wrack my brain, flicking through anyone I've come in contact with like a Rolodex. I can't recall anyone who was recently pregnant. Then, a sharp breath. What about the woman at the coffee shop? I'd commented on her adorable belly a few months ago. I try to pinpoint how far along she was. Could she be Henry's mother? It seems farfetched. I was just a random customer.

I've spent far too much time searching birth records far and wide, looking for anything that will click. But there's too many, and I don't even know when his actual birthday is.

Whoever it was, and why they chose me, I have no idea. But it's thoughts like this that put my conscience in a wrench. What if she was doing the best thing for her baby? What if I could somehow help in reuniting them? I try to form a picture of Henry's birth parents. Does he have his father's strong brow? His mother's dimple? Who are these people who could bring a life into the world and then abandon it so quickly?

I shake the unease from my mind and reach up under my shirt to run a baby wipe over my armpits. The past is the past—there's no changing it. Time to look forward. In the grand scheme of everything, we both did wrongs—she left her baby, and I took him in—but whose wrong is worse? I'm picking up the job she wasn't able to carry out, and in a way, I'd like to think she'd thank me.

One son, two mothers, and a whole lot of mess in the middle.

FOURTEEN

"I LOOK GOOD WITH A BABY, DON'T I?" RYAN HAS HENRY IN the carrier affixed to his chest. He grabs a wooden serving spoon and circles it above the stove, the chef of an imaginary meal. "See? I could totally do this."

I snort. "Very Mr. Mom."

"Work, cook, parent—I'm basically a pro."

"What's stopping you then?" It's a rhetorical question.

He gives me that you-already-know-the-answer look. "Someday," he says.

"Someday might never come if you don't just do it. You've got to be proactive. If it's something you want, then just do it. That's what I did."

In a roundabout way. Henry didn't come to me in the way I always envisioned, but here he is, and I wouldn't have him at all if I'd called the authorities. Can't Ryan see how great it all is?

"Maybe you're just braver than me."

"Oh please."

He jabs my arm. "Fatherhood's in my future, somehow. Hopefully sooner than later. I just need to figure out all the logistics."

"Like a man?" I put a hand on my hip.

"A man would be nice. Bonus points if he wears a size-twelve shoe."

"Well, take it from me, you don't need a partner to be a parent. Not in today's world anyways. Look at Henry and me—we're doing it on our own, and I couldn't be happier. This could be you too. We could be the single parents at the playground. The ones everyone whispers about."

Ryan says he's waiting for the perfect time. What I've tried to tell him is the perfect time doesn't exist.

"Anyway," I say, "there's a shitload of leftover chicken in the fridge. The neighbors are keeping us well fed. Help yourself."

He takes a cookie from a full Tupperware container someone dropped off. "This place is like carb central. Thank God you don't have baby weight to lose."

I give my belly a jiggle. "Yeah, just regular weight."

His shoulders shake with laughter, in turn rustling Henry from his sleep. "Oh, sorry, little man," Ryan says, lulling Henry with a few smooth sways.

We take our plates to the living room, where Ryan unhooks the carrier and lays Henry in the bouncer on the floor. This is so nice, the three of us, an easy night in. I could totally get used to this. Unless of course Ryan were to find someone. But I don't want to think about that now, not with how good this feels.

Ryan flips on the TV. The screen comes alive to a Lifetime movie.

"Oooh, I love this one," he says, pulling his feet up under him and balancing his plate on his knee. "It's the one where the nanny steals the baby. Can you even imagine?"

My heart plummets out of my ribcage. I can almost hear it splat on the floor. The real world is nudging its way into my little fantasy land and I don't like it. I've convinced myself this is real because I've had to—the lie is too deep now. But things like this—movies about women and babies who don't belong to them—remind me of the truth, and my part in it. This is real. This baby isn't mine, but I'm pretending he is. How much trouble could I get in? I imagine the punishment intensifying with each passing day. Keep the baby for a night, get a slap on the wrist. Keep the baby years, spend a decade in prison.

I try to steady my runaway heart rate. Play it cool, Cate. "Yeah, I've seen it. Let's watch something else." *Please. Anything else.*

"Aw, come on. It's so good. The dad looks just like Rob Lowe." There's a long pause while Ryan's engrossed in the film. Then, "Yup, here she goes. Can you believe she just takes him? Ahhh, I can't handle the tension!"

I clamp down on my tongue so hard I taste blood. Fuck, fuck, fuck. This wasn't how I envisioned it all. I thought my worries would just quietly go away. Or maybe I didn't really think it but hoped they would. No one's come looking for Henry yet, so who's to say anyone will?

I can't watch this. I reach for the remote.

"Let's change it," I say.

Ryan yanks it away. "Wait, we're just at the good part."

I shift uncomfortably. My eyes dart around. I look to Henry and stare hard, as though he'll defend me. *You did the right thing, Mama.*

Ryan's transfixed on the TV, as if this fictional movie were a live news conference. One of those true-crime stories that everyone gets wrapped up in, even more so when there's a child involved. The pregnant woman who's murdered, the young mom who smothers her baby and claims insanity. We're all drawn to the horror of it, putting ourselves in their shoes and declaring how it could never happen to us.

Until it does. Until a baby appears on an infertile woman's doorstep and she passes him off as hers. Until you start a lie without considering how big it could grow.

That's it. I snatch the remote and flick to another channel.

Any channel—anything but that. My hand is so sweaty, my fingers slip right off the button.

"Hey!" Ryan says.

"I can't watch that. It's too..." But I don't even know how to finish the sentence. Too what? Heart-wrenching? Soul-crushing?

Guilt-inducing?

"You used to love those movies," Ryan says.

I shake my head, unable to form the words, and do everything possible to accept the truth: Somewhere out there might be a family looking for a newborn baby boy. If I hadn't kept him, he could have been reunited with them.

Or would he have?

I flip the script. If it weren't for me, Henry would have frozen to death. Loving parents don't leave their baby alone in the cold and the hands of a stranger. There are always two sides to every story. I'm choosing to listen to the one where I'm not the monster.

A chill creeps up my core. All of a sudden, I want to feel Henry close to me. I need him in my arms, a justification for everything. I feel as though there's a big flashing sign above my head: It's me! I'm the one! The baby is here!

I swoop over to Henry and lift him from his seat. Ah, there. That's the reassurance I needed. We settle on the couch, and I tuck my legs up under me, nestling Henry into a little swaddle. He's safe. I'm safe. I'll do anything to keep it this way.

And yet...

Morality sits heavily on my shoulder, whispering in my ear. Liar, liar, liar.

Ryan flips through the channels, landing on an old Reese Witherspoon flick. "Hallelujah," he says. "Give me a man proposing in a Tiffany store any day."

I like this movie too, but I can't tear my gaze away from Henry enough to watch. His eyes are closed, his long dark lashes lying against his skin like a blanket. Where'd he get those lashes?

Something tugs on my conscience. Words are forming on my tongue—an admission. Do the right thing. Do it now. Nausea swirls like a hurricane.

I open my mouth to speak. "Ryan, I—" But then I stop. I brush my finger along Henry's palm and he instinctively grabs it.

"What is it?"

A long pause. A battle of good and evil. I can't win. "Never mind."

Ryan returns to the movie. "Your chicken's getting cold."

"It's fine."

The truth is, I no longer have an appetite.

FIFTEEN

Mom's voice floats through the house a little before ten. She's early, which should come as no surprise—Marcia Connally doesn't do late.

"I'm here!" she calls. "Cate?"

"Upstairs," I manage with a mouthful of toothpaste lather. I'm always two steps—or thirty minutes—behind this woman. Got asked to prom but wasn't prom queen. Stood in line for Adele tickets but wasn't first in line like she was for Carole King in 1973.

"There you are," she says, coming around the bathroom corner. Her perky smile drops. "Is that what you're wearing?"

I give myself a once-over. "Yes?"

"Oh."

"What's wrong with—"

"No, nothing." The smile returns. "You look... comfy."

The idea of leggings as pants is something Mom just can't quite wrap her head around. The only pull-on pants she owns are a crisp pair of striped pajama bottoms—and even those are nicer than most of my wardrobe. I'm pretty sure she irons them.

"Does Target have a new dress code I'm unaware of?" I say,

trying to keep my tone light, though my teeth grind. She provokes my defenses so easily.

Mom purses her lips, giving me that look she does so well. Drop the attitude, Cate. I hear one of her favorite phrases in my head: Appearances are a direct link to mindsets. Look good, feel good, do good. If only she could grasp my complete disinterest in appearances. After years of trying, I've lost the drive to impress anyone with what I look like. And a newborn certainly doesn't care.

I pull my hair into a ponytail and swipe on some Chapstick. Mom eyes me. I know she wants to say, "That's it?" what with her matte lipstick and color-matched eyeshadow. But some act of grace keeps her lips sealed. Hallelujah—I really didn't want to start the day on this foot.

"Let me just answer this email real quick and then we can go," I say, tapping on my phone.

"You're still working?" The look on her face is as if I had three heads. "You're supposed to be on maternity leave."

"I am. It's just a few emails here and there. Darci's been picking up most of my load, but I don't want to put everything on her. Plus, that promotion is coming—I can feel it. I have to stay connected so I'm not too far behind when I go back."

"But that's not for weeks, right?" She brings a hand to her heart. "I can't imagine going back to work after having a baby."

Grind. Clench.

"Not everyone has that luxury, Mom."

"Oh sure, I know that. I just mean, it must be so hard. I loved being home with you girls is all."

I want to point out that she had Dad—and his comfortable salary—which allowed her to stay home, but that would only reinforce my husband deficiency, my solo-by-choice status that's somehow equivalent to a felony.

Instead, I change the subject. "I can't forget to grab the next-size diapers—he's already growing out of newborns. Can you believe it? It's only been a week. And he could use a couple more sleeper sets."

"Blue!" she calls, halfway down the hall toward the nursery. "Enough with the gender-neutral stuff. Too much gray and cream."

I roll my eyes and take a deep breath.

Her voice elevates in pitch, and I know she's talking to Henry now. "Boys wear blue, don't they? Yes, they do. Oh, come here, you sweet angel. Grandma's going to take you shopping."

I poke my head around the door frame. Mom has lifted Henry from his crib and is holding him out in front of her, cooing to his face. She leans forward and plants a string of kisses on his head. My heart actually inflates. Somehow my highly critical mother has turned into a doting grandmother.

Must be nice, kid.

"Okay, this is a definite yes." Mom holds up a miniature dress shirt and suspender set. I wrinkle my nose, but she flings it in the cart anyways.

"Where is he going to wear that?"

"Oh, who knows. But it's just too cute not to get."

"It's twenty-eight dollars."

She dismisses me with a wave and keeps shopping.

So far, I've found three zip-up sleepers and a six-pack of onesies—the blue-and-green color palette appeasing Mom although I would have preferred the trendier gray ones. It's all Henry needs. All these fancy clothes are for looks alone—there's nothing easier and more functional than a footed sleeper.

Mom tosses another tiny knit sweater in the cart.

"Mom!"

"Okay, fine. Let's browse the women's section," she says.

"I don't need anything." Though I'm happy to move away

from any more infant clothes I'll never put Henry in. It's funny, I thought I'd be the type to play dress-up and photoshoot with my kid, but this past week has shown me how impractical all that is.

"Need is subjective, honey. Everyone can use a new top." She gives my college sweatshirt a harsh eye.

My days of frivolous shopping are behind me. I have a child now, and I'd rather spend any extra money on him—even if it means my whites are a bit yellowed in the underarms and my leggings pill at the thighs.

Mom leads the way, and I dutifully follow, pushing the bright red cart that holds my sleeping son. I'm flying high on good spirits, until a woman passes and does a double take, popping my euphoria cloud and making me scoot behind a display stand. Could it be the person who left Henry? I peek out with one eye, but the woman is gone.

I breathe hard to calm myself. It's just everyday people out shopping. They're allowed to make eye contact. Relax, no one is out to get you.

While Mom grazes a rack of cardigans ("When you find something you love, you should own it in every color"), I run a hand across a table of sweaters I don't need, pretending to shop but really keeping a lookout. My positive self-talk isn't working. Is this ever going to feel normal? I wish I could get rid of the slow-blooming dread swirling in my core.

It's not long before I feel the weight of someone's eyes on me—again. I look up to find another fifty-ish woman with a short bob at the next table over. She's looking in Henry's direction. Then she takes a step toward us. Shit. My chest constricts. Instinct propels me in front of the cart, blocking her view. It startles the woman, and she abruptly stops.

"Sorry," she says, hands up defensively. "I have a staring problem when it comes to babies." Her face is friendly, her mouth pulled into a warm smile, and I retrace my thoughts to determine if that's how she looked before or if this is a coverup. Is she a good guy or a bad guy? Am I being paranoid? I give her a once-over. She seems too old to be a new mother—it can't be her.

This is getting out of hand. I need to relax.

"It's okay."

I can feel my shoulders soften, and I step to the side.

The woman comes forward again and leans to peer into the cart. "He has your little chin. Lucky you. None of my kids looked like me—my husband's genes are strong."

She smiles again, so I do too.

"Thank you," I say.

Henry has my chin—huh! It must be the angle, or the fact that newborns all look the same, their features not yet defined enough to tell who they resemble. Still, I take the likeness gladly. I momentarily let myself imagine what Henry might look like as a child, a teen, an adult. Maybe he really will have my pointy chin.

The woman stares for another beat, in that way baby-crazed women can't help. I should know—I'm one of them. I wonder what she's thinking. Me, this very white woman with a clearly darker-skinned child. There are pockets of the world where this is far from uncommon, where families look all sorts of ways. But not in upper-class, suburban Ohio. Not here. Henry and I, we stick out like a sore thumb—and that's scary. Maybe she thinks I'm in a mixed-race marriage. Without thinking, I curl my hand so she can't see my naked ring finger.

"Isn't he a doll?" Mom comes up beside me and looks lovingly into the cart.

"Adorable."

"Cate adopted him. She's a single mom."

My eyelids drop, unable to process my mother's need to highlight these facts of my life on a public stage. Thank you, Mom, for stating the obvious.

"Good for you," the woman says, though there's a rightful awkwardness to her tone, as if this personal information was handed to her like an unrequested stick of gum.

Mom gives my arm a little rub, and I open my eyes again. Inhale, exhale. Does Target sell alcohol?

"Henry's going to need a bottle soon," I say by way of getting out of this now-painful conversation.

"Okay, best be going then."

Mom tosses a yellow cardigan into the cart—I'm pretty sure she already owns an identical one—and we make our way to the checkout. I put the items on the belt and go for my wallet.

"I've got this," Mom says.

"What? No, I can get it." I'm perfectly capable of affording supplies for my own child.

"Don't argue, Cate. Let me buy something for my grandchild."

I hold out the suspender set. "You can get this. I've got the rest."

We're in a standoff, and finally Mom relents.

"Fine." She playfully rolls her eyes and pays for the adorable yet completely impractical outfit while I load the rest of my things on the belt. I engage my rhythmic breathing with each item. Why is it so hard to enjoy a simple outing with my mother?

Only lunch separates Henry and me from being home free. I can do it. I can handle Marcia Connally for another hour. In my heart, I know she means well, but that doesn't negate the fact that I start to itch after we've been together for more than fifteen minutes.

Cart loaded, we head to the automatic doors. Henry's still sound asleep. There's a lightness in my step—another successful outing. We're getting the hang of this. A man passes and, instead of darting my eyes, I meet his face and smile. I'm proud. I'm normal. He smiles in return. See? You've got this.

"Oh!" Mom says. "I almost forgot to tell you. I ran into Dr. Handrian yesterday and told her all about Henry."

"Mom," I say, slightly miffed.

"What? She was thrilled." She shrugs in defense of her good deed.

"It's my news to share, not yours."

She dismisses my concern. "Speaking of doctors, when is Henry's first appointment with the pediatrician?"

My body tingles. "I, uh... I'm not sure."

"Not sure?" She gives me a sharp look. "You called, didn't you?"

"Not yet."

"Cate, newborns have a very strict vaccination schedule."

"Right, of course. It's just been a busy few days and I forgot to call."

"Didn't the agency give you all his medical information? They should have done his first round of shots at the hospital, I think. What was his Apgar score?"

My heart rate is climbing again. "What are you, a doctor now?" I say as light as possible, yet with an undeniable edge to my voice.

Mom gives me a look. "These are normal questions, Cate. I don't know why you're getting all worked up about it."

"I'm not getting worked up."

"Well, I'd just think you'd know these things about your son, that's all. I would have been sure to ask—"

I cut her off. "Yes, I know. You would have asked all the right questions and got all the answers."

I push the cart faster, walking a few steps ahead, and can sense Mom's hurt over my shoulder. I don't mean to snap, but I can't help it. And the truth is that she's prying into dangerous territory. What happens when she wants to know more about that day? What if—God forbid—she ever ran into Kathleen?

"I'll call tomorrow," I promise. *After I get the birth certificate.*

I've walked past the pediatric office countless times on my way to obstetrics and fertility, the hospital layout a wicked reminder. I used to avert my eyes from the door covered with cartoon jungle animals. Now I'll be able to walk through that door, to the land of bubblegum-pink walls and superhero stickers. But despite the elation that comes with this thought, it's met equally with fear, as I keep coming back to the same question: Who would leave a baby on a doorstep? As much as I try, my mind won't let it go. I wonder what situation they must have been in and, more poignantly, will they be coming back?

I dismiss the dread with a long exhale. Focus on the positive, I tell myself. Henry is here, and he's yours. Our future is set. There are just a few technicalities in the way—but I don't have the mental capacity to think of that now. Marcia Connally has a way of draining me, and I just want to finish this outing and go home.

When we reach the car, I clip Henry's seat into its base and give him a soft kiss on the forehead. The smell of him relaxes me. But not for long, because as I'm rounding the car to the driver's side, I hear Mom say something about sending a thank-you card to the adoption agency.

SIXTEEN

My stomach crashes. "You what?" I say. I'm suddenly dizzy, my vision narrowing to a pinpoint. Is the car tilting?

"I said I'm going to mail a card to the agency. They've done so much for you. And finally, we all have our happy ending."

"No!" I shout, and she recoils, eyes wide. I soften. "Sorry. I mean, I'd rather you didn't."

"What? Why not? It's the polite thing to do." She's aghast, the woman who sends handwritten thank yous for just about everything.

A sparrow dives out of the sky and lands on the side mirror of the car next to us. It perches there, looking at me, its head tilting this way and that like it's scrutinizing me. I shiver and look away.

"It's just that..." I'm grasping for some veneer of an excuse, but nothing makes sense. What's the harm in sending a thank you? Nothing. "It's just that I already sent one." There. I hope it will not only suffice but also impress her.

"Well, there's nothing wrong with me sending one too, don't you think?"

"*Mom*," I snap. "Can't you just..." I'm clearly aggravated

now, but this is nothing new. In fact, it's par for the course with her and me.

Mom purses her lips. "Fine, fine. So much for a little appreciation."

The subject dropped, we pull from the parking lot in tense silence. Nausea replaces the dizziness. I'm getting tired of feeling so on edge all the time. Will it ever go away? Or is this my new life?

"Olive Garden?" Mom says.

"Actually," I say, "I'd rather just go home and get something to eat there." There's about zero food in my house—at least nothing Mom would consider a substantial meal—but the thought of being in public any longer makes my head spin. Our little safety bubble calls.

"But I thought we were having a lunch date, the three of us." She frowns and physically deflates in her seat. The disappointment sends a javelin through my heart. Why does it have such a hold on me? I know why: Because she can't just accept me at face value. Because I'm not a carbon copy of her.

"I'm whooped. Henry was up a lot last night. Can we just grab takeout instead? My treat?"

"Don't be silly."

She concedes, though I hear her mumble something about breadsticks as we turn toward home. I give a silent prayer of gratitude. I can't take any more paranoia today.

I watch Mom's car disappear down the road, heading back to her picture-perfect home where the closest thing to breaking the law is an episode of *Law & Order*.

I close the curtains with a swoosh then let out a long exhale. Henry's restless and fussy tonight. I give him gas drops and lay him on his back to bicycle his legs like Becky showed me ("Helps break up the bubbles"). After an hour he finally calms against my chest, his body my own personal heater in the dead of winter.

I want to bask in this moment, to really feel the glory of motherhood, but there's a massive stone wall blocking my way. I thought I'd be able to hurdle it. I thought I could let the "rights" of this situation outweigh the "wrongs." But here I am, baby on my chest, little fingers curled around the edge of my shirt's neckline like he's holding on for dear life. A phone in my hand, ready to dial.

A tear slips down my cheek. I need to turn myself in. Put an end to this before it gets any worse. What will be the repercussions? My chest tightens thinking of the possibilities. The massive fallout, not just for me but for my family. I cling to any thread of hope. They'd know it was all fueled by good intentions, right? I saved him. I am a good mother. It was all for him.

How long I hold my phone open to the dial pad, thumb hovering. I know this is the right thing to do, but why does it feel so unfair? My castle in the air is crashing down around me inch by inch, the closer I get to calling.

9—

Crumble.

I sniff. I don't want to do this, but I need to do this. Oh, but just a little bit longer. I inhale Henry's sweet hair. Close my eyes and rock some more. It's complete silence here in the nursery, the only sound the gentle whoosh of the rocker back and forth. It lulls us, this rhythmic motion. My eyes are tired, my mind weary.

1—

Crumble.

One more button. One more tap to finish this call, and then it'll be all over. A shudder runs up my spine. Then it will be all over! Henry, taken from me. Gone. I can't imagine not having him with me anymore. It's like he's always been here, always been my boy.

I hover, finger trembling. The last bit of my fortress stands. I either let it crumble completely, or I hold on, build it back up. Before I can tap that last button to seal my fate, my phone rings, startling me as much as a boogeyman hurtling from around the corner.

"Jesus," I breathe, letting my heart rate come back down. It's only Darci. Seeing her name flash across the screen is bittersweet, reminding me of the job I love but also that I won't be able to bask in maternity leave for much longer.

"Hi, Darc," I say. Aside from the flowers my team sent, it's been mostly quiet, them giving me the time and space a newborn requires.

"How's motherhood treating you?" she says. "Too bad we're all the way in Chicago—Henry will have to make his inaugural Zoom appearance as soon as you're back!"

I give a light laugh, though it feels forced. More people exposed to the lie.

"Listen," Darci continues, "I'd love to talk babies all day, but the truth is I have other news to share and don't want to take all your time."

There's a pause, almost like she wants me to guess it. "Okay," I say, to fill the silence.

"Congratulations, Cate. Your promotion was officially approved this morning and takes effect immediately. I signed off on it just a bit ago."

"Oh! Wow, thank you, Darci. I'm—I'm honored." I'd been hoping for this call, but now that it's come, it's met with an unexpected internal response. A slimy feeling comes over me with the clash of such recognition and reproach. There's deceit at the center of my character now, the kind of thing that doesn't get rewarded with a fancy new title.

"You deserve it, my friend. It's been an amazing decade working together."

I don't know quite what to say, so I merely murmur and

hope Darci equates it to new-mom debility. We exchange a few more niceties, until she says she'll let me go, for which I'm thankful.

When I hang up the call, the screen returns to the dial pad and I'm reminded what I was about to do when Darci interrupted. 911. There are two numbers still on the screen, the last one waiting to finish the magical code.

A yawn escapes my lips. I'm so, so tired. One more number. Push it, Cate. Push it.

Henry coos in his sleep. Turns his head so it's nestled into my collarbone. Another minute, just give me another minute. He's so peaceful. I close my eyes. My phone drops away.

SEVENTEEN

Three weeks later

THE THERMOMETER BEEP SOUNDS LIKE A PANIC BUTTON. Warning! Warning! Something is wrong here! Hundred and two point five. That's not good, not for anyone, but especially not for a human this little whose immune system is still developing. It kills me that I don't know Henry's exact age. But with my experience as an aunt, along with some deep Google research, I've guessed that he's probably about six weeks—which means he was born early January. A New Year baby. My perfect belated Christmas gift.

I think back to Ryan and I ringing in the new year and wondering whether it would be *the* year.

In the end, it was.

Only now, my New Year baby is screaming his head off and nothing I do soothes him. Not a bottle, not a diaper change, not hours and hours of pacing the house with him in my arms. How did I not consider this, the fact that he would eventually need medical care?

It's been four weeks and he's yet to see a doctor. I've rationalized it all away with the justification of the delayed immunization schedule. Google tells me it's a thing some parents opt for. Henry would have had the initial shots at birth. He could catch up once I got everything sorted and we got into more of a rhythm. Plus, he's been nothing but healthy this whole time. Not even as much as a runny nose or blemish to his perfect skin. But now, everything comes barreling at me, and I worry that maybe he should have been seeing a pediatrician all along. Suddenly I feel like the bad mom, instead of the woman who left him in the first place.

Sometime around one, Henry woke with piercing screams and that's when the witching hours began. I tried everything. But his cries were different than normal. More acute, with an edge that told me it wasn't just hunger. And along with it, fear. Fear in a new form. Fear that something was wrong with my baby.

By the time the sun rose this morning, I was delirious and Henry had popped a blood vessel in his right eye from crying. My T-shirt was drenched, his body like a little oven up against me, and it finally occurred to me to take his temperature.

Then I kicked myself for waiting so long. Maybe I'm not as natural at this as I thought.

The thermometer trembles in my hand. What is it they always say? Anything over one hundred degrees warrants a call to the doctor? This is significantly over one hundred. I hear Mom in my ear: *Call the pediatrician immediately!* An unwanted thought enters my mind: What would Becky do? In all her annoying perfectness, I still can't help but follow in the path she's already forged. If the boys were this sick would she have already called? Gone to the ER?

I bounce Henry in my arms. Sing a melodious lullaby. I offer another bottle, and he suckles for a moment before spitting it out with a fury that screams, *How dare you. This is not what I want.*

We should go. But here's the problem: I haven't established him with a pediatrician, nor do I have all the information to do so. Won't they need details of his birth? His vaccine history? Mom was right: I can't even answer the most basic questions about my own child. And how to pay? He's not on my insurance —that would require proof of adoption too. I don't think most doctors' offices take cash from walk-ins.

How was I even going to make this all work? Was Henry never going to see a doctor in his life? I think about all the documentation I'll have to forge. A false identity. I gag and put a hand to my mouth to stop anything from spewing out. I suddenly feel like this plan of mine wasn't so well thought out.

Think, Cate. Think. Your child needs medical attention. I pace the room.

Henry lets out another wail. His tears have long dried up so now he just looks like he's in agony without the salty proof. Where his eyes are dry, mine now well. "Please, Henry," I beg, desperately trying to get his pacifier past the thrust of his tongue. "Come on, buddy. We're supposed to be in this together." A drip of sweat travels down my cleavage, but since there's no bra there to catch it, it continues down over my belly and settles into the waistband of my sweatpants.

I dash to the medicine cabinet and grab the infant Tylenol— one thing Becky insisted I have. I read the dosage instructions and draw out the tiniest amount into the syringe before squirting it into Henry's mouth. About half makes it in, the rest dribbling out the side, down to his chin. The flavor must shock his senses because he stops crying, eyes open, and smacks his lips for only a few heavenly seconds before picking up where he left off, somewhere between alto and soprano.

"Please work, please work," I chant to myself.

We bounce through hours of early-morning infomercials selling Proactiv and ShamWow. His cries lessen with each minute, until finally his little body is all out of fight and he falls asleep. It's six forty-five in the morning and we've been up since one. Maybe the Tylenol will work. Maybe he'll sleep and wake up a happy baby again. Fevers come and go, right?

I don't dare try to put him down for fear he'll wake again, so I inch down onto the couch, lay my head back and close my eyes. If this isn't exhaustion, I don't know what is.

Our nap is short-lived. Henry's eyes fling open at the same time his cries start all over again. I jolt up, check the clock. Seven twenty-five.

No, no, no. How long will this go on? What happened to my content little angel?

I take his temperature again. Still at a hundred and two. Shouldn't the Tylenol be working by now? A sinking feeling takes over my body, like I'm slowly being sucked down by quicksand. I can't do this alone. Maybe I should call someone. But who? Mom? No. Becky? Hell no. I gulp away my fears. Just take it minute by minute, hour by hour. You've got this. Give the medicine time to do its job.

When lunchtime has come and gone, and I've still yet to eat anything all day, and Henry is still running a high fever, I admit defeat. This solitude is too much, and I'm sick knowing I've put off help for Henry based on my own selfish fears. What kind of mother does such a thing?

I call Mom. Each ring pulls on my heartstrings: I don't need you, but I desperately need you. She answers just before her voicemail picks up.

"Hi, sweetheart, you barely caught me—your father and I are just leaving to catch a matinee."

Henry's cries pierce through the line, and I don't even get a word in.

"Oh my! Sounds like someone's not very happy today. Poor guy, does he need a little grandma time?"

"He won't stop crying," I say, my chin quivering. I hate that I'm so vulnerable right now—that I can't handle this on my own.

That everything in my body wants to plead for my mother's help. The woman who knows how to fix anything.

"Well, that's what babies do, dear." I hear car keys jangle.

"No, I mean he's been crying for twelve hours straight. He has a high fever. The Tylenol's not helping."

"How high?"

"Over a hundred and two."

"Hundred and two?" The alarm in her voice makes me feel even worse. I shouldn't have let it go this long.

"Point five, to be exact."

"Cate, that's really high for a newborn. He seems irritated? You should definitely take him in. Fevers are dangerous. They can cause seizures and—"

"Don't scare me, Mom!"

"I'm not trying to—I'm just telling you the facts. Don't mess with fevers. Take him to see a doctor—today. Now."

I clamp down on my lip. The thousand reasons why this is impossible run through my head. "What, like the ER?"

"Just call the pediatrician—they should be able to get you in." The tone again—Cate, don't you know anything? "Do you want me to come over? I can go with you."

"No." I say it too fast. "We're fine. I'll call." The last thing I need is Mom to be witness to me stumbling through intake... or worse.

"Are you sure?"

"I'm sure."

"Keep me posted, okay? And don't let him out of your sight. If he starts shaking, make sure he can't hurt himself on anything, or swallow his ton—"

"Okay, Mom. Got it. I'll call you back later."

I hang up, feeling no better than before I called. Maybe that was a mistake. Now Mom's going to be paranoid and checking up on us every hour. She'll insist he sees a doctor—and then what's going to happen?

But Henry's not calming. His face is red, and I can feel the heat coming off his body. He needs to be seen. A good mother would do what it takes—even at her own detriment.

A good mother.

"Okay, little one," I say. "Okay."

If I'm going to take Henry in, I need to at least put a bra on. A shower would be preferred, but there's no time for that. Instead, I lay him on my bed while I pull a sports bra over my head, put on a fresh shirt, and slap on some deodorant. A baseball cap hides wildly greasy hair.

There's a lump in my throat, and it stings. I have to do this, have to get him help. Oh, why can't kids just be healthy all the time? I shake my head. There's no sense in useless wishing. Henry's clearly sick, and I don't want it to get worse. Heaven forbid Dr. Marcia is right. Some risks are too dangerous to take.

I dial the pediatrician's office. A recording answers, giving instructions on extensions, and finishes with, *if this is a life-threatening emergency, please go to your nearest emergency room.*

Is this a life-threatening emergency? Could he ride it out and be fine tomorrow? I don't know and I can't wait to find out.

It sounds like one big ominous hint. Like the movies when you know something bad is lurking in the basement, but the dumb actress goes anyway. Don't mess with fevers. Okay, Mom, I won't. I may have already done some dumb things, but this won't be another.

Without control, my mind goes to the gut-wrenching obituary I remember reading years ago in the paper. A toddler in a horrific accident. Far too young to die. Seeing that little face—it was so unnatural. I'm sick thinking of Henry being anywhere close to that.

I press "3" for the receptionist, and she answers in a sing-song voice. When I relay Henry's symptoms, the tone changes, and she replies with the three words I was dreading but knew I'd hear: *Bring him in.*

My breath is shallow. Like I could choke on it at any second.

But there's Henry, innocent and hurting, his very existence dependent on me. He wins. He'll always win.

"Okay, sweet boy," I say, picking him up from the bed. "Let's go."

EIGHTEEN

I DRIVE WITH ONE ARM STRETCHED BACK TO HOLD THE
pacifier in Henry's mouth. I've found my new talent: Contortionist. My leg—the one that's leveraging me, making my back
arch so I can reach—has cramped twice to the point I've had to
let go and sit properly enough for the pain to go away. Each
time, Henry promptly spits out the pacifier and screams. So I
reach back again. It's a talent I didn't know I'd ever need in life.
It also can't be safe to drive this way.

I don't care. It's better than the screaming.

"We're almost there, bud," I say as upbeat as possible,
though I'm sweating through my clean T-shirt again. Henry
doesn't give a shit about my tone or the words coming out of my
mouth. I could be cursing to the heavens and he'd still be wailing. Why did I wait so long? Guilt isn't strong enough a word in
a moment like this. A moment when your child's cry is piercing
daggers. I think of the note again and the mysterious person
who left it. They trusted me. Maybe they shouldn't have.

"Okay, here we are," I say, hoping he'll sense help is near.

We pull into the lot after what feels like an hour of road-
rage driving, where I'd weaved in and out of traffic. It's a

wonder I didn't get pulled over for speeding. I send up silent thanks to the sky. It's a small token, not adding a ticket on top of everything else, but feels like a win nonetheless.

I fling the car into park and open the door, letting out pounds of built-up pressure. When I dash around to get him, I stop in my tracks, fingertips on the handle. "You've got to be kidding me." He's passed out, pacifier dangling from his open mouth.

Murphy's Law of parenting. Becky's lamented all about this. When you want something to happen, it doesn't. When you don't, it does. Sort of like how a kid won't play with a toy for months then asks for it the minute you throw it away, or how your normally obedient child gives themselves bangs the night before picture day. Or how a baby cries the whole drive only to fall asleep two minutes before the destination. I used to think Becky was just being dramatic. Now I get it—it's real. I swear, if we go in there and his fever is suddenly gone, I'm going to be pissed. Relieved but pissed.

I pop the car seat out, hang it on the crook of my elbow, and walk toward the door. With each step, I question whether to keep going. He's calmed now—do we really need a doctor? Yes, I remind myself. Remember the twelve hours of crying and the dangerous fever? I draw a full breath and open the door.

To my surprise, there's only one other parent in the waiting room, a man with a curly-haired, snotty-nosed toddler on his lap. The girl coughs every five seconds. Her dad nods at me as if to say, *Great way to start the week, huh?* I thought this place would be packed. The lack of people is a welcome gift. Fewer eyes. Maybe we can slip in and out.

I go to the desk, set the car seat on the ground, Henry facing away from the man.

"What brings you in?" the receptionist asks. She looks up at me through purple-framed glasses attached to a beaded strap.

"He, uh—My son, he's got a bad fever. Seems really uncomfortable. Was up all night."

"How high?"

"Hundred and two point five."

She types on her computer, unfazed by the number that shook Mom. She must see a lot of really sick people come through these doors. Or maybe it's not as bad as I thought?

"Name?"

My tongue is stuck to the roof of my mouth. I force myself to speak. "Henry Connally." It's the first time I've said the two names together for anyone besides Dad, and something in me explodes like a firework. It sounds so right, so beautiful. The name living on.

Even though it's a lie.

My face flames. The room feels hotter than seconds ago. Should I have given a fake name? I'm reminded that Henry isn't even Henry. But Connally is very real. Connally is me. It's my family. It's traceable.

"Age?"

Focus, Cate. "He's, uh... six weeks."

"Did you bring his insurance card?"

Here we go. Hurdle number one. I squeeze and release my fist. At least I prepared for this one thing on the ride. I knew it would be coming.

"He's not on my insurance yet," I say like I'd practiced. No hesitancy, no doubt.

The woman looks up like I'm crazy, and I give a little laugh. "I sort of forgot about it, you know, after he was born. It was an adoption—the second actually. And this is the first time he's been sick, so..."

Ditzy blonde mom. I may be dumb, but dumb is not a crime. At least in her eyes.

She's back to typing, acrylic nails doing a tap dance across the keys. I hope she doesn't refuse to see us. My nerves stir again thinking of being turned away. Can they do that? Aren't they obligated to treat a sick child?

"Can I pay cash?" I ask. I'll gladly pay double if we can just see a doctor with no questions asked.

She tilts her head. "We don't usually do that."

"I know. I'm sorry. It's just—he's so sick, and—" I'm grasping for something, anything. But it's not fake desperation in my voice. This is real. I'm begging for the sake of Henry. Please let a doctor see him. "I'm planning to call the insurance today. Please..."

Then I see it, the thing I recognize so well: Pity. "I can check with the physician. Why don't you have a seat? Someone will be with you shortly, and we'll figure this all out before you leave. You can fill out the intake form after."

"Thank you," I say with the most genuine smile my tired face can manage. If I could reach through the window and kiss her, I would. "I really appreciate it."

Gratitude goes a long way. Maybe if I'm extra compliant, extra thankful, this will work. People are willing to help kind people. You scratch my back, I'll scratch yours. Only, I'm not giving this woman anything, and she has no obligation to appease me. Still, I let myself hold on to hope. Is it conceivable for Henry to get what he needs and the two of us return home all in one piece? It's the only thing I can focus on.

We sit a few seats down from the man and his toddler. The vinyl makes a squeak. I scan an array of tri-fold brochures. RSV, Covid-19, walking pneumonia, flu shots. Everything's anxiety-inducing. I turn my attention to *Dora the Explorer*, playing on a small flat screen fixed to the corner of the ceiling. The curly-haired girl is mesmerized.

"Vamanos!" Dora says with animated enthusiasm I can't quite stomach right now.

Yes, let's go, I think. Let's get this over with so I can help Henry and get us home.

I take a peek at him. His poor little cheeks are red and clammy. I think of what Mom said. I hope this fever hasn't done real damage. Landon and Owen had tons of fevers over the years and they're perfectly fine. Fevers are a normal part of childhood. But what if...? The thought of it being something worse, something really serious, makes my insides clench. I couldn't bear it if—

My phone rings and Mom's name flashes on the screen. I groan. As predicted, she's checking up every hour. If I don't answer, she'll panic. I'm already panicked enough; I don't need her to be the same.

The curly-headed girl's cough is so loud and repetitive it's like nails on a chalkboard. I need to answer Mom's call, if for nothing more than to assure her we're getting help, but I can't even hear myself think.

I stand and lift Henry in his car seat and go back into the hallway.

"We're at the doctor's," I say without a hello first.

"Oh good, I've been worried to death."

Henry jostles awake, drowsy still, and starts to whimper. "It's okay, buddy, we're almost there. Help is coming," I say. Best-case scenario, they send us home with a prescription and he gets his first dose within the hour. I can see the light at the end of the tunnel. Just need to get through this last thing.

Mom is going on about home remedies. Did I try a luke-warm bath? Am I making sure his clothes aren't too tight? How I should really get one of those advanced thermometers that are more accurate, because am I sure the one I have is sufficient? I try but can't get a word in. And that's when my attention is pulled in a different direction.

A door down the hall opens, and a young woman in scrubs comes our way. Her dark hair is piled on her head in a messy top-knot. The uniform pulls tight across her midsection. Her name tag bounces at her hip, but I don't need to see the name to recognize her. It's Dr. Handrian's nurse—what's her name? Marcia Connally never forgets names—the same one who'd heard my sob story time and time again. How surprised she'll be to see that my motherhood goal has come true!

"Mom, I have to go," I say. "I'll call you after." And before she can reply, I hang up.

I turn back to greet the nurse with a smile, but she's stopped halfway down the hall, like she'd stepped in quicksand and couldn't move her feet another inch. Her lips are parted slightly and, even from a distance, I can tell her face has paled.

"Hi," I say with an awkward wave. Why is she just standing there? Her eyes go back and forth between me and Henry, so much so that I look down to see if there's something wrong with my son. Then I realize—she must be surprised to see me with a baby. "Oh!" I laugh nervously. "Yes, I... The adoption agency called last month." I gesture to Henry and back to myself, like we're a pair from one of those children's matching games. We go together. "Can you believe it?"

She comes closer, slowly, each step careful, eyes locked on Henry. When she's mere feet away, she brings her hands to cover her mouth. And that's when I see it—a tattoo on her inner wrist. My heart stops. I've seen it before, this dark shape with its unique artistic strokes. A bird in flight.

A deep, black sparrow.

PART 2

NINETEEN

JADA

Five weeks ago

MY STOMACH SEIZES IN A MASSIVE CRAMP AND I BREAK
out into a cold sweat. Fuck, I knew I shouldn't have had
Chipotle for lunch. I stand from the desk and stretch, but then
it's like a knife stabs through my abdomen. I think I'm going to
be sick.

"Are you okay?" Lexi asks. She drops the stack of charts on
the desk and gives me a look that says, *Don't you dare puke right
here.* The look also says, *Maybe if you didn't eat Chipotle twice a
week you wouldn't have gained those extra pounds.*

They're not pounds, I'd reply, *they're healthy Puerto Rican
curves,* but instead I say, "I don't feel very good. My stomach."
But then I'm lunging for the trash can and proceed to vomit up
black-bean burrito.

"Shit, Jada." My co-worker hands me a wad of tissues. "Was
it lunch?"

"I don't know, but—" I wince as another wave of pain
comes. "I'm super crampy."

"You better go home before it all starts coming out the other end." Lexi escorts me to the bathroom, saying she's going to go find Dr. Handrian. I cup my hands under the faucet, fill them with water and take a sip, swooshing and spitting the acid from my mouth. Fucking food poisoning—great.

Not two minutes pass before there's a quiet knock at the door. "Jada?" Dr. Handrian says as she enters. "Are you all right?"

"I'm sick. I think it was something I ate." Another shooting pain, like period cramps but worse. If I'm going to explode, I don't want to do it here in this tiny bathroom with a shitty exhaust fan.

"Why don't you take the rest of the day. We're closed tomorrow, so you'll have a long weekend to recoup." She gives me leery eyes, and I'm sure she's wondering if this is really a stomach virus or whether it's a side effect of using again.

"Okay," I manage, thankful for her offer but steaming at the thought of this being anything more than a twenty-four-hour bug. I'm supposed to be off next week, and I'll be damned if I use vacation days just to be stuck at home hugging the toilet.

The office staff keeps their distance as I gather my coat and purse, like I have the plague instead of just eating Mexican fast food. "Get better," Dr. Handrian says.

The twenty-minute drive north into the city sucks, as the pain travels from my belly to my back, and all the way around. I have to breathe through it and stay focused not to shit my pants right here in my little Toyota.

I throw the car in park at the curb outside my apartment and hurry as fast as I can inside, thanking God that I'm on the first floor. Another jolt of pain makes me howl, "Damnit!"

On the toilet, I lose everything, and the cramping is so intense, I have to double over to fight off dizziness. This is one bad case of food poisoning. I swear I'll never eat Chipotle again.

Once I've emptied out my entire insides, I'm met with a brief moment of relief. Whew! But it's short-lived. As I'm walking toward the bedroom to change out of my scrubs, another wave of pain crashes through me, and I have to brace myself against the wall. This time, it feels different, and there can't possibly be anything else that needs to come out. It's like a vise clamping my stomach, rising in strength, then letting go. I guess I'm in for a rough night.

I throw on sweatpants and an old high school T-shirt, and crawl into bed. For hours I toss and turn, trying and failing to find a position of comfort. The ache is rhythmic and repetitive, and eventually I start to wonder if this is something else, if Chipotle isn't to blame after all. I remember having eaten a bad salad once and throwing up an ungodly number of times. But not this abdominal pain, not like this.

Then, as one of the cramps surges, a new sensation: I think I have to poop again. I press myself up to sit at the edge of the bed, and that's when a gush of warmth escapes.

"What the..." I spread my legs and look down. There's a wet spot on my pants like I've peed myself. But I don't have time to think about that, because the pain is at an all-time high now, no longer easing back down, just staying, throbbing, and with an unbearable urge to push.

I hobble to the bathroom and collapse on the toilet. Sweat has made the baby hairs on my forehead curl. My whole body shakes. Something is happening. I can't control it. My body acts on its own, and before I know it, I'm holding my breath and pushing. I look down and scream. The toilet bowl fills with blood, and something is coming out of me.

A baby. I'm having a baby.

What the...? A string of expletives fly from my mouth. I can't think straight and definitely don't have answers to the million things flying through my head, most notably *how*? All I see is white and all I feel is piercing pain, like I'm being split in half.

I scream again, a low, guttural howl, and somehow I know to reach down. There's a head between my legs. Another contraction—I know that's what these are now—and the shoulders come out, followed by the rest of the slimy body, dropping into my trembling hands.

I'm panting and crying and panting some more. Each exhale comes out in wobbly *ooooohs*. I slide to the floor with the baby on my chest and frantically glance around the room in disbelief, my eyes blinking rapidly. This can't be happening. This can't have just happened. A baby? I didn't even know I was pregnant.

The room swirls as lightheadedness comes on fast. My legs are numb. The shock is so great, it feels like I'm in a dream.

The baby lets out a cry, and it's the first thing that solidifies it: Yes, this is real. The room comes back into focus.

"Oh my god," I say again and again in swift succession. I can't form any other thought. Simply, oh-my-god.

My bath towel hangs to the left of the toilet and I reach for it, yanking it down and covering the baby, whose cries subside to a whimper. I'm still so dumbstruck, so completely mind-blown, I don't feel the pain again until my hand instinctively goes to my belly. It's like I want to press away the spasm. Seconds later, my body expels another warm gush and I lurch in horror as a deep purple blob lands on the honeycomb tile. I give a sharp inhale. What the fuck is *that*?

The shaking is so intense, my adrenaline levels through the roof. I'm living in a blur of shock and confusion and fear. Tears stream down my face, mixing with sweat to form new paths and land on the now-bloody T-shirt.

I manage to reach my phone from the counter. Mom—I should call Mom. But something stops me. How can I possibly explain? And what's more, how can this possibly be anything but a mistake?

Instead, I dial 911 with trembling fingers. When the dispatcher answers, I blurt out in sobbing hysteria what must sound impossible: "I didn't know I was pregnant, but I just had a baby in my bathroom."

TWENTY

WHEN THE PARAMEDICS ARRIVE, I'M IN THE EXACT SAME spot. I managed to wipe some of the goop from the baby's head and face, and pulled the towel aside enough to see that it's a boy.

"In here!" I call, when I hear them come through the door.

The two men fly into action, rushing at me with blankets and medical equipment. One jabs my arm with a needle to start an IV, and my first thought is I'm surprised he can even find a vein. My arms have seen a lot of damage.

I'm naked from the waist down, covered in blood and who knows what other bodily fluids, but all sense of modesty has gone out the window. The men each have their role: one attending to me, the other to the baby.

"How many weeks were you?" one says.

"I... I don't know. I didn't know." I feel delirious, body and mind still trying to catch up.

"Didn't know?"

"Didn't know I was pregnant. I never felt— And my periods — I have PCOS."

They share a look, and I get it. This is absolutely, wildly

unbelievable. How does a woman go nine months without knowing she's pregnant? But here I am as proof. I never once had so much as a single symptom. My stomach no bigger than a post-Thanksgiving dinner bloat. Sure, I'd been more comfortable recently in pants with a stretchy waist, but who isn't?

"Well, looks like you did a good job," the wider of the two says, lifting the baby from my chest, placing a clamp on the umbilical cord, and giving it a quick cut. "He's small but not a preemie. And he looks okay, but we need to get you both to the hospital."

All I can do is nod.

The men lift me onto a stretcher and place the baby, now wrapped in a sterile white blanket, in my arms.

This morning I was a twenty-five-year-old with a rough past. It took everything in my power to get through each day. And now—now my somewhat stable boat has been rocked, and that scares the shit out of me. Because I know what happens when anything rocks my boat. My life's already a mess, and now this? I can't handle it—I don't have it in me. No baby deserves to have me as its mother.

Is it possible to feel like you were just hit by an eighteen-wheeler? Because that's what I feel like. My belly still cramps, and even though the nurse told me it's normal, I have a brief moment of panic that there's another baby about to come out.

"It's just your uterus shrinking back down," she explains. "It'll be crampy for a few days, especially when you're breast-feeding."

Breastfeeding? Whoa, lady, this is all happening too fast. I can't wrap my head around the fact that a human just came out of my *vagina*, on the floor of my *bathroom*, and now I'm expected to feed it like a *cow*?

She takes my temperature and then pulls down the blanket

covering my lower half. "Just need to take a peek down here. Okay, yep. Everything looks good. Swollen, but that's also because of the sutures. Don't worry—you'll be back to normal in a couple weeks."

When they'd brought me into the emergency room, the doctor had taken one look down there and given a swift nod. "Even little babies can cause pretty big tears," he'd said, much to my horror. Thirty minutes later, I had five lovely stitches to prove it. And now, after being transferred to the labor and delivery ward, a massive ice pack between my legs and red Jell-O next to me, I'm still struggling to process the last five hours.

There's a swaddled baby boy in a bassinet on wheels an arm's reach from me. How is this possible? And more importantly, what the hell am I supposed to do now? I lean my head back against the pillows as a tear rolls down my cheek. I want Mom but can't bear the disappointment she'll certainly feel. Birth comes with baggage in our family—it's not been something to celebrate.

A knock on the door makes me lift my head again. The same doctor who'd attended to me upon arrival saunters in. "Just wanted to check on you," he says. "I'm sure it's been quite a whirlwind."

I give a nervous laugh, as though this were some sort of lighthearted comedy, when in fact I'm fucking terrified. This man has no idea how shitty my life is.

"Believe it or not," he says, coming to the foot of the bed, hairy arms crossed, "I've seen this before."

"This?"

"A patient going into labor without knowing she was pregnant. I've been practicing thirty-six years and you're my second." He says it like I'm a freak attraction at the circus. Like he gets a high from the unconventional. "Pretty wild, huh?"

That's one word for it.

My voice hitches. "But how is this possible? How could I have been pregnant this whole time and not had a clue?"

"It's possible. In fact, about one in twenty-five hundred cases. That's not such a small number when you think of it. We call it a cryptic pregnancy. Most women eventually discover they're pregnant after the halfway mark, once they feel the baby move, but some, like you, go the entire gestation period without knowing. It's rare but not unheard of."

"I never even felt anything. I barely had a bump."

"Your uterus was likely retroverted, which means it was tilted backwards and very deep in your pelvis." He uses his hands as a diagram against his own abdomen. "And if you had an anterior placenta, it would have acted like a cushion, explaining why you didn't feel the baby's movements. Plus your polycystic ovarian syndrome and irregular periods. It sounds crazy, I know. But all of these things combined into the perfect storm."

I listen carefully, trying to process what he's saying. So I'm not the only one. It's happened before—he's seen it himself. Then why do I still feel like an absolute idiot? How clueless could I have been? Everyone's seen that show on TLC, and everyone laughs at it. Now I feel like the laughing stock.

"Anyway," the doctor says, "you're lucky. It doesn't always end up this way. You had zero prenatal care, but your baby still passed all his tests. He's perfectly healthy."

A shrill tremor works its way down my spine. What have I been up to for the last nine months? Not regular exercise and healthy eating, that's for sure. More like parties and enough weed to make me forget. How this child is healthy is beyond me. I say a silent prayer of thanks that at least I'd managed to lay off the hard stuff after my last trip to rehab.

The doctor pats the footrail of the bed. "All things considered, you should be cleared for discharge tomorrow."

That's it? I want to say. I can just leave here with a baby in my possession? One I'm in charge of? But I don't say these things for fear of sounding even more childish than I already feel. Instead, I watch the doctor leave, off to deliver more babies to parents far more prepared and worthy than me.

I don't sleep, not much anyway. There's a steady stream of nurses in and out, checking my vitals, massaging my belly, administering meds. A newborn, greedily chomping on my nipples every two hours, making me wince each time. And all I can think is how I managed to make my life harder than it already was.

TWENTY-ONE

THERE ARE NO BAGS TO PACK, NO FLOWERS TO CARRY OUT, just me and a brand-new baby boy wearing a plain white onesie the hospital provided. After explaining that I didn't have a car seat, nor the means to get one, a middle-aged woman shows up to my room.

"Hi there. My name's Peggy. I'm one of the medical social workers here." She has a light pixie cut that's so thin I can see her scalp and a sugarcoated voice that makes me think she must have been born to work in a field that helps people. Peggy comes to the side of my bed, charted folder in hand. "We just like to check in on all the new mommies before they leave. I understand this delivery was a bit of a surprise?"

I arch my brows. "A bit."

"Something so sudden can bring on a lot of feelings. Traumatic births also lend themselves to postpartum depression and anxiety. You've heard of these?"

I nod, thinking of the new moms who show up for their six-week follow-up at our office with lifeless eyes, and how Dr. Handrian listens intently before prescribing a little white pill. Is that going to happen to me?

"Do you have a support system in place?" Peggy asks. "People who will be there to help you?"

When I don't answer right away, she follows up with, "Does anyone else live with you?"

"No."

A look of concern crosses her face, sending me into a small panic. I said the wrong thing.

"Well, I mean, my mom's around a lot," I clarify even though that's not exactly true. Mom works sixty hours a week. "She'll be staying with us for a while."

It's a bold-faced lie, but I've perfected the art. I can lie to anyone's face without so much as a blink.

"Great," Peggy says. "Babies are a lot of work—it's important you have someone you can turn to for support."

She gestures to an infant car seat near the door. "This is for you. Can't leave the hospital without one."

"For free?" I say, thinking of how much this baby is going to cost me.

"We get donations. Buckle Up for Life has donated close to ninety thousand car seats across the country—isn't that wonderful?"

"Mmm."

"Let's practice buckling him in."

She brings the car seat close then stands back like she's about to assess my parenting skills. I'm still for a second then get up gingerly from the bed and unswaddle the baby. He grimaces and makes a little squeak, to which Peggy smiles. I pick him up clumsily, never having held a newborn before yesterday. The nurses taught me to support his head. When I lower him toward the seat, Peggy stops me.

"If you put the handle back first, it's easier to get him in," she says then presses a button on either side to recline the arm.

"Oh... thanks." I lay the baby in the seat, bring the straps over his shoulders and clasp the buckle across his belly. I sit back on my heels. There, see?

"Don't forget the other ones," Peggy says, waving a pointed finger.

"Oh," I say again, feeling and sounding incompetent. My face flares. Two pointed buckles hang from the straps but I can't tell where they're supposed to go. I pull this way and that way, trying to look like I know what I'm doing. Finally, Peggy steps in.

"It's under his bum," she says, not unkindly, but like I'm a child playing with a doll. I reach under the baby and pull out the final buckle, clipping the two sides in. Peggy nods. "There you go."

The whole thing has worked up a mild sweat. If getting him buckled into a car seat is enough to fluster me, how can I expect to get through the really hard things? I give a long exhale and wave the collar of my shirt to get some air to my damp skin.

"Don't worry—you'll be an expert in no time," Peggy says.

I wish I believed her, but there are serious doubts in the way. I can barely take care of myself, let alone another human. Her smile provides only so much warmth as the thick layer of mercy is enough to be seen a mile away. She doubts me too. My defenses spring up. I just want to get home.

Peggy rests a neatly manicured hand on my shoulder. "You've got this. Women have been doing it for millennia."

No pressure.

"We need to schedule his first appointment with the pediatrician. Does next Wednesday work?"

"Sure," I say unconsciously, still trying to adjust to the thought of a baby coming home with me. The last thing on my mind is a pediatrician, but I agree to appease her. I have a lot to figure out between now and next Wednesday.

"Now," she says, making a note on the file. "There's just one final thing. You'll need to fill out information for the birth certificate." She hands me a paper form. "Have you decided on a name?"

Until now, the dry-erase board on the wall has said "Baby Morales," and try as I might, I couldn't come up with a name. Most people have time to think about it, months and months to make lists and feel them out. But I'm getting discharged any minute and this child is still nameless.

I stare hard at him, his skin now smooth and cleaned of gunk. When they brought him back from giving him his first bath, I'd run my hand through his dark hair and smelled the powdery scent of his peach-fuzzed skin. There are red veins running across his eyelids. Who is this little human I unknowingly created? He has my wide eyes, but the full lips are someone else's. Someone I'm embarrassed to even say I knew, let alone slept with. Felix was a fling, and once he tired of me, he moved on. But oh, those early days when I fell hard. He told me I was beautiful and that's all it took. Now, I don't even know if he's still in Cleveland let alone the state of Ohio. He's a loser whose mission in life is banging chicks and dealing coke. I would never list him on a birth certificate.

Peggy clears her throat, and I realize I never answered her question. The baby's name.

"Nicolas," I say, surprising myself. I don't know where it comes from, but the second it leaves my mouth, it sounds perfect.

"Little Nicolas," she clucks, leaning over the car seat where he's fallen back to sleep. "That's lovely."

I fill out the form and hand it back to her.

"Is there someone coming to get you?" she says, and I'm ready with my prepared response.

"I'm just going to call an Uber."

"An... Uber?" She looks aghast, and again, that pity. Who leaves the hospital completely alone after giving birth?

"My, uh... my mom's waiting for us at home," I say quickly.

Another lie. My apartment is empty, and that's exactly the way I want it. The truth is, I don't want anyone to know about Nicolas. Not yet. Not until my mind catches up to reality. As far as my work is concerned, I'm home recovering from food poisoning. As far as Mom knows, I'm sleeping in on my day off. I'll deal with all of them soon.

I put on my best fake smile. I can tell she's reluctant with this plan, but I push forward, lifting the car seat from the ground. It hurts to move—every step feeling like my entire reproductive system is falling out into my huge, mesh underwear. My nipples abrade against my bra, even with the nursing pads the hospital gave me.

I give Peggy a quick nod—"All set"—and she wheels us down four floors, through the lobby, and to the spinning door where we wait seven minutes until a small black car comes to take us home. My stomach is in knots the entire way. I can't help but feel like I'm starting a new journey I didn't ask for.

TWENTY-TWO

WE GO TWO WHOLE DAYS WITH NO ONE BOTHERING US. Nicolas cries and I change him, and then he pees out of his diaper, and I google why and learn I should tuck his penis down. There's so much I don't know. In fact, I feel like I know nothing, that he and I are just figuring it out hour by hour. Between the hot flashes and the racing thoughts, I feel so out of control in my own body. I've asked the internet a million questions and second-guessed myself even more.

When Sunday morning rolls around, I wake up to rock-hard boobs fit for a porn star. The skin is pulled so tight, with grotesque, criss-crossing veins, Nicolas can't even latch. He screams bloody murder, which only makes me cry in frustration. The hospital sent me home with ready-made formula samples just in case, and I cry out in release when he takes it willingly. But that won't last long; nor will the single pack of diapers.

I can't leave this apartment. Stepping out from the safety and privacy of this tiny space scares me. What if I see someone I know? What if we bump into Mom? The idea of her discovering this latest fuck-up is enough to crush me. Haven't I disappointed her enough? Haven't I been enough of a burden in her life? I cancel Nicolas's appointment for Wednesday, saying something came up and we'll reschedule. I'm just not ready.

The newborn phase is nothing like I would have imagined. Nicolas screams so much his whole body convulses.

"What? What do you want?" I plead. It's the first time I've spoken out loud all day. I've tried everything—new diaper, food, swaddle—and he just won't stop. I try bouncing him, swinging him, burping him. Nothing works. We walk around the apartment, but standing too long makes my hemorrhoids swell, and so we retreat back to the bedroom. I lay Nicolas down on the dusty rose comforter. His arms shoot out to the sides. I didn't know it was possible for a baby to cry so much. In fact, I've googled that exact thing.

"What do you want from me?" I say, flinging my hands around wildly. If I had a white flag, I'd be waving it. That's it, I give up! SOS! There must be something wrong with him—this is not a baby from a Gerber commercial. On second thought, it's probably me. Something's wrong with me. I'm deficient in so many ways, why would motherhood be any different?

The cry-sleep cycle goes on for what feels like an eternity but is actually only three hours. It's like when he's awake time slows down, every minute dragging by in agony. Then when he's asleep, I barely have time to shut my own eyes before his spring open again, demanding something new. I don't jump immediately. It takes me a minute to dredge up the effort, like I'm moving through quicksand.

During one of his short-lived quiet times, I get on my phone, pull up the delivery app, and place an order. Diapers, wipes, formula, a five-pack of pajamas for Nicolas, and a navy blue diaper bag that's fifty-percent off just for the hell of it. I should be thinking long term—I'll need way more than this—but there's something in my brain preventing that. It's like I can't think beyond the current moment. Everything is whizzing and vibrating, and I'm fuzzy from lack of sleep. A fog has settled in the apartment. It's thick and comes with a heaviness that makes me think it will never lift.

We've camped up in the bedroom—Nicolas on one side of the bed, buffered with pillows, and me on the other. I leave only to go to the bathroom or kitchen. Last night, it was ramen. Tonight it will be... well, probably ramen again. People like me don't have the luxury of ordering takeout every night. The thought of having a second mouth to feed beyond my own makes my head hurt. I try to do the math—diapers, food, all the baby essentials—but then my breathing is out of control and I throw the comforter over my head.

Nicolas wakes again, and his face pinches into what I know is about to be a scream. Before the sound comes out, I'm already wishing I were anywhere but here.

My phone rings at seven-thirty, startling me awake from a post-dinner nap. I barely have a sense of time and only know that if Nicolas is asleep, I should be too. We have another long night ahead of us, and I mentally prepare to be awake when the rest of the world is shut down.

I check the screen. It's Mom. My insides constrict. I'm surprised she hasn't called before now. Usually weekends are when she's more paranoid about me. More free time. More opportunities to get in trouble. A thick blanket of guilt piles on at the thought of keeping this all from her. Then again, it's just another layer to a life filled with missteps, so what's one more? A quick glance at Nicolas to make sure he's still sleeping—and therefore quiet—and I answer.

"Hi," I try to sound normal.

"Hi, mija. Just checking in."

I stifle a groan. I hate when she says this, like I'm still a strung-out junkie. It's been two years since I've used heroin, and that's not to say I'm squeaky clean, but the hard stuff is long gone.

"All good," I say with the passive-aggressive tone I've perfected.

Nicolas squirms next to me, a couple of writhing twists followed by the release of gas in three quick *putt, putt, putts*. He smiles in his sleep. I bring a hand over my mouth not to giggle. What odd creatures babies are. It's the first moment of levity I've felt since leaving the hospital.

"What did you do this weekend?"

"I haven't been feeling good," I say, because it's not a lie. Childbirth ranks pretty high on the not-feeling-well chart.

"You're sick? Why didn't you call me? I would have brought over food or something."

"Don't worry about it. I took a half day Friday and have just been lying low."

"Well, why don't I stop by and—"

"No," I interject with more force than intended. "I mean, I don't want you to catch it. I've been pretty lousy."

"Okay," Mom says, not totally assured. She's always been the one to take care of me, even when she shouldn't. Running a cold shower when I came home plastered on cheap beer in high school, making excuses to my boss when I was too high to go to work. We're a funny thing, us two—codependent to a fault. I guess that's what happens when you're a single parent. In truth, I've never understood why she hasn't given up on me when she didn't even want me in the first place.

That's a whole other saga I can't unpack right now.

The last two years have been better. I moved out, got my own place, promised Dr. Handrian I'd get my shit together so she wouldn't fire me. Everything was on track... until I met Felix, and slowly, my weaknesses won out. Ten months later, and here I am alone with his baby, living a very out-of-body experience I never planned for.

"Well," Mom says, "I guess I'll call you tomorrow to see how you're feeling."

"I'm sure I'll be fine. Just another work week," I lie, not needing her to know I'm off all week. Surely that would be suspicious, and surely that means she'd be snooping around. Once an addict breaks trust, it's nearly impossible to gain it back.

We hang up just as Nicolas starts to stir. I try to regulate my breathing—it feels like my heart rate has been stuck at a runaway pace ever since we got home from the hospital. I tent my legs and lay him on my thighs. His big brown eyes open and it's as though we stare into each other's souls, forming opinions and conclusions about this new person we're still getting to know. But then the sweet moment bursts, and Nicolas lets out a wail. I sigh. Here we go, an endless loop. My life raft is almost completely flat, just a layer of plastic unable to hold me afloat. That storm? It's over my head now, pummeling rain from a starless sky.

I feed Nicolas again, and he promptly spits up all over me, a milky white shower I didn't ask for. I google if that's normal. My laundry basket is filling up with wet, sour clothes. He cries more. I groan and throw my hands into the air. "You wouldn't be hungry if you didn't throw up everything you ate," I say, like he can understand. I seriously don't know if I can do this. My previous life calls to me. *Come back.*

A thought weasels its way into my head: What if there were a way to get there? To rewind nine months and make it so this never happened. It's impossible. But is there another way? Could I... give him up? We're past the point of adoption. That's too complicated, and anyways, it would expose me and this whole mess. But what if...

It's so vile, so shameful, I shudder an audible "No," as though there were someone else in the room to sway besides myself. I shake my head. No, I can't do *that*.

A familiar longing circles inside me, a voice I thought I'd blocked out for good. But it's so comforting, so convincing. Nicolas screams in my ear, but the voice is even louder. It makes me want bad things. Bad, bad things.

I close my eyes, trying to tune it out, willing it away. Don't go back there, Jada. I've come so far and have managed to fight off the occasional temptation. I think of those years when things were at their worst, how close I came to death on more than one occasion. I told myself I'd never let it happen again. But this time feels different. This time the voice is more persuasive than ever, offering promises on a silver platter.

TWENTY-THREE

THIS IS SO HARD. HARDER THAN I EVER EXPECTED—NOT that I expected to be doing it at all. And definitely not how I thought I'd be spending my week off work. So much for sleeping in and Netflix binges. What am I going to do when Monday rolls around?

Nicolas is one week old and the noisiest human I've ever met. He grunts and snorts even when sleeping, which keeps me in a light level of sleep (at best) or fully awake (at worst) all night long. It's taken me the full week to be able to grasp his presence here. I have a son. A *son*. I'm a mom. But the swell of love you see in movies or read about in books is far different to what I'm feeling.

Sometimes I stare at him and get a tiny twinge, like my heart being zapped. It must be love. I think it's love? It's definitely something that connects me to this tiny person. However, those moments pass faster than a sneeze, and the majority of the time I pass the hours in a sleep-deprived state of desire for my old life. Not the one just leading up to Nicolas's birth—the *old* old life. The one where I didn't feel anything at all. Those years come back to me in full, vivid color, and I get lost in the memories. The way the drugs took away all the hurt. How I didn't have to worry about anyone but myself.

Plain and simple, I want to use.

Nicolas is lying in the middle of my bed, crying and writhing, arms jerking around in figure-eights. But instead of going to him, instead of soothing him, I'm backed into the corner, wishing the wall would suck me through. I slide to the floor and pull my knees in. I feel like I'm in the middle of the sea, a dark cloud approaching, and a slow-leaking hole in my life raft.

Water fills my eyes, and I brush the tears away with the backs of my hands. I've never cried so much in my life. My body is a hormonal mess. Loneliness has descended the last few days, and I'm desperate for adult interaction. I never thought I'd miss Lexi and her constant talking, which usually drives me nuts while I'm trying to work. Now, I'd welcome the stories about her cousin's neighbor's dog. Anything to keep me from doing what I know I'm about to do.

Hugo's number is no longer saved in my phone, but that doesn't mean I don't remember how to contact my dealer. Seven digits that important are not something you easily forget.

I feed Nicolas, the whole time my mind envisioning the needle pricking my skin, then lay him on the bed. I'm not *actually* going to do it—I just want to call. There's nothing wrong with a phone call, right? I swipe my phone alive and go to the dial pad. My fingers tap the numbers with ease, a combination with the power to unlock the only thing that matters. My best friend in poison form.

It rings. My body shakes.

"Yo, Jada! Where you been?" Apparently he still has my number, and he greets me like I've been quiet for two days instead of two years.

"You got any stuff?" I say, my mouth wet.

"Whatchu looking for?"

"H."

"Yeah."

I'm buzzing, everything in me aflame, knowing it's within reach. I can't wait any longer. "Now?" I say, with all the hope in the world.

"Sure."

"Where?"

"Casey and Smalls are here if you want to come party."

The angel in my ear gives its warning: Don't do it. Hang up.

"'Kay," I say and end the call. My body hums. Forget a shower, forget everything—I take one quick look at Nicolas, asleep in the middle of the bed, and then I leave. He'll be okay. I'll be right back.

TWENTY-FOUR

I DON'T COME RIGHT BACK.

I wake up the next morning, slumped on Hugo's couch, hair in my face, mouth as dry as the desert. I blink, roll my head. The crook of my arm is sore from not being poked for so long. But it's a good tender, a welcome home. This is what I know. This is my life.

Needles and bent spoons litter the coffee table. A line of unused blow atop a round mirror. The others must have passed out before getting to it.

I sit up, look around, then down at myself, still in the same clothes from yesterday. And then my breath stops. Two seeping wet spots spread on my shirt where my slowly diminishing milk has leaked.

Nicolas. Fuck.

I scramble for my keys and fly from the house, fishtailing in the snow and speeding back to my apartment. What have I done? Dark possibilities attack my mind: Nicolas smothered against a pillow. Nicolas face down on the floor, having rolled off the bed in the night. I fight off a sudden wave of nausea. It was supposed to be a quick pick-up. Get the stuff and go back home. But the escape of Hugo's house felt like bliss, and I told myself I'd stay for an hour. Then an hour turned into two, five, the whole night.

I throw the car into park and dash into the apartment. "Nicolas!" I holler, as though he might respond.

The cry hits my ears before I'm fully inside, and I reach the bedroom in seconds. "Oh my god, I'm sorry. I'm so sorry," I sob.

He's perpendicular to how I left him, body running alongside the headboard, a large pillow trapping his left arm. His face is pinched and red. The scent of feces fills the air.

I swoop him up, and my hand feels something wet. He's peed out of his diaper, leaving a wet spot on the sheets where he lay. My first thought is to feed him. It's been over twelve hours since he last ate. I rush to make a bottle and plop it in his mouth. He takes it greedily.

Crying ceased, I try to steady my breathing, but the grief is too much. I fold forward into him, remorse-filled tears dropping onto his already-wet onesie. I can't do this. I'm a terrible mother. He doesn't deserve this life.

And then the idea returns, as swift and sure as anything I've ever felt. The dark, ugly thing that I'd refused to entertain just a few days ago. But that was then. That was before I just left him overnight alone so I could get high. Now, the idea doesn't seem as shameful as it does necessary. I need to give him up. Not for me, but for him. I can already feel the drug grabbing hold of me again, and, as much as I want to deny it, last night won't be a one-time thing. If my past has taught me anything, it's that addicts will do anything, hurt anyone, to get what they want.

I stare down at his little face and know what I'm going to do. But where? And how? I want to make sure he's safe, that he's with someone who will love him like I wish I could. Someone who deserves him. It doesn't take long, and maybe I've known it since the day he was born. There is someone. The perfect person. I know her story—the tragic medical condition, the crushing desire for motherhood.

Her name is Cate Connally. And if there's one thing I know, it's that she wants a baby more than anything in the world.

I don't think, because thinking means feeling, and feeling means the possibility of second-guessing. I can't chicken out, not with everything that's on the line. And the saddest part of it all is that while I'm buckling Nicolas into the car seat, blue hat on his head and dinosaur blanket draped over his legs, I'm thinking about getting high again. The shame is a heavy ball and chain, shackled to my ankle, destined to follow me around forever. I want to be a better person, a good mother, but it doesn't seem possible. I can't. And the truth of the matter is it's not fair for Nicolas.

With twitchy fingers, I call Dr. Handrian's office. Lexi answers.

"How's your week off? Feeling better?" she asks, to which I give a believable enough response. But I'm not calling to chit-chat. If I don't do this now, I might never—and then something bad could happen to Nicolas.

"Can you look up a patient for me?"

"Sure. What do you need?" There's a hesitancy in her voice, and I worry she's going to become suspicious.

"Cate Connally. I need her address."

"What for?"

I roll my eyes. "I, uh... I need to drop something off to her." This, of course, makes no sense, and in no world would I have any connection to Cate Connally outside the office, nor the need to drop anything off at her house. But Lexi isn't the brightest, and chances are she's watching a TikTok video as we speak.

"Okay, just a sec."

My spirits lift and I feel light. This is going to work.

After a few seconds, Lexi's back. "Seven-four-five Maple," she says.

"Thanks, Lex," I say and hang up before she has a chance to ask any more questions.

Address plugged into my GPS, I go to the kitchen and pull open a drawer where I keep random office supplies: an assortment of pens, loose paper clips, a roll of scotch tape. There's a stack of white stationery cards with matching envelopes, a high-school graduation gift from one of Mom's friends, as though we were back in the fifties and I were the type to send handwritten letters. I remove one and write two simple sentences from the deepest chamber of my heart:

Take him. Please forgive me.

I'll leave this with Nicolas, a request of both him and the woman I'm trusting to take him in. Forgive me for what I've done and for what I have to do. Tears collect in my eyes as I hold the note in my hand. Nicolas will never know me, but maybe that's for the best.

I can't sign it, can't have any link that could be traced back to me. But still, something urges me to leave my mark, like a goodbye kiss, proving he once was mine. I take the pen and draw the shape of a bird at the bottom, coloring in the wings until they're as black as the tattoo on my wrist. A sparrow, Aphrodite's favorite bird, and symbol of love. I hope it will be enough to show I loved him as much as I knew how. A final reflection of how hard I tried.

I drive on autopilot, no time to get cold feet. My mind's made up.

Cate Connally lives thirty minutes outside the city, in the suburbs where houses go out instead of up, and where mailboxes line the streets instead of cluster boxes on walls, numbered for the entire building. There are snowmen in yards and lingering Christmas lights on trees.

I feel out of place driving through these nice neighborhoods. There aren't people like me here. I'm struck with the thought of what Mom's life might have been like before I came along. Could she have ended up in a neighborhood like this? Hers isn't the life she planned either—she didn't expect at seventeen to be thrown onto a bed by a friend of a friend, whose name she didn't even know. Or for him to shove himself inside her while she begged him to stop. Didn't expect to have a fuck-up for a daughter. Certainly never predicted twelve-hour days waiting tables at a subpar Italian chain.

But I can't change the past; I can only change the future. And that's what I'm doing—changing Nicolas's future. He'll be better without me. Just like Mom would have been better without me. I say it over and over in my head, willing it to stick.

Finally, the GPS instructs me to turn onto Maple Street. And there, halfway down on the right, is a modest house, gray with black shutters, and a driveway with a silver Jeep. Is this Cate's car? Is she home on a work day? It occurs to me I don't know what she does for a living. What makes me think she even has the means to support Nicolas? But that fear quickly fades—money isn't everything, and Cate's pure yearning for a baby outweighs any dollar amount in the bank. Besides, this neighborhood is safe, it's clean. I imagine Cate running beside Nicolas down the sidewalk as he learns to ride a bike.

My throat tightens. I look over my shoulder to the car seat in the back. How can I do this? I play the what-if game. What if he stays with me? What if I leave him here? I mumble, convincing myself of both sides. "It's what's best," I say, followed quickly with, "No, I can't." I pull on my ear, physical anguish making me jittery. The internal debate goes back and forth, but in the end there are far more pros on one side of the argument. Resolve comes, and I give a strong, decisive nod.

We park across the street, adjacent to the house. I do a quick glance around but see no one. Are there people watching from windows? What if someone sees me? I can't analyze it or I'll never move. So instead, I take a deep breath and zip my coat up to my chin. I go around the car and lift Nicolas's seat out. The air is freezing and his face scrunches from the assault.

"Shhhh," I say. "It's going to be all right."

I keep my head down as we cross the street. The walkway is clear, only little beads of salt from where someone has de-iced the sidewalk. *See?* I think. *This woman cares. She's thoughtful.*

I'm as quiet as possible, going up the few front steps and placing the car seat facing the front door and the diaper bag next to it. I pull the blanket up so only Nicolas's face is free, then give it a tuck around his body. I pray she'll find him quickly. Then, before I turn to leave forever, I slide the notecard in next to him, run my hand along his cheek, and whisper the same three words: *Please forgive me.*

Back in the car, I'm paralyzed. My hands grip the wheel but don't register any touch. I wait and watch. How long will it take her to find him? Is the blanket warm enough? I didn't dare ring the doorbell for fear of being spotted. This was always meant to be a secret mission, and I fight the urge to dash back across the street and knock with a heavy hand.

The minutes stretch. "Please come. Please come," I whisper. There are no more tears—they've dried up just like the milk in my breasts. I can't watch the clock because it just seems cruel, and that was never my intention. Maybe she's not home. Maybe this isn't going to work after all. If I don't do it now, will I have the courage to do it again later?

Is that what this is—courage? It feels like anything but. It feels more like disgrace.

I watch the front door like a hawk. After an unbearable eternity, a shadow passes by the window, and I gulp a quick breath. She's here. She's going to find him. And that means I have to leave. Now. Before she sees me.

I right myself and throw the car in gear, overtaken by full-body shivers. The gray house shrinks to a pin behind me.

TWENTY-FIVE

SOMEONE'S SHAKING ME OUT OF THE BEAUTIFUL SLEEP I'D been enjoying.

"Wake up, Jada. Wake up."

I know this voice. It's the first voice I heard upon entering this world. Only, why is Mom in my apartment?

My brain pounds inside my skull. I look right and left, and the muscles in my eyes strain. I've never felt cotton mouth quite like this. Worse than any hangover, worse than the stomach flu. Mom's hovering above me, dark locks pulled back into a ponytail, baby hairs neatly styled on her forehead. When she sees I'm alive, she steps back, folds her arms across her chest. There's no, *Oh thank God.* No tears of joy.

Maybe she wishes she wouldn't have found me in time.

Maybe I do too.

I open my mouth to talk but struggle to find the words. The look on her face doesn't help. The sad eyes, downturned mouth. The too many worry lines for someone who's only forty-three. I've seen pictures from her younger years when Mom was bright and hopeful, a wide-eyed teen who didn't know what was about to come. Now, she wears life's hardships on her face. It's far more weathered than those of other women her age. I guess being a single mom to a junkie will do that.

We stare at each other for a long minute, so many things unsaid but understood.

"I'm sorry," I whisper, an apology for what I know is happening: I've relapsed. Again.

There are no tears, only a matter-of-fact resolution stemming from years of stress. She shakes her head, and even that is sad. "I can't do this again, Jada. I just can't."

"It was just a—"

"Just a little? Just once? Is that what you were about to say?" Her voice elevates now. "What, like you can just do a little bit of heroin and that's okay? So long as it's not enough to kill you?"

She's an animal ready to pounce. I clamp my mouth shut. That's exactly what I was going to say, though when she does, it sounds ridiculous. A little bit of heroin is no better than a lot. Doesn't take much to snatch a person and never let go. It's magnetic, one of the nastiest things to ever come from Pandora's Box. I think of her phone call a few days after Nicolas and I got home from the hospital. The skepticism in her voice, and how I'd deceived her so easily.

Mom leans forward, eyes drilling into me. "Do you know how lucky you are to be alive?"

"I'm sorry," I say again, and I mean it. I'm sorry I can't fight this addiction, and I'm sorry for the secret I'll now have to keep from her. I'm sorry for the toll my life's taken on my mother. She deserves better than me. And I certainly don't deserve her.

"You keep saying you're sorry," Mom says. "But actions speak louder than words. We're in a vicious cycle, and one of these times will be the end. I'm scared, Jada."

"I know." Regret floods me. I'm so, so sorry. Hurting the one person on earth who loves me—nothing could make me feel more like shit. Remorse is a heavy burden. But addiction gives you superhuman strength, because at the same time the barb of guilt pushes into my conscience, the wheels are turning as to where I can get more dope. I don't know how to get off this fucked-up ride.

"You have to go back."

"Back?"

"To rehab. Before this sucks you in even further. How long has it been going on this time?"

"Twice, that's all. I swear."

This disappointment kills me. I'm such a fuck-up.

She shakes her head. "I can't keep loving you into sobriety."

This is Al-Anon talking, the meetings that preach about how to live with an addict. Still, her face is stern, harsher than I'm used to.

"What's that supposed to mean?" I say with just as much attitude. Our fiery Latina personalities are ready to pounce on the other to see who will win.

"It means I'm done paying for this place." She sweeps her arms wide. "I've covered your rent long enough. It's time to grow up, Jada."

"You wouldn't."

"Watch me. You're using again. I made a promise to myself that I—"

"What? Mom, no—"

"It's the only way to keep you alive. A risk, but one I have to take." She won't look at me now.

I'm speechless, mouth agape at what she said. She'd actually kick me to the streets? She knows my paycheck is enough, but not when I blow hundreds a month on drugs. My head's all twisted; nothing's making sense. So I say the meanest thing I can think of as a way to throw my guilt onto her. "You're a horrible mother."

The insult cuts deep and her mouth drops open. What she doesn't know is that I meant it equally for myself.

Mom straightens herself up, like she's smoothing out her

dignity. "There's one exception. Go back to treatment. Get help again. You've done it before—look at these last two years. Go, or I cut off everything."

"I'm out of here," I say, standing on wobbly legs and pushing past her.

"You're not going anywhere but rehab," Mom says, holding her ground. "This is it, Jada. I'm putting my foot down." She's rigid as a soldier, but I see her bottom lip quivering ever so slightly. A crack in this new Al-Anon persona. "I can't keep enabling you."

"That shit never worked before, why would it work now?" The stints did nothing—their power never trumping the pull of the drug. Last night was proof. We're trapped in a never-ending loop that I don't know how to break.

"Your choice," she says, like she doesn't care. But then, with compassion: "Please."

I think of the last two years I've been clean, how good it felt to be an upstanding person, just regular, no secrets, no crimes. I was on my way, and for the first time in my life I could see a future. It's amazing how quickly that can all go away with one choice. I'd traveled so far, only to be brought back to square one.

Mom must be reading my mind because she comes to me and leaves a light touch on my forearm. "You can get there again," she says. "I promise you can."

A fresh set of tears well in my bloodshot eyes.

Go. Don't go.

You can do it. You absolutely can't.

There are so many uncertainties, so many things I can't predict. But one thing I know is that I did the right thing by leaving my baby with Cate Connally. And now, sobriety stares me in the face. Getting clean is so hard, I honestly don't know if it's possible. But Mom's face brings up memories of the past, all the times I've disappointed her, just like now. If I know one thing in this life, it's that she deserves more. I don't want to let her down again.

When my lips part, nothing comes out at first, only an uncertain breath. I'm so mad at myself for letting this happen, and also overcome with the thought of the work ahead of me. One tiny choice comes with a marathon of effort. I make myself no guarantees. Mom urges me with her eyes. I owe it to her as much as I do myself, which is why I say, ever so quietly, "I'll go."

TWENTY-SIX

THE WOMAN ACROSS FROM ME LOOKS LIKE AN OLDER version of Pam from *The Office*—thin brown hair not even mousse can thicken, washed-out skin against a lavender button-down shirt. Mom would call her "mousy." She has a legal pad and case file on her lap, my name in thick Sharpie on the manila tab: Morales, Jada.

I'm just another druggie up in this place.

"Are you feeling better today?" Karen asks.

Yes, that's right, Karen—the whitest name for the whitest lady. I can already feel her pressing her belief system on me from her soapbox. Though she's not the typical blonde Karen, she probably still drives an SUV and gets all her news from Facebook. I can't believe this is who they put me with.

"You look better," she adds warmly.

She's referring to the last forty-eight hours of detox, implying I no longer look like garbage without saying I looked like garbage when I got here. It's a charity I don't need. I own a mirror—my skin reflects when I'm using. Still, she's going for tact, taking baby steps. She doesn't know me, doesn't know how I'll respond.

I want to tell her I threw up twice this morning if that means anything, but she probably already knows this. Detox is predictable and ugly. It's days of hell. I sweated through my shirt hourly, couldn't stop shaking long enough to run a brush through my hair. Cramps seized my legs, urging me to walk, but dizziness kept me chained to the bed. The physical pain of detox is worse than the mental pain of life. Please, just snip that thread, Three Sisters of Fate. Take those shears and put an end to it all.

Worst of it were the nightmares. The ones where Cate Connally never opened the door, never found Nicolas. I woke up to my own sobs more than once.

It's been a miserable forty-eight hours. Sleep is still a bit restless, as are my legs. But I'm nearing the other side. I've done this before; I know how long it lasts.

"Yeah, I feel better," I say, though the nausea hasn't gone away. At least I'm no longer convulsing.

"It's like a bad case of the flu," Karen says, giving me a sympathetic smile. "But the symptoms should subside completely soon."

Before I ask how she can possibly know, she reads my mind (or my skeptical facial expression). "I went through the same thing. Been sober for almost twenty years now. Trust me, I know how you're feeling."

Her confession shocks me. Karen, a recovering addict? Something shifts inside me—a rearrangement of assumptions. I hear Mom's words in my head: *You know what they say about assuming...* So Karen was once a junkie. Interesting. I never would have guessed we had something in common. Doesn't mean we're about to start braiding each other's hair.

"Detox is the worst of it," she says. "Each day will get better."

It's cheesy to a gag-worthy degree, but she's right. The withdrawal sucks everything from you but replenishes with a whole new set of functions. The scent of waffles coming from the kitchen was so strong this morning, so completely sweet and real, my mouth watered before I'd even opened my door. My senses are awake again.

I shift in the chair, hug my arms across my chest. These feelings, they're raw and uncomfortable. I don't want this to turn into some sort of cry fest. Thankfully, Karen gives her pen a click. Back to business.

"Now that your head's a bit clearer, I'd like to start some of our one-on-one sessions." She props her pen up, ready to capture all my fucked-up glory. "You've been through facilities before, is that right?"

"Two." I can't help it—my eyes lower. What a failure. I turn my Crocs inward. They're the preferred shoes here. Hard to hurt someone by slinging a piece of soft rubber.

"Nothing to be ashamed of. The average person sees rehab five times before recovery."

The average person. She means the average addict. I'm not an average person.

"Well, looks like I'm over halfway there," I say. "Only this stint and two more to go." Self-deprecating humor has served me well, so why stop now?

"My point, Jada, is that sometimes it takes the right program to click. I'm confident we can work on not only your drug dependency but also any traumas from your childhood. There's a link, I'm sure you know. Solve one, you have a better chance at solving the other. This isn't a surface-level issue. You have to dig deep."

At the words "childhood trauma," goosebumps break out over my arms. Is my love of dope linked to my entry into this world? Probably. Do I feel like spilling my guts to this uppity woman with bad teeth? No. There are some boundaries too strong to break. I fidget with the hem of my shirt.

Karen puts out a hand like a stop sign. "Let's just take it slow, huh? Start at the beginning?" She nods, a question.

I nod back. I don't want to do it, but what's my alternative?

"Tell me when you first started using," Karen says, sitting back in her chair.

"It was my seventeenth birthday." I know this because birthdays will forever be a reason to want to die, not celebrate. Turning seventeen is not something Mom or I are particularly fond of remembering. Seventeen is when bad things happen.

"So," she calculates, "about eight years ago?"

"Yeah. It was at a party at some house in North Broadway. I went with friends, and there was a guy who kept talking to me, flirting I guess. We hung out the whole night. I was drinking—everyone was—and then we did some lines of coke off the table. A bit later he said, 'You think you like this, I've got something even better.'"

"Did you know it was heroin?"

"I'm not an idiot."

"But you went along with it anyways?"

"I didn't have anything to lose."

Karen pauses then writes a short sentence on her notepad.

"We went to his car and he pulled out a little kit, like a small toiletry bag with a zipper. When I saw the needles, something in me said to get out, to go home, but I didn't. I said fuck it and let him stick it in my arm." The memory of that first time fills me with a euphoric warmth, as though I am getting high again right here in this tiny office. A fictional high. "That first time made me so sick, but it wasn't enough to stop me from doing it again. And then I was hooked."

"And how often would you say you used after that?"

"As often as I could. I guess maybe a couple times a week at first, but it quickly escalated to daily, then multiple times per day. Whenever I had money."

"Mmm-hmm. Okay. And after the two times you went to rehab, you were able to stay clean for a period?"

"The longest was two years. Just up until this past weekend." My shoulders slump at the admission. I was doing so good. What a fucking loser—just another thing I've failed at. Something hitches in my throat. Damnit. My voice goes small. "The drug—it's just too fucking strong."

"I know," Karen says, lowering her pen and meeting my eyes. "I know. That's why you're here. That's why we're going to work on the root of it all. But in order for it to work, you're going to have to trust me and trust the process, okay? It's one day at a time around here."

Oh, the cliché. This woman is delusional. Can't she see I'm beyond help? One day at a time—can't she see I'm one minute at a time? But reason takes over. Just say what she wants to hear, and you can be out of here soon. I nod. "Okay."

"Tomorrow I'd like to talk a bit about your family."

What family? It's just me and Mom, the woman whose life I'm slowly destroying. A pang, followed by a fleeting thought of Nicolas. I squeeze my eyes shut, as though I can scrub away the image of him. These memories, they haunt me. But again, I agree. I nod. Whatever you want to hear, lady.

We're finished—for now. Karen ushers me to the door and sends me off with a soft hand to the shoulder. I return to my room and flop onto the twin bed, depleted an understatement. The weight of it all hits with a different force than before. Stronger, with more sting. A tear rolls from my eye, over my nose and drops onto the pillow. My core temperature heats up again and within minutes my shirt is damp. I can't tell if it's the detox or postpartum sweats. My body is so confused with everything that's happened to it.

A familiar pang shoots through my chest, like a bullet. It might as well be one—my heart is completely bleeding. Minutes drag by, hours even slower. Being here is torture in more ways than one. I toss and turn, trying to distract myself with something, anything, to dull the pain. But the only thing that works, the only thing that's been able to mask the burden of existence is far away in a needle I can no longer reach.

TWENTY-SEVEN

BETWEEN INDIVIDUAL MEETINGS WITH KAREN ARE GROUP sessions—the ones where I can choose whether to sit next to a guy with god-awful B.O., or a girl who looks like she wants to kill everyone in the circle. Fun times. It's day three and I'm over it.

We're in our usual circle formation, taking turns answering the counselor's question: What are your main triggers to use?

"Whenever my dad opens his mouth," a girl with purple hair says. "Before he even speaks, I want to shoot up."

"Being around any sort of substance," another adds. "Doesn't matter what it is—alcohol, cigarettes—the idea of the high is enough to make me use."

B.O. guy speaks next. "Failure is my trigger. Flunking an exam. Losing a game." He looks like a college athlete—strong legs and broad shoulders. Maybe he goes to one of the schools around here, or maybe he's from another state completely. Just because I was able to stay local doesn't mean others don't travel far and wide to try to beat their addiction. He talks in the present tense, like losing a game happened just last week. I wonder how he's managed to stay in school. Then again, I did—at least for the two-year associate's degree.

"What about you, Jada?" Our counselor looks to me. She's round and matronly with blunt-cut bangs. The type that's given up on trying to be trendy. I can't say I blame her.

I pick at a scab on my forearm. What's my trigger? What's *not* my trigger? All eyes are on me, and I want to curl into a ball. My teeth grind together. I stare through her to the far wall, find the shape of a baby in the wallpaper pattern. Nicolas. If I can zone out enough, it'll be like I'm just talking to myself, not sharing all these private details with a bunch of strangers.

"Being alive," I say, my voice flat. My trigger is life itself.

There's a beat of silence, like she didn't expect quite a severe response. "Oh, okay, well... Thank you for sharing."

The group claps like they did for everyone else. Yay, congrats to me.

A girl around my age, maybe a little older, goes next. Her name tag says Mary Francis, which surprises me since it sounds like such a proper, religious name and I didn't think proper, religious people were drug addicts. She twirls a piece of wavy brown hair around her finger while she talks. Annoying. I don't hear what she says because my mind is elsewhere. The rest of the session blurs like one big mirage. I'm in a room full of people, but I'm utterly alone, lost in my thoughts.

There have been no news reports of a dead baby, as far as I can tell. Nothing at all about an abandoned newborn, which means Cate found him. She's taking care of him. She's loving him. A small voice in my head: *You did the right thing; you did the right thing.*

The screech of chairs against tile snaps me back to reality. Session is over, and everyone stands. I stand too, give my legs a little shake, and try to push away the nausea. I feel weaker than normal, my appetite completely suppressed.

"Want to play cards or something?"

I turn to find Mary Francis spinning a Claddagh ring. She's short and muscular and reminds me of a gymnast. I'm jealous of her nose stud, which Mom forbade, saying it would highlight my minority status even further. I pierced my belly button at sixteen instead.

"Oh, I—" It catches me off guard, and at first I'm not even sure she's talking to me. I wheel around to see if there's someone more appealing standing in my shadow.

"Never mind," she says quickly. "Forget I asked."

"No, it's just—I mean, I just got here. Well, just got done detoxing. I'm not used to... doing things, I guess."

"You'll go crazy if you just sit in your room the whole time. Trust me, I tried to do that for the first two weeks. Take my advice: Find something to do. I started offering hair styling to the women. It's sort of my thing. Even some of the staff has taken me up on it."

She's talking like we're best friends instead of meeting for the first time. It's kind of jarring. Still, I don't want her to leave. Dare I say it's nice to talk to someone aside from counselors? I keep the conversation alive. "How long have you been here?"

"This is day eighty-four for me." Her chin goes up a little, like she's proud.

Damn. Eighty-four days? Girl must have been *bad*. I'm thankful I'm only here for two weeks. "I can't imagine," I say.

"I couldn't either. But you go one day at a time, and pretty soon, you're at day eighty-four."

Okay, Karen. One day at a time—that must be this place's motto or something.

"So...?" she says and mimics dealing cards.

"Yeah, sure." What the hell? There's nothing else to do.

She gives a nod of approval. "I'm Frankie, by the way."

"I thought it was—"

"Mary Francis?" She laughs. "Yeah, no one calls me that besides my parents."

THE BABY LEFT BEHIND   163

"I'm Jada. Just Jada."

Mom said she almost named me Carlita after herself. Little Carla. It's now something we laugh about, the way a name fits a person. "You were always meant to be my Jada," she tells me. Now, those words burn. Is there really destiny in life? Are we born at exactly the moment the world intended? As much as I resist, I can't help but think of Nicolas.

Frankie and I walk to the common room that houses a ping-pong table and bookshelf full of creased-cover books and board games that look like they've been around longer than any of us. Two tables, a half-moon of chairs, and a couch frame a TV in the corner. We take the table on the right.

Frankie shuffles a deck of cards. "Rummy?"

I shake my head. "Don't know it."

"King's Corners?"

I shrug. "Nope." It's not like I grew up with family game night. When Mom wasn't sleeping, she was working two jobs to keep a roof over our heads. Cards are about as foreign to me as another language.

"Well, I guess I'll teach you then."

Why is she being so nice to me? Can't she tell I'm a terrible person? Apparently not, because Frankie acts like we've been friends for years. Like we're just two twenty-somethings in the prime of our lives gossiping about guys and which concerts are on our bucket lists. It's unsettling at first, but then I give into the distraction of it all. Whatever this is, it'll end the minute we leave here.

"What's the story behind your tat?" she says, dealing us each a pile of cards.

I flip my wrist, exposing the underside. "It's a sparrow. Supposedly a symbol of love. They were Aphrodite's favorite bird." I run the pad of my thumb over the black ink and think about drawing the same distinct image on the notecard I left with Nicolas.

Frankie raises her eyebrows. "You know Greek mythology?"

"Apparently you do too."

We smile. None of my other friends would have known who Aphrodite was.

"I took a class in high school and have loved it ever since." My face burns a little; I feel like such a dork. While most of my classmates bitched about reading Homer, I saw myself in the stories of fate and flaws. Reading them gave me hope that I, like Odysseus, would have a triumphant outcome.

Too bad nothing about my life is worth celebrating.

"Okay, so there are four suits: hearts, diamonds, spades, and clubs..."

But I can't focus on Frankie's instructions. The mention of my tattoo, remembering the note, has sent me back to that day. The internal push and pull. I wonder what he's doing. If Cate has kept him like I hoped. I try to conjure his face, but the edges are blurred. Maybe I could see him again, from afar, once I'm out. Little check-ins can't hurt, can they?

TWENTY-EIGHT

Frankie taught me to play poker this morning, and now I see how gambling can be addicting. Granted, we only played with blue plastic chips, not real money, but the excitement was the same. When I went all in and won, doubling my "cash," I got the same blissful lightness I've only known when junk hits my veins. Makes sense. Poker, shopping, heroin—it's all just a substitute for something else. Maybe I'm just predisposed to addiction of any kind. What did my last rehab call it? Addictive personality. Apparently, that's what I have. It's a fact but not an excuse.

I check the clock on the wall. Almost time for today's session with Karen. I think about what I would be doing if I weren't here. At work, checking in patients, bullshitting with Lexi between calls. When I agreed to treatment, Mom called Dr. Handrian with yet another plea: *Hold her job for a couple weeks. She's getting clean again. Please.* Like some sort of saint, Dr. Handrian agreed, but not without a firm warning. As much as she sympathizes, this will be the last time.

Begrudgingly, I hoist myself off the bed and head down the hall, arms crossed against my chest. My boobs are flatter now, and I no longer need nursing pads to catch the leaks. My head hurts today, a stubborn pain behind my eyes. Wonder what Karen's going to drag out of me this time.

I pass Frankie's room. The door is shut. I can't believe she gets out in three days. She says her stay flew by, but here I am on day seven. I didn't come expecting to make friends, and yet— I now know how to play poker.

A thin redhead leaves Karen's office as I approach. Her eyes are bloodshot. There's a lot of crying around here. Shame crying. Fear crying. Homesick crying. I give her a small smile, but she keeps her head down. I get it. We're all navigating our own shit.

"Jada. Come on in. How are you feeling today?" Karen's as welcoming as ever, her sweet voice the perfect match to her knack for humanity. I wonder if she ever gets tired of being so upbeat all the time. Doesn't she have problems too? A shitty day once in a while?

I shrug. "Same. No worse, I guess."

"That's great! A clear head is the perfect starting place for healing."

She always uses philosophical phrases like this. I imagine she's the owner of many notebooks and bookmarks plastered with inspirational quotes. It's a good day to have a good day. Mindset is everything. Be the reason someone smiles today. I hate that bullshit. Life's fucking hard and there's no way around it.

Karen flips her notepad to a clean page then crosses her wrists in her lap and waits for me to begin. When I don't— because I'm not sure what she wants me to say—she jumps in head first.

"Last time, I mentioned we should chat a bit about your family, your upbringing."

The familiar tangle in my stomach squeezes. I press my lips together.

"Can you tell me a little about your parents?" she says. "Do you have any siblings?"

"I'm an only child. It's just me and my mom."

"Has it always been?"

"Yeah." It's a roundabout question, and I know what the next one will be. My gaze hits the floor.

"Do you know anything about your father?"

Yep, I was right. I bite the inside of my cheek until I taste blood. It's hard enough to admit the truth to myself let alone share with anyone else. This is the one thing I've kept locked away, like a dangerous artifact that should never see the light of day.

Karen cocks her head. "This is a safe space, Jada."

I take a breath, a heavy thumping in my ears. Just say it. Then she'll understand why you are the way you are. My lips part. "He raped my mom."

She nods slowly, willing me to go on. Does nothing shock this woman? Apparently nothing is too disturbing when you're working with drug addicts. So much trauma, so many stories.

"She was seventeen," I say. There's that number again. "Doesn't know who it was. He was never caught."

"I'm so sorry, Jada." Her eyes are sad now, but it doesn't feel like an act—it feels real.

I pick a piece of lint from my pants. "Whatever. I mean, it is what it is. He's a loser, and Mom and me are better without him."

"But I'm sure knowing this has affected you internally, no?"

"What, like wishing I had a dad?" I snort a laugh. "Nope."

What I don't tell her is how I study every man I pass, looking for features like my own. How I've perfected the quick up-and-down. Are you my father? Are you the man whose DNA I carry? I have no idea if my mother's rapist still lives around here, or if he ever did for that matter. She doesn't talk about it, says she's erased that part of her life from memory.

Still, I search, not knowing if I even want to find him. But like a car wreck you can't help but stare at, I'm drawn to this self-destructive behavior. He could be alive, he could be dead. He could be in jail or be a reformed family man with other kids. It's the uncertainty that drives me. What will I do if I ever identify him? No clue.

Karen shakes her head. "No, not just wishing you had a dad. I mean deeper than that. Your identity, your self-worth."

A dry burning courses up my throat, like I might breathe fire. She's chipping at a wall I've held up—albeit barely—my whole life. This is not something I want to dive into. The pool is empty, and all that waits for me is a crash into concrete. Careful, Karen. You might not want to go there.

The room is quiet, but the silence is deafening. I interlace my fingers and squeeze.

"Let me rephrase," Karen says. "How about I make a statement and you just answer yes or no. Okay?"

I nod. I can do that.

"You feel unworthy of love."

I stare silently.

"Remember. Safe space," she says. Then, again, "You feel unworthy of love."

"Yes." The response comes so quick, I blink a couple times after hearing it leave my lips. It's the rawest truth I've ever admitted. I'm exposed.

"You sometimes think the world would be better if you were dead."

"Yes." My eyes prickle. My throat tightens.

"You think your mom's life would have been easier if she would have aborted you."

Right to the jugular. My chin's quivering now, and tears fall freely from my eyes. "Yes."

"You feel guilty for being alive."

I can't answer through my sobs. My body folds forward, my

shoulders heaving. This is all the answer Karen needs. She's up and at my side in seconds, rubbing my upper back, whispering soft words of comfort I can barely hear.

How does she know these things? These things that have been my secrets? I thought I'd hidden them so well.

We stay like this for what feels like a long time, until my cries slow and Karen returns to her seat. I don't know how it's possible to feel lighter and heavier at the same time. It's as though we've had a breakthrough yet have so much more work to do. This is just the tip of a really big iceberg.

Lethargy seizes me, and I wither in the chair. I wonder if I'll even be able to make it back to my room when we're finished.

"I'm so proud of you," Karen says. "That wasn't easy, I know. It takes courage to speak your truth."

I wipe my eyes with a tissue—I brought makeup from home, but there hasn't been a reason to wear it. I've always liked hiding behind the layers of foundation, bronzers, and highlighters, as though with a full face of makeup, I'm a different person.

"But," she continues, "those truths are all false beliefs. Your fears and responses are tied to disillusioned thoughts. They're lies, but they're powerful enough that you believe them. That's where your emotional wound lives." She searches my face to make sure I'm following. "You're worthy of being alive, Jada. You're not defined by the man who helped create you. I won't even use the word 'father' here—that's not a father."

My gaze floats around the room. These words—what she's saying—they sound nice, and I want to trust them, but instead my brain says, *Nah, girl.*

"You've been self-sabotaging for years. Searching for safety and acceptance that's been there all along. Your mother loves you, does she not?"

"Yes," I squeak. So she says, at least.

Karen gives me a pinched-lip smile. How many other girls

like me has she counseled? How many have heard these exact words? Break the cycle. Treat the trauma.

"Do you see what I'm saying? I know it's hard to hear, and probably goes against everything you've ever told yourself. But trust me. It'll take time to reprogram these thought patterns, but that's what I'm here for. We're going to get you healthy, Jada."

She waits for a second to see if I'm jumping on her bandwagon, and then, "Close your eyes. Go ahead—close them. Now, I want you to picture your ideal future. There are no barriers in your way; anything is possible. What does it look like? Sit there for a minute. Can you see it?"

At first all I see is a dull wall of eyelid. But I try, I really try. And an image forms. One where I'm clean and sober from this moment forward. Living somewhere with sunshine. A job that not only pays the bills but one I enjoy. The temptations gone. A little boy by my side. But no, I gave that little boy up. I can't take him back, can I? I'll be limited to driving by Cate's house to sneak peeks of my son. As soon as I'm out of here, it's what I'll do.

"Now open," Karen says. She gives a hopeful nod. "Did you see it? It's possible."

My heart swells. I'll forgive Karen's horrible clichés only because she's the first counselor I've ever connected with. Can I really be a whole new person? When Karen talks, it all sounds so clear, so... easy. I want to believe her. I visualize myself clean —actually clean, forever.

But there's a devil screaming in my ear.

She's lying to you. You're trash.

TWENTY-NINE

KAREN POPS HER HEAD INTO THE REC ROOM. "TEN minutes till Group, ladies."

I nod then, once she's out of sight, groan. "Does she always have to be so... up?"

Frankie smiles. "Right? I know." We're playing chess, and I'm losing. "I remember feeling the same way, like stop being so damn happy when my life is falling to shit."

"Exactly."

"But Karen's—"

"Nice."

"Nice."

"I didn't want to like her," I admit. The other counselors are so detached, like they're just going through the motions with yet another addict. Karen is different. Or maybe... I'm different too?

"Same. She has a way."

"Even if it's always chipper as hell."

Frankie laughs. "I get it. But better than being just *blah*. There's enough depression around here to sink a cloud." She moves a pawn to a black square on the board. "Checkmate."

"Bitch," I joke. It's the third game in a row she's trapped my king. I really need to up my gaming skills. Is this what normal people do for fun?

"You'll get the hang of it."

I sit back in my chair. "You know, I didn't plan on doing this while I was here."

"What? Play chess?"

"No. Talk to people. Like, real talk."

"You don't achieve recovery alone, Jada."

It sounds like something Karen would say, which would normally annoy the piss out of me but coming from Frankie is more tolerable. Maybe because we're similar in age, or because we're going through the same thing at the same time. Either way, it comes off less preachy and more like support from a—dare I say?—friend. Plus, Frankie's been here a lot longer than me. She must know what she's talking about.

"I've never been alone," I say, looking down at my nails. "At least not physically. Whether it's my mom, or friends—well, before I lost all those—or fake friends who only care about getting high, there's always someone around."

"Yeah, but are they the right people?"

I give her a look. We both know they're not the right people.

"Being alone and being lonely are two very different things."

"Jesus, what are you, a shrink now?" Is this girl really in her twenties?

Frankie laughs. "No. Just someone who's worked the steps and come out the other side. No one wants to hear this stuff when they're in the depths of it, but it's all true. I was just like you a few months ago and look at me now." She puts her hands under her chin like her face is on a pedestal. "You'll get there too. You'll keep improving and learning. Just like your chess game." She punches my arm playfully.

I let myself smile, even though something is pulling at me. This—whatever this is—makes me want to spill it all, lay everything out on the table, like I'm confessing dark secrets to my big sister. Frankie will understand, I tell myself. Let her in. Release some of the burden. And maybe, just maybe, she'll validate what you did, convince you not to change your mind. Tell you not to stalk Cate Connally's house.

I open my mouth to speak. It comes out more muffled than I intend. "Frankie, have you ever done something bad?"

She doesn't look up as she continues to pack the chess pieces away. "Ha! Don't you think we all have? I mean, look where we are."

"No, I mean, something... wrong. Something you regret."

"Yeah, sure."

She's definitely not thinking the same thing as me. Whatever shameful thing she did in her past could never live up to mine.

"I sold some of my mom's jewelry for money once," she says. "They were my great-grandmother's pieces, prized possessions. My mom was livid. I probably only got a fraction of what they were worth."

There it is. Jewelry. Nothing more than a *thing*. My "big wrong" involves a human life, and in that instant, I know I can't come clean as much as I want to. She'll never understand why I did what I did—what normal person would? My muscles harden and my defenses go back up. This is a secret I'll have to carry alone. Something stings in my eyes, but I'll be damned if I'm going to cry in front of some chick I just met, regardless of any feelings.

I change the subject. "So tomorrow's the big day, huh?"

Frankie takes a deep breath. "Yep. North Carolina, here I come."

"Sober living."

"Sober living. It's a transitional facility. Helps make the process a little easier until we're ready to live independently again. You should consider it."

"Think you'll be able to stay clean?"

"I hope so. I pray I can." She shrugs. "I feel strong. I really think I'm making the right steps this time."

"But why so far away?" I'm surprised by the emotion in my voice. I haven't felt friendship for so long, I forgot what it's like when you're about to lose it. The feeling takes me by surprise. Surely there must be places closer.

She shakes her head. "I can't go back to my old life. Those same people, they'll just suck me back in. I need a fresh start, somewhere new. I might go back to school. Maybe someday open my own salon. Plus, I'm ready to get the hell out of this weather."

I can't fault her there. Northern Ohio winters blow—no one would argue that. A bit of sunshine would be amazing, but I couldn't imagine leaving Mom all alone. Then again, maybe her life would be better if I were a thousand miles away.

Something must register on my face because Frankie reaches out and squeezes my hand. "One day at a time." Then, "Let's go. Don't want to be late for Group."

The next day, a soft knock on my door makes my eyes flutter open. It's midday, but napping has become as much a part of my daily routine as breathing. My body is finally catching up on hours of lost sleep. I've been here ten days and I've slept at least ten hours each night.

The door inches open, and Frankie's face peeps through the crack.

"Already?" I say, checking the alarm clock on the nightstand. No, not yet.

"My flight's at three."

She pushes the door open the rest of the way, and I stand. A large duffel bag lies on the floor by her feet, a tasseled hobo purse slung over her shoulder. We stare at each other like we're kids again, arms folded across our chests like dams bursting to break free. It's an awkwardness—her wanting to leave, me wanting her to stay. I clench my toes to keep it together, but on the inside I'm screaming.

"You can do this," she says. "Don't think too far ahead, just take it one day at a time. Remember, you're not alone."

I nod, feeling like an imposter. Frankie has so much more confidence in me than I do in myself.

"Here." She extends a scrap of paper. "My number. Call me when you're out, huh? Maybe you can visit Wilmington. Get yourself a little sun and sand."

I give a twitch of a smile, imagining walks on the beach, waves crashing around my ankles.

"Let me give you mine," I say, tearing a page from the spiral-bound journal Karen gave me. Who knows if either of us will ever dial these numbers, but it feels nice to pretend. The likelihood is slim. This is all just polite manners, a way to say goodbye. Frankie's leaving and starting a new life. She'd never want to stay in touch with someone like me.

From down the hall, a woman calls her name, and my chest cramps.

"My ride. I better go," she says.

We shift awkwardly, until Frankie reaches out and wraps me in a hug. She smells like sweet mint and cucumber. We stay like that for several long minutes. Neither of us is in a hurry to let go.

"Take care of yourself, okay?"

"You too. Good luck." I bite back the tears.

She lets go, and we share a final smile. With a cleansing breath, she turns and leaves. In her absence, a familiar emptiness roots down, like she's taking with her all the sunshine or oxygen from the world.

She said I'm not alone. But I look around and see otherwise. No Frankie. No Nicolas. The fire inside me burns.

Use. Use. Use.

THIRTY

THE FOLLOWING MONDAY IT'S MY TURN. IT'S MY LAST DAY here, and I have to admit, the cravings have eased. Not completely—I don't think they'll ever go away completely—but they're definitely less strong than when I first arrived two weeks ago. I've survived without Frankie. My sessions with Karen renewed all the teachings I learned last time. None of it's new. It's so easy to fall off the wagon and much harder to get back on. *Work the steps*, they tell us. That's easier said than done. All I can do is take it one day at a time and hope to God I don't relapse again. But hope's a bitch and it hurts.

Before I leave, I take one last look at my room, where I've spent the last fourteen days. It's minimal, but it's been a home of sorts, providing a sense of safety when I never felt that on the outside. My breath hitches, and I pause for a minute to interpret this feeling. Sadness? Eagerness? No, it's something darker. It's fear. Part of me is scared to leave here.

I picture Nicolas and imagine how he's changed since that day I left him at Cate Connally's door. The image is fuzzy, but I do my best. Are his cheeks fuller? Does he still fit into newborn clothes? The emotions are conflicting—regret mixed with certitude. My belly knots. Even if I really did want him back (which I still can't determine for sure), it's too late now. She'll be a better mother than me. If my track record has proven anything, it's that I'm weak and selfish, two things a parent can't be.

No, I just want to get back to my life. Back to work and saving money and staying on the right path. Forget about this latest bump in the road, the shameful things I did.

I yank open the dresser drawers and shove all my belongings into the canvas bag I brought with me from home—two pants, couple shirts, my toiletries. The little fan I use as white noise, as though it would bring me a speck of comfort. I didn't come with much, and I'm leaving with the same.

In the lobby, a new girl enters through the sliding doors, guided by one of the male counselors. She looks rough, hair matted, makeup smeared, like life's been mean to her. It probably has—life isn't our best friend before coming here. The girl looks at me then darts her eyes quickly away. Dodgy—I get it. That was me too. I briefly think back to those first two days here and shudder. The detox, the pain. You couldn't pay me to trade places with her. Nope, no thank you.

Karen is here, next to me in a seafoam-green blouse. This lady and her pastels. "Day fourteen," she says proudly.

"Day fourteen."

"I'm proud of you."

I'm not used to warm and fuzzy, so I just shrug and look down. My face warms.

Karen places two hands on my shoulders. "Remember the things we've talked about. You, your past, your present. What brought you into this world. You're valid. You're worthy. Okay?"

I nod again and pray that one day I'll be able to believe the things she says. That a day in the distant future, I won't carry around such a heavy mental load. Truthfully, I can't imagine it.

The woman at the front desk hands me my phone, which they'd confiscated when I'd arrived. I power it on to find several texts from Hugo: Do I need any dope? Do I want to come party? I delete them on the spot.

Karen walks me to the door, like I'm a kindergartener being escorted to the first day of school.

"Be well, Jada," she says, and we exchange smiles.

Mom waits in the parking lot for me. I exit the double doors to a cold, gray February day.

"Hi," Mom says.

"Hi."

She gives me a kiss on the forehead, and we get in the car. I study her face. It looks so much like mine, only older. What must she think of me? Are we about to jump on this wheel again? Will I continue letting her down?

I stop the thoughts with a firm *No*. No, this time will be different. I'm going to pretend there isn't a little boy out there, carrying my genes and half of my heart. I'm going to silence the voice that says to find him. It's better this way. I just have to trust it.

THIRTY-ONE

Two weeks later

A BABY SCREECHES IN THE NEXT AISLE, AND MY BOOBS tingle like there's milk that wants to let down even though it's been dried up for weeks. Will it ever stop? Despite shrinking, my breasts are heavy in my bra. I hate this feeling, my body reacting to something against my will, not giving a shit that there's no baby here to feed. Fucking nature. I'm just trying to check out with a salad for lunch and mind my own business, but the world seems to be thrusting babies in my face wherever I go.

I glance over and see the frazzled mom, attempting to console her infant. That would have been me, a clueless parent who can't even soothe her flesh and blood. But the cry does something to me, and I can't help but analyze it. Regardless what people think, they're not all the same. This one's shrill and chopped, where Nicolas's was more insistent—I think. It's been a month, and I'm already starting to forget what he sounded like. It's the worst kind of shame.

The middle-aged man working the register has thinning hair and fat fingers. I give him a once-over. Not my father.

I check out faster than the other woman and let out a long breath as I speed-walk across the parking lot, shaking my hands and telling myself to focus. Forget the past. Stay present. I've stayed clean in the two weeks since I left treatment. I can't let dark thoughts pull me back.

At work, I find distraction. It's more of the same: patients and charts and scheduling. Lexi trying to get me to sign up for a new dating app, Dr. Handrian asking if Mom's going to their reunion this summer. They were high-school friends once, a lifetime ago, before circumstances sent them on very different trajectories—one to medical school, the other to changing diapers at eighteen. I'm lucky Dr. Handrian is not only kind but tolerant, that she's given me *another* chance. It's something Mom never fails to remind me of.

We close for lunch at noon. Lexi pushes back from the desk, and we walk to the small staff breakroom with a mini fridge and microwave. "Want to hit up Subway? I'm dying for a BLT."

Who dies for a BLT? I think, but reply instead with, "Thanks, but I brought a salad." I open the fridge. "Wait, where *is* my salad?" Then, "Shit, I think I left it in my car." That crying baby in the grocery store really distracted me. Ugh, it's too cold to trudge back outside. I groan, annoyed, then huff out of the office, down the hall past other departments and toward the exit of the building. Pediatrics is the last one before the sliding doors, and I plan to avert my eyes like I do every time I enter or exit this place. It's just too painful to see the little faces and wonder about an alternative life. Only today, my path is blocked. There's a woman in the hall, phone to her ear and a baby carrier hung on the crook of her arm. I don't think much of it—it's a pediatrician's office after all—until I get a bit closer and stop suddenly in my tracks like I've hit a wall and can't move an inch further. Every ounce of air leaves my lungs.

This isn't any woman. It's Cate Connally.

And if this is Cate Connally, that must mean the baby is...

I choke on a cough and feel the blood drain from my face. Oh my god. It's Nicolas. It's my son.

Cate must recognize me, because she lifts a hand and says hi. I blink, back and forth between her and Nicolas in the car seat. He's so much bigger! So... so... beautiful. I'm gaping, I know, but I'm far too stunned to speak. All the people in this city, all the moms and babies who I could have bumped into, and it's them. The timing—is it a sign? Or my penance?

I'm stuck back in the memory of that day, leaving him at the house with the pine-cone wreath and carefully shoveled sidewalk. I had no more tears then, but now I feel like a fire hydrant ready to surge, as though all my emotion has been withheld for weeks.

How could I have given up my baby? Something powerful and maternal kicks in, much more than those early days. An undeniable pull. My eyes are glued to him.

"Oh!" Cate laughs nervously. "Yes, I... The adoption agency called last month. Can you believe it?"

So this must be the story she's telling. An adoption. That would make sense—I recall Cate telling Dr. Handrian about her adoption journey, how she'd been in the delivery room and everything, ready to take the baby home, when the birth mother changed her mind. The whole office had sympathized with Cate at that time. How horrific, how wrong. It's why I chose her. Now, it seems to the outside world that Cate Connally's dreams have finally come true. They look perfect together. Cate is a natural. And that is the most bitter thing of all.

Only it's a lie. This isn't an adopted baby. It's my baby. And seeing him here for the first time in a month brings up emotions I thought I'd squashed. A flame ignites, something savage, and with a force that feels involuntary. I have the urge to reach for him and never let go. My baby, my son, he should be with me. What did I do?

I bring two hands to my mouth, as water floods my vision.

But not enough that I can't see Cate's face drop and go as faint as mine. She looks to Nicolas, then back to me. Not my face, something a bit lower. She's eyeing my tattoo.

I can't stop my arms from reaching for him. I know what I need to do.

PART 3

THIRTY-TWO

CATE

"Nicolas," she whispers, and my stomach goes sour. She reaches for him.

"No." I take a step back, holding the car seat as close to me as humanly possible. "This is Henry."

She looks to me. "Cate, it was me. That day, I— He's mine."

I'm shaking my head furiously, panic bubbling to the surface with each passing second. If you'd have given me a thousand guesses, I never would have picked the young nurse from Dr. Handrian's office. But now, this woman—I see her ID badge says Jada Morales in big, black letters, and the name comes back to me from all those office visits—stares at Henry with a grief-stricken face. This is the woman who left Henry at my door? Now, my vision of the hooded woman has a face.

"No," I say again, but she's not listening.

"He's so beautiful." She keeps coming closer, and I keep backing away. Tears fall down her cheeks now. She reaches toward him. "Nicolas, I'm so sorry. I made a mistake. I—"

I don't let her finish. "I don't know what you're talking about," I say, putting my hand out to stop her. My arm shakes. "You must have me confused with someone else."

Even as I say it, I feel stupid. We each know who the other is. There's no denying the unfathomable triangle we find ourselves in. But instinct tells me to deny, deny, deny.

And fear makes me run.

"Wait!" Jada calls behind me. "Stop! My baby!"

I bolt from the building, holding Henry's car seat like I'm a robber running away with an armful of loot. Henry screams from all the jostling. His face is scarlet, eyes sealed shut, gums exposed. My mama instinct wants to stop and console him, but there's no time for that.

Ohmygod, ohmygod, ohmygod.

How is this possible? It can't be.

But it is.

That tattoo. It's her. Henry's mo—

No, I can't say it. Can't even think it.

Without even the quickest glance backwards, I throw the car in gear and fly into the street. Henry lets out a wail.

"It's okay, sweet boy," I say in my most soothing voice, though there's an edge of disbelief even I can't ignore. Nothing's okay. This has all suddenly gone very, very wrong—and the thought of what's coming next makes me want to pull over and get sick.

Turns out I do pull over, not to vomit but to attend to Henry. I can't let him scream the whole way, trapped behind a five-point harness, and my binkie-contortion trick isn't working. I steer the car to the side of the highway and slam it in park, then climb through the seats to the back, bumping my head on the overhead light, next to where Henry's in a full-blown melt-down. He's still in pain, lugged here for treatment he never received.

"I know, I know," I say, tearing through the diaper bag as fast as I can—the last few weeks with Henry have taught me to be prepared. I pour water into his bottle, dump in the formula packet and give it a shake. My whole body is vibrating. "Okay, buddy. It's coming—let's get you out of there."

I unbuckle and lift him out of the car seat, cradling his sweaty body in my arms. He takes the bottle instantly, suckling interrupted by receding gasps as his body calms.

That's one of us at least.

His wails have stopped, but there's still ringing in my ears. This is dangerous. A car on the side of the road is like a flashing neon sign. Look at me! Look at me! Did Jada call the police? Did she watch which direction we left in? There could be cops swooping in on us at any second, yet here I wait like a sitting duck, desperate to comfort Henry even at the risk of getting caught.

I look ahead, then back, every direction I can. I listen for sirens. Nothing. Just cars passing as normal. No one stops.

Yet.

Breathe, Cate. Stay focused. My gaze drops to Henry, whose incessant sucking is putting him to sleep. One of his tiny hands wraps around my pinky finger, squeezing for dear life. My nose prickles. As I watch him, I'm overcome with sadness. What will happen to him? To us?

I'm hot, sweat running down my back and chest. The whole thing has me worked up on so many levels. The way Jada looked at Henry can't be described in words, yet her complicated eyes said everything. It's something I'll never understand, and that both devastates and scares me.

As Henry takes his last gulps from the bottle, water crests my lids. He's all I've ever wanted, all I've ever dreamed about. After so many shitty deals, I finally got a good hand. He feels like my blood, like I was meant to be his mom. My sole purpose is to give him a life he deserves. I can't let her take him away from me. This isn't just about me; it's about Henry too. He needs to be taken care of—loved and protected. Not with someone who would leave him on a doorstep in the freezing cold.

Then a thought, like the strike of a match, hot and fast: What if we disappeared? Left town, left the state, the country even. He and I could start a new life somewhere. We'd both be safe. I could come up with a story—a battered wife, seeking safety for herself and her child. False identities, a new haircut, the works.

I cover my mouth to stop myself from throwing up. What am I thinking? It's asinine. Not only digging my own grave but burying myself in it as well. I've completely lost it. I hiccup a sob. My conscience pulls tight, but my heart pulls even harder. We might not run away and disappear, but I'm not giving up. This isn't over, not yet.

It's scary how powerful delusion can be.

I feel the hairs lift from the nape of my neck. As much as I wish we could stay right here like this forever, enclosed in safety, two bodies heart to heart, I need to get moving. I can't just keep sitting here, a car on the side of the road. The inevitable is a sticky web I'm resisting. No one likes to touch a cobweb, especially when it's so thick you can't see through to the other side.

Scenarios spin out of control in my mind. What am I going to do? What is *she* going to do?

For now, I ease a milk-drunk Henry back into his car seat and buckle him up without protest. The bottle has appeased him for the moment. Get home—that's all I can think. Home is safety. I'll figure it all out there.

I look around before getting Henry out of the car, as if my neighbors don't already know about him and I'm smuggling in a forbidden object. I guess, in a sense, he sort of is.

Mercifully, he's asleep, finally giving into that post-meal

nap he desperately needs. I don't think I could handle any more crying right now. My brain's already short-circuited. I'll re-dose the Tylenol when he wakes and figure out where and how to get him medical help. The thought of going to another doctor's office or the ER has me spooked, but Henry's health will always win. He's the trump card, even at my downfall.

I leave Henry in his car seat in the middle of the living room. And then I pace. Back and forth, hands to my temples. Think, Cate. Breathe and think. Call and turn yourself in. Get the upper hand. Admitting defeat must bode better than being caught.

I replay the encounter. Jada might not have recognized Henry, but she certainly recognized me. He's no longer the scrawny, wrinkly newborn that first came into my life. In just a few weeks, his face has filled out. There's a double set of rolls on his thighs, and his nails grow so fast I have to cut them twice a week. A cowlick on the back of his head means there's always a fluff of hair that won't lie flat. These details weren't there before. She wouldn't know these things. She hasn't comforted him in the middle of the night or been on the receiving end of his first smile. These are privileges reserved for mothers who don't neglect such a sacred role.

Then again, mothers and children are connected with an invisible thread so strong it can never be broken. I get it: she'd recognize him anywhere. And once she saw my face, she put two and two together.

I breathe hard and fast, a plummeting in my core. It's over. Time's up.

But then fear flips to anger, and I stop mid-stride. I remember all the reasons I took him in the first place. The fear of what would happen to him otherwise, the canyon he filled in my life. No, I won't call. Maybe there's still hope. I sit down next to Henry and lean in to smell him. I can't give up on this.

THE BABY LEFT BEHIND   191

But the more I sit, the more the fear creeps back in. I'm a yo-yo.

Call, don't call.

Run, don't run.

Regardless of what happened that day, what's happened over these few blissful weeks, the reality is that it's about to all come crashing down. Jada knows where I live. She's been here before, unbeknownst to me, and something tells me she'll be back again.

My stomach roils. The house is quiet. Too quiet. Fake quiet. As if someone's about to jump out and scare me. I look around and am suddenly afraid of being alone. Instinct tells me this is not going to end well. And as much as my earlier thoughts were on an escape plan, it now sounds utterly foolish. How the hell did I think I could pull this off?

THIRTY-THREE

AFTER TWO, THEN FOUR, THEN SIX HOURS PASS WITHOUT the doorbell ringing, I start to consider the possibility I'm in the clear. Was this all just a misunderstanding? Jada must have had reasons for leaving him—did those justifications resurface? Did she talk herself out of motherhood a second time? I could spiral into a tornado of what-ifs, but instead I keep the curtains drawn as though a layer of embroidered cotton will protect us from everything.

Frantic Google searches bring up little about Jada Morales. I find her Facebook and Instagram accounts, but they're set to private, so all I can see is a car selfie as her profile picture. I go to the hospital's website. There are headshots and bios listed for all the physicians, including Dr. Handrian, but nothing for the rest of the staff. My fingers dance across the keyboard; I'm frantic to learn anything I can about this woman.

It's five o'clock when I hear the hum of a car engine outside my house. When it dies and a door shuts, I'm filled with so much dread I can't even get myself to the window to see. I don't have to wait long though, because within seconds there's a firm knock at the door. I peer through the peephole and everything crashes around me. It's her—Jada Morales. She wrings her hands and sways from side to side. And those eyes, they're determined.

I tiptoe back, just as she knocks again. And again. Then the doorbell, and finally: "Cate, please. I know you're here. Let me in—we need to talk."

Talk? About what? About how she abandoned her child and now wants him back? I don't think so. I'll stay inside this house forever if that's what it takes. Maybe if I don't answer, she'll go away.

"Cate." *Pound, pound, pound.* "Cate!"

I bite my lip to keep from crying.

"He's my son! Cate!" *Pound, pound, pound.*

The knocking has elevated to banging, and her voice is now more of a shout. What if the neighbors hear? I can't risk anyone knowing the truth.

"Please, open the d—"

I fling the door wide, and then we're standing face to face. Jada's eyes are red-rimmed. Blotchy hives crawl up her neck. Her nails are painted a shocking blue. She's still wearing her medical scrubs, but the ID badge has been removed.

"What do you want?" I say, breathing hard. At any moment my legs might give out from under me.

"I... I don't know. I just... I want to see him. Is he all right? Is he..." She's blubbering, can't catch her breath or make any semblance of a coherent sentence.

I glance around to make sure no one's watching. This girl is falling apart on my front steps, and despite every urge I have to slam the door in her face, something tells me that would cause even more of a scene.

"Come in," I say, and she barrels through the doorway.

Henry is asleep in his bouncer chair on the floor—I couldn't bear to put him in the nursery so far from where I held watch.

Jada dives for him, falling to her knees. She caresses the air around him, like she's afraid to touch him, afraid to wake him. "Oh, Nicolas, I'm so sorry. I should never have left you. I love you so much."

I stand back and watch in utter horror as she weeps and begs for forgiveness from an infant who knows nothing. She takes a finger and strokes the top of his hand.

"Don't touch him," I say.

She turns. "He's my son."

"Okay, but..." I'm frantic, willing to say anything to appease her and make her leave. But then the anger bubbles up. "You left him."

"You don't understand." She sniffs and wipes her nose with her forearm. "I was messed up. I wasn't thinking straight."

"It was freezing."

"I knew you'd care for him."

"Why me?"

"All those times I saw you at the office. Your story. I knew how bad you wanted a baby, and how unfair it was that you never got one. You seemed like a good person. Someone who would love him."

"Like you couldn't?"

"I didn't even know I was pregnant!" she hurls. "It's not like this was some premeditated thing for nine months. I literally had him in my apartment, by myself, and no one even knew. Not my mom, not my friends, not my boss."

I stare, wide-eyed. Is this some sob story to make me feel bad for her? If so, it's not working. "I don't believe you. How could you not know you were pregnant?"

She cocks her head. "Have you been pregnant before?"

"No, but—"

"Then you have no idea. I didn't think it was possible, but guess what, it is." The redness on her neck crawls up toward her face. She's agitated, defensive, and then as if something washes over her, a realization perhaps, she closes her eyes. Her tone softens. "But it was too much. It was too hard. I couldn't do it."

"Motherhood is *supposed* to be hard, Jada. That doesn't mean you just give your baby away and pretend like it never happened." I momentarily cringe—it's something Mom would say.

"I relapsed."

"Relapsed?"

"Heroin."

I shudder, but then she follows it up quickly with, "Don't worry, I went back to treatment. I'm clean now."

"You're not taking him," I say, surer than anything in my life.

"I was clean for two years before this. I can do it again—I know I can." Her words are a contrast to her expression, which reads much more uncertain.

Little by little, the strong exterior cracks. She looks back to Henry, gently touches his face, and then droops. "I don't know what I want. I thought I could move on knowing he'd have a better life with you than with me. But when I saw him today, everything came flooding back, only stronger. Something changed. I had to have him. I can think clearer now, but at the same time, I'm not sure what's right. Nothing makes sense anymore."

"I won't let you take him," I say again.

She stands, comes close to me. We're in a face-off. "But he's mine. I gave birth to him. I have the documents to prove it. All it would take is a DNA test and..."

My mind drifts to the very real consequences I could face. Is this kidnapping? No, I didn't steal anything. The note said to take him. So I can't really get in trouble, can I?

I can't go to jail. But I also can't lose Henry.

"I'll let you see him," I blurt, instantly hating it but desperate for something. I feel trapped, backed into a corner. I don't want her to take him away from me, but I also don't want her to turn me in to the police. Could there be a happy middle?

"What do you mean?"

"Supervised visits. You can come here and spend time with Henry—"

"It's Nicolas."

"—but he stays with me."

Jada's eyes are locked on mine, and we stay like that for a long minute, both tossing around my proposal. *She'll never agree to it*, I think, but still, I cling to any thread of hope.

Finally, she looks back to Henry. "I can be a good mother," she says softly.

"Can you though?" I have to persuade her with everything I have. "I love him and will continue to love him. He's happy here."

Jada falls to the floor again. Her shoulders shake and she drops her chin to her chest, runs a hand over the track scars lining her arms. The wrestling isn't just internal, because she physically rocks, knees pulled to her chest.

"Do it for him," I say.

Jada lays a hand on Henry's belly, like she's feeling for a heartbeat. I'm teetering on a ledge. One breath and over I'll go. *Please.*

It's a long minute before she whispers an answer. "Okay."

THIRTY-FOUR

WE AGREE TO MONDAY AND THURSDAY EVENINGS. JADA will come over when she gets out of work, spend some time with Henry, then go. I refuse to leave the room when she's here. Instead, I watch like a hawk, torn in a million different ways, and wishing I'd never stepped foot into that hallway to take that call. Jada would have walked right past the pediatrician's office and been none the wiser. That, and Henry would have been treated sooner for what turned out to be a nasty double ear infection diagnosed by a young doctor at a walk-in clinic who bought my story about Henry getting on my insurance imminently. Now, three days later, my boy is back to his pleasant self, the antibiotic doing its job.

It's Thursday, which means Jada will be coming over tonight. I've spent the morning with a steady case of mild nausea at the thought. When Ryan called asking if Henry and I wanted to meet him for lunch, I jumped at the chance for a momentary distraction. Work was slow, and I spend most lunches in front of my computer with a cold-cut sandwich. Today feel like a good excuse for something a bit nicer.

We go to the little Italian place halfway between our

houses, not only because the service is quick, but because Ryan knows I love the garlic bread.

"Who doesn't love pasta in the middle of the day?" he jokes as we both order the lunch special of spaghetti and meatballs—half of which will make a nice, leftover dinner later.

While we wait, I get Henry out of the car seat and hold him on my lap.

"Handsome boy," Ryan says.

"He's drooling like crazy, even though it's way too early for him to cut a tooth." I adjust his bandana bib to protect his shirt.

"When do teeth come?"

"Gosh, I think Becky's boys were at least seven or eight months."

"Soon he'll have a whole mouthful of chompers."

"Yeah, I'm already saving for braces." I rub my fingers together like one does when something's expensive.

"Cha-ching," Ryan echoes.

As the conversation naturally continues—dates, and the latest Netflix must-watch, and upcoming travel plans—it hits me that I haven't once thought of the big lie. We've been sitting here for half an hour and it's felt as normal, as everyday, as possible. No guilt-ridden cluster in my stomach. No constant worry about spinning my narrative. And that—the realization of how easy this charade has become—puts a bad taste in my mouth, so much so that I take a big gulp of water to wash it down.

We take turns holding Henry as we eat, and he's the best little boy. When Ryan holds him, I stare at Henry's little face, and when Henry's with me, Ryan gawks back.

"Now that he's here, can you even imagine your life without him?" Ryan asks.

"No." I take another sip from the straw.

He shifts in his chair. "Hey, listen, there's something I wanted to tell you—"

But his sentence is cut off when Henry lets out a string of gas, so audible Ryan's mouth falls open in amused revulsion. The smell that quickly follows tells me it was more than just gas.

"Did he just—"

I lift Henry by the torso and one leg and am met with a lovely gift: A large yellow-brown stain halfway up his back and down to the backs of his knees.

"Explosion," I say, holding Henry aloft, then turning him to show Ryan.

"Holy shi—"

"Yep, holy shit. A lot of holy shit."

Henry's face turns red and he lets another one rip.

"Good Lord!" Ryan says, and we both laugh.

"I'm going to go change him really quick," I say, trying to grab the diaper bag without getting baby poop all over myself. We head to the restroom, where I lay Henry on the fold-out changing table and use half a pack of wipes to clean him off. A fresh diaper and outfit later, we're back at the table.

I let out a breath. "Sorry about that. What were you saying before poopgate?"

Ryan looks at his phone. "Shit, I have to get back. It was nothing. I'll call you later, okay?" He gives Henry a kiss on the head, we pack up our food, and head back home.

Five hours later, Jada sits on the floor next to where Henry lies on a playmat, staring up at dangling rings and colorful circus animals. He kicks and swats at them, making Jada laugh.

"Can you reach them?" she says to him. "Here." She unlinks one of the plastic rings and puts it in his palm. His fingers instinctively clench around it. At six weeks, he's not old enough to bring it to his mouth yet, but I know that phase will be coming soon. This thought prompts me to open my mouth from the chair in the corner where I've been hovering.

"When's his birthday?" I say, feeling embarrassed to ask. The date I've been using, the day I supposedly went to meet him at the hospital, isn't right, but there was no way for me to know the exact date he was born.

"January twelfth. It was a Thursday."

So he was seven whole days when he came to me.

She continues talking to Henry as though I'm not here. "Your grandma's name is Carla. Maybe you'll meet her some-day. When you're older she'll make you mofongo. It's my favorite Puerto Rican meal. I know you'll like it too."

I cringe, hearing her talk about the future—one she plans to be very much a part of. My mind drifts to what her upbringing was like. Were her parents at every sporting event? Did she get to go school clothes shopping every August? Was the skating rink rented out for a private party on her twelfth birthday? I don't need concrete answers to make a general conclusion. Something tells me Jada has had a very different life than mine.

How am I going to get her away from him? What can I say to make her realize the best thing is for him to be with me? First things first, I need to set up some parameters if this is going to continue—and as an out for when she will inevitably break.

"This arrangement isn't without strings," I say, and Jada gives me a look.

"What's that supposed to mean?"

"Henry needs stability. He needs to be around people who are... you know... good." She stares, waiting for further explana-tion. "You say you're clean. But if that changes, if you relapse again, this deal is over."

Her eyes narrow. "Are you threatening me?"

"No, I— Look, I'm just doing what's in his best interest, okay." Because in my mind, she'll surely relapse again. And when that happens, *poof*—visitation over.

"I could walk out the door with him today and there's nothing you can do to stop me," Jada says with a smug air.

I put a throw pillow in a chokehold, knowing she's right but terrified to enrage her any further. I don't want to be mean or greedy, and part of me aches for her position. But that sympathy only goes so far. This is a fine line to balance.

Henry tires of lying on the playmat, like he always does after fifteen minutes or so, and makes a noise of displeasure. I go to reach for him, but Jada beats me to it. She lifts him up, resting him in a cradle hold. He squirms, back arched, gives out a few unpleasant grunts.

"He doesn't like to be held like that," I say.

She adjusts him, without looking my way. "I got it."

"No, he prefers to be—"

"I said I got it."

I clamp my mouth shut and bite so hard my teeth might break.

Eventually, Henry dozes off and Jada lays him back down. She drapes a light blanket over his legs and gives his tummy a gentle pat. My skin crawls when she touches him. These three hours are excruciating, and I just want the time to be over and for her to leave. But even then, the reprieve will be short-lived, as the next visit will roll around. I'm nauseous just thinking about it.

"How many ounces is he drinking now?" Jada asks, jolting me from my thoughts.

"Uh, about four or so."

"How often?"

I give her a look. What's this line of questioning for? "Usually every three or four hours, sometimes longer through the night if he sleeps well." I can't help it—my defenses pique: "Why do you care all of a sudden?" She better not be getting any ideas. I'm not letting Henry out of my sight. He's not leaving this house unless it's with me.

"I'm just curious about my son, that's all. I missed out on the last month of his life."

"By your own doing," I remind her, and she looks down.

"Listen, I said I was sorry. Maybe I didn't do the right thing. Maybe I did. It's all very conflicting. All I know is that I'm trying to make up for it."

The silence hangs there awkwardly. I've dug at the skin on my hands so much it's left marks. Time for this to be over. Time for her to leave.

"He'll probably sleep for a while," I say as a cue. It's nearing eight o'clock and I'm so drained I feel like I could fall asleep standing.

"Okay." Jada stands but not without first leaning down to plant a soft kiss on Henry's head. "Bye, Nicolas."

"Please don't call him that."

Her brows scrunch. "It's his name."

"Maybe at first, but he's been Henry for longer. It'll just confuse him."

"I'll call him what I want to call him."

I grip the edge of the chair. It takes everything in my power not to fight her on this, but I worry that if I push too hard, she'll take him away. I have to let her think she's getting the best of both worlds in this situation.

Jada puts on her coat. "We should exchange numbers. You know, in case of an emergency or if one of us need to get in touch with the other."

Is she crazy? I don't want her knowing anything about me. We're not co-parents. She's not who I would call in an emergency. "I don't think that's necessary," I say.

"But what if—"

"No." I shake my head vehemently then wave a finger between us. "This is fine for now."

Jada gives a final look to the sleeping baby. It seems laborious for her to move, but she slowly takes one step, then another, toward the door. "Monday then?"

I don't respond because even though it's what we agreed on, I don't want to think about it. Don't want it hanging over my head all weekend long. How is this going to work?

Jada eyes me hopefully, but all I can do is give a curt nod and shut the door.

THIRTY-FIVE

THE VISITS CONTINUE IN THIS SAME PAINFUL FASHION FOR the next two weeks. Every Monday and Thursday I wake up with knots in my stomach just thinking about Jada coming over. It's so uncomfortable, watching her interact with Henry. But more than that, the visual is what really hits me: he looks just like her. Their skin tone, their dark hair, all of it a contrast to me. When she's here, it's sorely obvious that she's his mother—at least on the outside. And if she's his mother, what does that make me? Nothing. It makes me nothing.

This morning, I laid Henry on the black-and-white monthly blanket to take his two-month picture. "Hey, you stinker," I cooed, giving his belly a tickle, then hurriedly snapped a burst of pictures when he broke into a gummy smile that melted my heart.

Mom, Dad, Becky, and the boys are coming over for dinner tonight, a ritual Mom tries to hold on to but one that is increasingly difficult to maintain, especially when Becky's perfect husband works seven days a week. "It's important," she chides. And while I would usually be irritated before they even arrived, it's recently served as a good distraction from the fact that tomorrow is Monday—which means another visit from Jada.

"Hello!" Mom sings as she comes through the door. "Where's that perfect little prince of mine?"

She gives me no option but to hand him over, which I do with a smile. Seeing her in her prime—with my child—gives me such a sense of purpose.

Dad comes in behind her and takes off his newsboy cap. "Hi, Birdie girl," he says, giving me a kiss on the cheek, like I'm a child with pigtails instead of a grown woman. I'd be lying if I said I didn't like it.

"Have you grown in the last three days since I saw you?" Mom exclaims with her dramatic flair. "What is your mama feeding you?" She holds him up and baby talks to his face before slathering him in kisses.

"Mom, your lipstick," I say, and we all chuckle.

Becky arrives just on time, as expected. Even with two kids in tow, she prides herself on promptness "like any decent person should." Landon and Owen blow past me to the bin of toys I've collected for Henry, all of which are far too advanced for an eight-week-old.

"Hello to you too," I joke. I've been upstaged by my son.

We stand around my small kitchen while Mom and I (mostly Mom) prepare meatloaf and a creamed-corn-and-pea concoction that tastes far better than it looks.

"Oh, Catie," Mom says. "I meant to tell you. Did you see that stroller recall? I think it's Graco. Something about a safety latch and pinching babies' fingers."

"I don't have a Graco," I say, "but thanks."

"Still worth looking into."

I inhale and exhale. "Why care about a recall that doesn't affect me?"

"It's called being cautious, Cate." Mom looks offended, like why in the world I would question such a thing.

"Did you tell your sister about your promotion?" Dad asks, saving us all from an unnecessary quarrel.

"Promotion?" Becky asks.

"Birdie got a promotion a couple weeks ago. What was it again—director of...?"

"Director of digital content," I say.

"Very cool!" Becky says, though none of them have a clear sense of what I do for a living anyway. The world of marketing that lives wholly online is beyond my parents' comprehension.

The conversation carries on in safer realms like Mom's friend's daughter who's getting married (but eloping, and how inconsiderate to the family), Dad's recent top score in Wordle (got this morning's on the first try), and Becky's foray into Ashtanga yoga (which gave her sore muscles she didn't even know she had).

Just as I'm about to pull the meatloaf from the oven, the doorbell rings, and we all turn.

"Did you invite Ryan?" Mom asks, which doesn't make sense because Ryan would never ring the doorbell.

"No?" I say, more of a question than anything. I'm still emerging from that newborn fog—my brain's not at its highest function. *Did* I invite Ryan?

I leave the kitchen, go to the door, and peer through the peephole. My body goes hot. Jada is on the other side of the door, anxiously twirling her hands. It's Sunday—what is she doing here?

She rings again, and I'm struck with panic. I can't not answer—she'll keep ringing until I do.

I open the door. "What are you doing?" I hiss. "My family is over."

"Oh," she says, eyes wide.

"You're supposed to come tomorrow, not today. That's what we agreed on. Mondays and Thursdays."

"Something came up and I won't be able to come tomorrow, so I figured today would be fine."

"It's not fine."

"But then I won't get to see Nicolas until Thursday."

"That's not my problem," I whisper, peeking back to see if anyone's followed me. For now, they've all remained in the kitchen.

"Please?" Jada begs. "I just want to hold him."

"Are you crazy? My *family* is here. How the hell would I explain that?"

I'm about to tell her to get lost when a voice from behind me makes me freeze in terror.

"Cate? Who is it, honey?" Mom comes up next to me, a hand on my back. "Hi there," she says politely to Jada.

"I, uh... This is..." I'm scrambling to come up with anything. Shit! What do I do?

"I'm Cate's friend," Jada says quickly and with a smile that would charm anyone, especially Marcia Connally.

"Oh!" Mom seems surprised to hear I have a friend outside of Ryan, especially one not my own age. Jada doesn't have grays sprouting along her hairline like me.

"I'm Jada."

"Nice to meet you Jada." She looks between the two of us. "And... how do you know Cate?"

"From, uh... from work."

I close my eyes and groan silently. My work is fully remote, with a company based in Chicago. But Mom doesn't seem to catch on because she simply smiles and says, "That's nice."

"I was just stopping by to say hello," Jada says. "I'm new in town."

"Oh, well you should come in and stay for dinner!" Mom says enthusiastically at the same time my pulse jumps through the roof. "Come, come! Cate, you don't mind, do you? There's plenty of food." She's all but dragging Jada through the door.

My eyes meet Jada's and I curse her for showing up here. This is a disaster. A shitshow that has no option but to end very, very bad.

Mom ushers Jada into the kitchen. "Henry, Becky, this is Catie's friend, Jada. Jada, this is Cate's father and sister." Then, gesturing to the baby in Becky's arms: "And this is my precious grandson, Cate's new little one, Henry." She beams. "Named after my husband."

Could she be more proud? Impossible.

"Hi," Jada says.

"Isn't he just the cutest thing you ever saw?" Mom says, running a hand over Henry's head.

"Without a doubt," Jada says.

I'm breathing so hard I feel like I might pass out. A baby that's not mine but whom my family thinks belongs to me, plus the woman who gave birth to him, abandoned him, and now wants him back. It's all too much. I falter and bump into the counter with my hip, making a loud *bonk*.

"Cate, are you okay?" Becky says.

"Yeah, I... I'm fine. Just a bit lightheaded for a second."

"You must need food," Mom says. "Let's set the table and eat while this little one is happy. Jada will be joining us for dinner. She's new in town and works with Cate," she adds to the rest of the room.

"I thought your company was based out of state," Becky says, picking up on the irony of two random employees of a Chicago company living in a small Ohio suburb.

"Coincidence," I say, trying not to let this whole thing run away from me. I breathe, in for three, out for three.

I could kill Jada. I'm not in the mood to put on a show, especially when anything I say could blow up in my face. I'd finally started feeling more at ease before Jada came into my life, and now my nerves are on serious edge. I pray she just sits quietly, eats her meatloaf, and leaves.

. . .

Jada doesn't sit quietly. At least she can't, not when Mom's throwing rapid-fire questions her way.

How long has she lived here? Does she have any siblings? Has she tried that new steakhouse that opened? Is her cable bill sky-high? (Because if so, there's a promo running this month.)

I sit there, biting my tongue and waiting for my head to pop off. Geez, Mom—are you going to ask her when she had her last pap smear too? It's Marica's way of being polite, but this is one time I wish she didn't care to dig into someone's personal life.

Jada doesn't miss a beat, and despite being a little "rough around the edges" (as Mom will no doubt describe her later), she's managing to fool my family with this newfound identity—I think. She's sitting directly opposite me, and every time I look across the table at her, I want to scream, *You're ruining this! Everything would have been fine if you'd have just stayed away!*

"What's your role at work?" Dad asks her.

I choke on my water, sputtering a bit down my chin. "Social media," I blurt, because I'm ninety-nine percent sure Jada doesn't even know what my company does.

Jada gives a nervous laugh followed by a simple nod. "Yeah, social media."

"Oh! Like Tic-Tac?" Mom says earnestly.

Becky laughs. "You mean TikTok?"

"Same thing. I can't keep up with all this hashtag and viral business. What the heck is a tweet anyways?"

We all laugh. Mom's sincere naivete is the perfect antidote to the tension I'm feeling. If only we could stay on this topic the rest of the meal.

I swirl the pea creation around on my plate, unable to stomach the meal I normally would devour.

"Why aren't you eating?" Mom says.

"Oh, I'm just full," I lie. "Had a big lunch."

She gives me a disapproving look, like why would I have a big lunch when I knew we were having Sunday dinner. I can never please this woman—eat too much or eat too little and you'll still get chastised.

From his bouncer seat, where he's been content for the last forty minutes, Henry begins to fuss.

"I'll get him," Jada and I both say in unison, pushing up from the table.

Everyone else looks to us, halfway standing, frozen in place at the sudden quandary. I expect Jada to immediately yield, but she doesn't, and we're stuck here in this awkward position, my family looking on in confusion.

After an agonizing moment, Jada clears her throat and sits back down, keeping her eyes low. Her face flushes from delicate gold chain to double hoop earrings. She doesn't look as I continue to Henry, picking him up and shooshing in his ear. I return to the table, baby in arm, feeling a certain pride when she raises her eyes again and looks at us. *See, he knows me.* She doesn't break her perpetual stare. It's just the two of us, gazes locked, exchanging all kinds of unspoken words.

"Do you have kids?" Becky breaks the silence.

Jada blinks, and our spell is broken.

This is it. The million-dollar question. The moment she could destroy everything if she wanted to. Right here, right now, over a pan of half-eaten meatloaf and King's Hawaiian dinner rolls. I hold my breath. All it would take is for her to come grab Henry from my arms and hold him up next to her face. Their resemblance is uncanny, and I can't quite believe no one has said anything to this point. It reinforces the power of the mind—we believe what we want to believe. We believe what we're told, even if it's a lie.

I meet Jada's eyes again, but this time I don't boast, I beg. *Please.*

There's another beat where no one says a word. The room is hot. Basil and pepper waft from the meatloaf platter.

"No," Jada says, all emotion sucked from her voice. And in that instant it's like she shrinks away.

"Well," Mom chimes in, "someday you will. Greatest blessing in life—right, girls?" She smiles at Becky and me.

My body trembles from what could have just happened, the adrenaline receding in slow motion.

At once, Jada scoots her chair back from the table. "I have to go. Thanks for dinner." She doesn't make eye contact with any of us, simply stands and drops her napkin onto her plate.

Mom gives a surprised *Oh*, and they all look around in confusion. But Jada is already hurrying from the room. I think I make out a muffled cry. A second later, the door slams.

Becky cocks her head. "What the hell was that about?"

"Don't say hell," Mom scolds without missing a beat. But they all echo Becky's question. What the heck just happened?

"She's a little different," I say, trying for nonchalance. I take a bite of meatloaf to prove everything is fine.

My family stares at me like I'm a stranger. A new "friend" they'd never heard of? Then a completely bizarre interaction, followed by her storming off? I can't deal with an interrogation right now. I need time to process, time to work tonight's events into my overall story. Please don't ask me anything else about Jada.

As if on cue, and like he knew what I needed, Henry gets the hiccups, causing us all to laugh and marvel and forget all about the strange newcomer who'd joined us for dinner. No one says another word about Jada, and I pray they've put the scenario out of their minds.

For now.

THIRTY-SIX

WHEN JADA SHOWS UP ON THURSDAY, I'M LIVID AND almost don't let her in the house.

"What were you thinking?" I demand, anger rising within the first ten seconds of her arrival. "Didn't you consider I could have had people here? And then the whole façade of being my friend? You're lucky they didn't see right through it."

"No, I'd say you're the lucky one," she replies, clearly unbothered by my agitation.

Doesn't she see how we're both part of this? Sure, I kept Henry, but she's the one who left him in the first place. I'd like to think her fault is bigger than mine. If I went to the police, wouldn't she face endangerment charges?

This was my first week back to work after maternity leave, and to say my brain is fried would be an understatement. Caring for Henry while trying to do my job has been harder than I imagined, forcing me to begrudgingly look up daycares. The promotion came with a fair share of kudos but also pressure and added responsibilities. Working-mom guilt is real. That whole work–life balance thing is way harder than I imagined. And because of all this, I don't have the mental capacity to deal with Jada and her attitude right now.

Henry is having tummy time on his playmat. I put him in a green onesie that says "Lucky Charm," even though St. Patrick's Day isn't until tomorrow.

Jada goes over and kneels down next to him, giving his butt a pat. "Look at you holding your head up," she says. "My boy's so strong!" Then to me, "Has he rolled over yet?"

"That's not until closer to four months," I say, annoyed. She wants to act like his mother, but she doesn't know anything about him, let alone babies in general. I can't help but think what his life would be like in her care. Lying around in soiled diapers, a crib full of sleeping hazards. What, is she going to offer him table food at three months? Does she know not to put a coat on him in the car or else he could overheat?

Henry lets out a string of gurgles, and Jada chuckles. "He's so stinking cute," she says. "I really see my mom in him."

I shove my hands into my pockets and tell myself to stay calm. I don't know how long I can take these visits. Are we going to do this for the next eighteen years? It's just too much. I'm going to have to tell Jada we can't keep doing this. She won't be happy, but maybe I can convince her it's for the best. After all, she's the one who initially wavered on her own ability. In her heart of hearts she has to know this was the right decision for her baby. It's been two months, Henry's used to me. Plus, she has so much to focus on with her own personal struggles.

Yes, I think now's the time to speak up. I'll persuade her.

"Listen, Jada," I say. "We need to talk. I—"

But my phone rings, and I glance at its screen to see Darci's name. Why's she calling after hours? I think for a second—do I really need to answer? I just put in an eight-hour day—can't this wait till morning? But my new position flashes in my conscience. The flashy title and pay rise must come with tradeoffs. I want to make the best impression possible, even if that means being available at six-thirty on a Thursday evening.

"Give me a minute," I say to Jada then step into the other room, not only for privacy but so Darci doesn't hear Jada in the background. There've been enough people questioning who this new person in my life is—I don't need my boss to be another.

"Hey, Darc, what's up?" I say.

"Cate, hi. So sorry to bug you this late."

"It's no problem. Is everything all right?"

She lets out a long sigh. "Ugh, not really. The Bower campaign hit a huge snag, and now I'm trying to find the original proofs we all agreed on, but the server is down and none of the files are opening, and—"

"Calm down—let me see if I can help."

She's a basket case. The Bower campaign is one of the biggest ones we've worked on this year, and everything is due to the client tomorrow morning. If it's true that the files are lost, we're screwed. But I know technology isn't Darci's best friend, which is why the team always comes to me when there are glitches.

"Have you tried the H-drive?" I say.

"Um, I think? Is that the one with the little computer symbol?"

Oh boy. I pace the room, trying to explain to Darci where to find the correct documents. It's a lot of *click on this, click on that*. And after close to ten minutes, Darci lets out a yelp.

"I found them! Oh my god, thank you *so* much, Cate. You're a lifesaver. It's no wonder you got that promotion."

I laugh. "It's no problem. Glad I could help."

"I'm sorry to have taken up part of your evening. I'm sure you're busy with Henry."

I stiffen, having completely forgotten about my son in the

other room. "It's fine," I say, though my voice has a new nervous sharpness to it. "Talk to you tomorrow."

I hang up and stand perfectly still for the three seconds it takes for me to hear it. Well, actually the absence of it. Nothing. The house is eerily silent.

I fling open the bedroom door and careen around the corner to where I'd left Jada lying next to Henry on the floor. My heart stops. The brightly colored playmat is empty. I dash to the window. Jada's car is gone.

And so is my son.

Something rises in my throat, and I'm afraid I might get sick, but then I realize it's just a scream. "Noooo!"

I dash through every room of the house as though they'll magically appear even though my gut knows the truth: Jada took Henry and I have no idea where they went. I go to call her then remember how I'd been adamant about not exchanging numbers. Damnit, Cate!

Sweat breaks out on my skin, and I'm on the verge of hyperventilating. She could be halfway out of Cleveland by now. Heck, she could be starting the short three-hour drive to Canada. I heave, arms outstretched. This can't be happening. I can't lose him.

Instinct tells me to call the police. My son was just kidnapped from my living room! But then what? The police come and I have to explain that well, actually he's not *really* my son. And the woman who took him is actually his *mother*, so...

I turn in a circle, hands on my head, feeling absolutely helpless. My brain's on one of those spinny rides, everything going too fast, everything blurring. Down is up and up is down. I have no phone number for Jada, no address, nothing. She could disappear into the night and there'd be nothing I could do about it.

I'm suddenly overcome, my leg muscles going limp, and I fall to the floor not far from where Henry was just minutes ago.

Why did I leave the room? How could I have been so stupid? My sole job as a mother was to protect him and I didn't. Now what will happen to him? My heart breaks for him as much as it breaks for myself. This was supposed to be my finish line. And now I'm all alone once again.

What am I going to tell my family? I try to imagine their reactions. Will they understand why I did it? Or will I sink to a new level of failure? I can't do this by myself any more. The last two months have been so much to bear, an impossibly heavy burden on the crown of my head. And now, the weight has broken me. I need help.

I look to my phone. If I do this, there's definitely no going back. The lie will be out, no longer just living in my head. But I have no choice. My parents will demand to know where Henry is. I can't explain this away.

I blink rapidly, trying to make sense of my options. Keep living the lie for as long as possible—hours? Minutes?—or let it start to crumble.

The answer comes faster than I'd expect.

I grab my phone. There's only one person I can think to call. It rings.

"Hi," I say, voice unsteady. "I'm in trouble."

THIRTY-SEVEN

RYAN USES THE GARAGE CODE HE KNOWS BY HEART. I WAIT for him at the table.

"What? What is it?" he says, before he's even all the way in. "Whoa, you look like shit. What's wrong?"

I'm sure I do. I probably have a river of black mascara under my eyes and a halo of frizz around my face.

"I fucked up," I say, placing my head in my hands. Seeing Ryan's face, knowing I'm about to confess something so horrible to someone I love, makes me want to crawl in a hole.

"Jesus, Cate, just tell me." He knows me. This is not a joke. Even Ryan's typical lighthearted nature is overcast with concern. He eyes me frantically. "What is it?"

I can barely talk. "It's Henry," I squeak.

He scans the room, eyes wide. "Where is he?"

I can only imagine what he's thinking. I lost it and snapped, did something horrible to my baby. It's nothing like that—the last thing I'd do is hurt Henry.

"He's gone."

"What do you mean, gone? Gone where?"

"I don't know," I cry. "She took him."

Now Ryan's face registers pure terror. "What? Who took him? Cate, what the hell is going on?"

"His... mother."

"His mo— You're losing me. I'm not following."

"He's not mine." I sniff. "I didn't adopt him."

There—that's it. The statement is dry and dusty, but it's out in the world. My body's on the verge of heaving, the words tasting vile on my tongue. It's the truth, but it feels incomprehensible, an impossible contradiction.

Ryan doesn't speak, just blinks and stares as he processes this bombshell.

Finally, he comes to sit next to me, puts a concerned hand on my shoulder. "Cate, this doesn't make any sense. What do you mean you didn't adopt him? The agency called you—you went to the hospital. We talked that morning. I don't understand."

"I lied."

"You never got a call from Kathleen?"

"No, that part's true. I did get a call. There was a baby, a boy. We were matched. I was all ready to go get him. But the next morning she... she..." I'm spiraling, the horrible memories whooshing back. How devastating it was to know another adoption had fallen through at the last minute. How I felt myself shattering into a million pieces. "The birth mother changed her mind."

Ryan sucks in some air. "Again? Oh, Cate, no." There's softness in his voice that I'm grateful for. I knew he'd understand. Ryan would never turn against me.

"I know, right? There's no way. But yes, again. I was losing another baby. I couldn't believe it."

He takes a few seconds to console me, and I can tell his heart too is crushed over my loss. When you watch your best friend going through hardships, it's difficult not to take on some of that pain. After a moment he pulls back, remembering the issue at hand.

"But... Henry." The meaning is there: If you didn't adopt that day, why has there been a baby here for the last two months? If he isn't the boy Kathleen called about, who is this child we've been calling Henry?

"He was a miracle." My face lights up, like this has all been nothing more than a fever dream. "I was broken, lost. I slept away most of the day on the couch when I wasn't crying. But then I heard a noise, and it sounded like a baby crying. I know... crazy, right? Just my imagination playing cruel tricks on me. But it was real. I opened the door and there he was."

"Wait, are you telling me Henry was just sitting outside your door? Alone? I don't get it."

"I know, I didn't either at first. I figured someone had to be around, but there was no one. He was crying, and it was so cold. I brought him inside to warm up. And then I saw the note."

"Note?"

"It said to keep him." I leap up and hurry to my bookcase, where I'd tucked the note between two thick novels on the top shelf. I hand it to Ryan. "Here, see?"

"His mother just abandoned him?"

"Yes. And she chose me. At first I just wanted to get him warm and comfortable and fed. But then he was so snuggly and seemed so happy. I took it as a sign. She'd basically given me permission! Then one day turned into two and three, and the lie was done."

I'm not sure I've ever seen Ryan's face like this, screwed up in a mix of disbelief and shock like I'm speaking Greek.

"Cate!" he says. "You can't just keep a baby that's not yours." He recoils like I'm no longer the girl with whom he choreographed talent-show dance numbers but an imposter.

"But she told me to. It's all I've ever wanted—you know that.

What kind of mother leaves her baby? I wasn't thinking—or maybe I was. I don't know. All I know is that the only logical thing in the moment was to protect Henry. And, well, I guess I was acting on pure emotion after the phone call from Kathleen. It's just not fair, Ryan. Why are there so many women who have children they don't love, when I'm continually deprived of having one myself?"

"Of course I know that, but..."

My best friend stands, wide-legged and on edge, running both hands through his hair. He stays like that for a long minute, and I want to reach out. I want to shake him and say, *You understand, right? You see why I did it?* He has to. He's my other half. If he doesn't get me, no one will. If I don't have him, I have no one.

"Fuck, Cate. What were you thinking?"

"It felt so right. Like it was meant to be." I don't dispute, only defend. There's desperation in my voice, like I'm trying to appease myself even though I've never been more certain of anything in my life. If I could go back and do it all again, I would.

And what does that say about me?

Then, like a lightbulb goes off, "Hold on, that's beside the point. Where is Henry now?" He scans the room again.

"She took him," I say again, and then realize that while I've known Jada's identity for a while now, this is all new for Ryan. So I fill him in about being at the pediatrician that morning Henry was sick, the nurse coming down the hall, the sparrow tattoo.

Ryan runs a thumb over the sparrow on the note. "So she just saw him and regretted it and decided to take him back?"

"I let her come here and spend time with him, and I thought that would be enough. She isn't stable. Said she has a drug problem, which is why she gave him up in the first place."

"But why you?"

I tell him about our connection through Dr. Handrian's

office. How Jada knew about my struggle toward motherhood. He nods along, like it's finally coming together.

"This is like something you see in the movies," he says, and I don't disagree. It's hard to even fathom. I recall the day the Lifetime movie came on and the immediate urge I had to change the channel, as though it would save my innocence.

A lump hitches in my throat and I don't even try to fight it. "What am I going to do?" I cry. I silently plead with him for the answer, any answer. Help me, my level-headed friend. "Everyone thinks Henry is mine. My parents, Becky..."

"And me."

I meet his gaze and there's hurt all over his face. A lead ball drops in my stomach.

"How could you lie to me?"

"I'm so sorry."

He stands and paces slowly, a hand to his hairline. "I never thought you'd..."

It's the worst feeling in the world, watching the betrayal I've caused. "Ryan, I—I don't know what to say or how to explain it. It snowballed so fast. And before I knew it—"

"But I'm your best friend. We've never lied to each other."

I hang my head. He's right, and I feel like nothing more than scum. "Can you forgive me? I need you, Ry. I don't think I can survive losing him, but I definitely can't survive losing you."

He doesn't hug me, doesn't soak up my tears like he's done on more than one occasion. A real fear creeps in: Am I really about to lose my best friend?

"Please, Ryan," I beg, hands pressed together. "I need your help. I can't do this alone."

He sits back down, runs his hand through his hair again.

After a long minute, he finds my eyes. "I could never desert you. But that doesn't mean I forgive you."

It's enough. There may be a long road of atonement ahead but, for now, I'll take it.

It feels like hours that we sit there in a silence that is blaring. I'm overwhelmed with thoughts of what I'm going to say to my family. How will they react? Will they understand?

"Am I a bad person?" I say quietly.

His response doesn't come as quick as I'd like. But eventually, he shakes his head. "No. You're not a bad person. You're a person who did something bad. You made a mistake, even though it felt like the right thing to do. And then—"

"Then she took him back because he's hers." It sounds so logical. Henry is her son and she has every right to take him. But that doesn't explain away what she did in the first place. How is it okay for a mother to drop her child on someone's doorstep without a word and then disappear?

A sudden urge propels me to my feet. I snatch my car keys and go for my coat.

Ryan looks perplexed. "Where are you going?"

"I have to search for him," I say in a fit of mania. "I could go back to the hospital where she works. Or to the shopping center, the baby departments. I could—"

"Cate."

"I could just peruse the streets. Check every neighborhood. He has to be *somewhere*."

"Cate." Ryan has a hand on my arm now. "Stop. You can't just go looking for him. You have no idea where they are."

"But…" I feel myself crumbling again. "I have to at least try."

"You need to call your parents," Ryan says. "They deserve to know the truth."

My stomach twists. He's right, but I don't want him to be right. I don't want this to be real, and telling more people will make it so. "Will you stay?" I ask, needing his support.

"Of course." He hands me my phone.

I dial, close my eyes, and hold my breath.

THIRTY-EIGHT

"DAD?" I SAY, VOICE SHAKING.

"Birdie? What is it?" I hear the concern in his tone and imagine him sitting up straight in his chair.

I sniff. Ryan squeezes my hand. "Something happened."

"What?" There's a slice of fear now, and I'm not surprised when Mom's voice comes through from the background: "Henry, what's wrong?" It's one of those phone calls parents dread, setting them into instant panic mode.

"Hold on, Birdie," he says, and I know he's putting me on speaker. "Okay, go ahead. What happened? What's wrong?"

"Can you come over? I don't want to talk about it over the phone."

"Cate," Mom says, low and serious. "You're scaring me. What's going on? Is it Henry?"

"Just come."

Then in unison: "We'll be right there."

They pull in my driveway less than twenty minutes later, and when I hear the two doors slam, my insides do a somersault. Here we go—this is going to destroy them.

Dad comes in first, wearing sweatpants and an old marathon sweatshirt. He probably had his slippers on and a bourbon in his hand when I called and threw a wrench in their evening. Mom has on jeans, which she probably changed into seeing as she'd never leave the house in anything close to pajamas, but her face is bare of makeup, hair spun up into a claw clip.

It's eight-thirty, and the sun has long gone down. I should be giving Henry his bedtime bottle. A sob catches in my throat.

"What is it?" they both say without so much as a greeting first or acknowledging Ryan, who sits next to me on the couch. Mom frantically scans the room, eyes blazing with worry. "Where's Henry?"

I take a deep breath and release it. "I have to tell you guys something." My voice trembles. "And let me start by saying I'm sorry, okay? I didn't mean for any of this to happen."

Their faces are ashen. Mom brings a hand to her heart. "What, Cate? Tell us."

I can't drag it out any longer. "Henry was never mine. I didn't adopt him. That morning, the adoption fell through— again. But then, this baby showed up on my doorstep with a note, and I brought him in. It was so cold outside."

I didn't know it was possible for their faces to register more horror, but they do.

Mom shakes her head, brows knitted together. "I don't understand." Then to Dad, "Henry? Are you following this?"

Dad tries to clarify. "You're saying you didn't go to the hospital that morning?"

"She changed her mind, just like the last time."

"Cate, no..."

"I named him Henry after you, Dad."

"Cate..."

"It was like a sign. His sudden appearance, right after my world crumbled for the second time. It was like the universe telling me this was right. And I imagined his life must have been horrible with a mother who would just desert him. Right? Who does that? So I kept him."

"How on earth do you know what his life was like?" Mom says, hand to her throat.

"Well, I mean, obviously—"

"No, obviously nothing. You don't know what his situation was. You took it into your own hands. You presumed, speculated."

I'm forty-one years old getting scolded by my mother. I deserve it, but the humiliation still stings.

Mom shakes her head in disappointment. "You lied to us."

A prickle bites at my skin. "I know. I'm sorry. I just wanted it to be real."

They look to each other then back to me with that awful expression: pity. Poor Catie. But even a set of unfortunate events doesn't give you the right to cross the moral line. I was raised to follow the rules, to be a good person. What I've done feels like anything but.

"There's something else," I say, because the story isn't over, and the worst part is about to hit them like a sucker punch. There's no way to soften it, so I just let the words fall out, past a ball of fire in my throat. "His real mother took him back."

Mom gasps and Dad's eyes go wide. "She *what*? No! She can't!"

"She did. A couple hours ago." I start to cry again, thinking about finding the living room empty.

"Why did you just let her take him?" Mom says as though I had anything to do with it. Like I willingly allowed it to happen.

"I didn't! I was in the other room, and—"

Dad puts out a hand and stops me. "Wait a minute. Back

up. We're missing something here. Some strange woman just came into your house and took your baby? This doesn't add up."

I pop all ten knuckles on my hands like a series of shotgun shells. The release does nothing. It's so much more complicated than that. "No," I say. "It was Jada."

It takes them a second, but then it registers. "The friend from dinner on Sunday?" Mom says. "She's... she's Henry's mother?"

I nod, head down.

"And you knew about this?" Mom shoots at Ryan.

"Not until tonight. Trust me, I'm just as shook as you."

Dad brings a hand to his forehead. "This is a mess. How could you get yourself into such a situation?"

"I don't know," I whisper. I look away and press a hard palm to my lips. The tension, the disappointment, bears down on me. Mixed with the pure grief I'm feeling, it's enough to make me want to curl into myself and succumb to everything.

Mom cuts the silence. "She can't just do that." And at first I think she's talking about me, that I can't just keep a baby that's not mine, just as Ryan had said, but then I realize she's not talking about me at all. She's talking about Jada.

"She left him, abandoned him with nothing more than a note? Then went back to her normal life like nothing happened? That's as good as giving up her rights." She's talking animatedly, arms flying this way and that, completely contradicting her earlier statement about assumptions. "You, Cate, you cared for him, you kept him safe and loved. There has to be some sort of retribution for that."

"What are you saying?" Dad asks.

"I'm saying we can fight this. We can get Henry back."

As she says it, something lifts inside me. Could we?

Mom marches to where she dropped her purse on the table like a punctuation mark. "I'm calling the police."

"Marcia, wait," Dad says, a voice of reason. "She needs a

lawyer. No one's going to answer this late. We'll call in the morning."

"But the baby..."

"She's not going to hurt him," I speak up, because despite so many unknowns in this moment, one thing I feel sure of is that Jada regrets what she did. I watched them interact. It's obvious how much Jada loves her baby. This whole thing might be the stuff of nightmares, but at least I don't have to worry about Henry being in physical danger—I think.

"You don't know that," Mom says.

I know where she's coming from—it's a place of anguish, where defiance outweighs good sense.

"I do."

Reluctantly, she concedes. "Fine. First thing in the morning we call."

And it becomes a deal, a plan to get Henry back.

Sleep is a faraway wish I cannot reach. How I'd love to fall into a dream and wake up to none of this happening. But that's not how it works. Instead, my mind grapples with itself in a game of guilt and contrition.

After my parents left, Ryan insisted on staying. I didn't fight him. He made himself a bed on the couch, even though I offered him my bed—I wouldn't be sleeping in it, not tonight.

I lie on the floor of the nursery, staring at an empty crib, and cry for what feels like hours, until the tears dry up and I'm left with nothing but a pounding head and a broken heart. Finally, when the first pink cracks of dawn trace the night sky, I fall into a fitful sleep.

THIRTY-NINE

GAIL MCCAFFERY IS A BULLDOG OF A WOMAN. SHE barrels into my house, dark head of hair bigger than an eighties Texas pageant queen's, lips matte pink and squeezed tighter than her blouse. The kind of face that doesn't invite people to talk to it. It's all I can do not to stare. She's... a lot. But she's the best—the billboards around the county say so.

"All right." She folds her hands on the table, her long red nails daggers for whomever crosses her. "I need to know everything. And I mean everything. Don't keep secrets from me—I don't like surprises." A pause. "Are you sure you want your parents here?"

"Yes," I say. This is the scariest thing that's ever happened to me, and I'm suddenly a child again, leaning on the security of my mom and dad. They came back first thing this morning, relieving Ryan, as though I were on a critical-care watch. Still, their presence is comforting.

She nods. "Start at the beginning. Give me the details."

She's all business, like someone asking about a simple day at the park. Calm, where I'm petrified. But I take a cue from her demeanor, and so I begin. I tell her everything, starting with the call from Kathleen only minutes before I was to leave for the hospital. The birth mother's change of heart, collapsing to the floor, the waterworks. Recalling it all brings all the emotion back to the surface. It's still so unimaginable—two failed adoptions. What are the odds? Mom assured me it wouldn't happen again. She said those odds wouldn't strike the same person twice.

She was wrong.

I continue. I tell Gail about hearing the cry, opening the door, finding Henry. When I get to the part about passing him off as mine, Mom closes her eyes. Blotches creep up her neck that not even her Hermès scarf can hide. Dad is sober, listening with no outward judgment, even though I deserve it all.

Gail takes furious notes on a leather-bound pad. "Did you consider going to the police? Turning the baby in to social services?"

"Yes!" I say it like I'm trying to convince myself too. See? I'm not completely heartless. "More than once. But I didn't know who the mother was, what kind of family he came from. Or if it was some other crazy possibility altogether. Whoever left him must have been in trouble, and so I figured Henry—the baby—would be thrown into foster care or something worse. I thought I could provide for him, show him the love he wasn't getting with her."

"Mmm-hmm." Gail nods to her paper. She's probably heard all kinds of horrific stories. Being a defense attorney must make a person numb to a degree.

We go back and forth with several more questions, until Gail is satisfied. She closes her notepad with a long exhale.

"What do you want to get out of this?"

I look at her like it's such an obvious answer. "I want him back."

"I can't lie, this is going to be tough. She's the birth mother. Our only angle is to really lean into child abandonment. We throw the blame on her—her decision, not yours. You saved him.

If it weren't for you, that baby could have died. You're the good person in this situation."

Good person?

"But that doesn't justify Cate keeping him all this time and pretending he was hers."

It's the first time Dad's spoken, and his voice has lost the vigor I know and love. He sounds deflated, flat. An old man who should be at home with his feet up watching football. We make eye contact, but it hurts too much and I look away.

"I'm sorry, Dad," I whisper.

"Now's not the time, Cate."

Cate? But no—I'm Birdie.

"You're right," Gail says. "She should have called the authorities. But she didn't do anything criminal, per se. It's not like people were looking for this baby and she was withholding him. The good Samaritan defense could help. You were doing what you thought was right. Saving an innocent baby from freezing to death. Or we could pull the M'Naghten Rule."

"M'what?" I say.

"The M'Naghten Rule. It's basically the premise on which the insanity defense stands. States that a person cannot be held accountable for the crime of which they're accused, based on mental defect. We'd say that you didn't know right from wrong at the time, couldn't comprehend the moral nature of what you did. The trauma of the failed adoptions, the call that morning."

"Insanity?" I blurt. "Wait, no. I'm not insane." Everything I've done in my life to this point has been to prove my competency, my adequacy. I got a 1450 on the SATs for god's sake. Being labeled as an insane person is the opposite of this. They might as well stomp on me with a steel-toed boot.

"Cate," Gail says like she's talking to a toddler. "Think about what you did. This is the only chance we have. Plus, it's not so far-fetched. Serious life upheavals can make people do things they otherwise wouldn't. You've been through a lot. Your emotional state was turned upside down."

Insanity. I roll the word around in my head. Was I insane then? Am I still insane for not believing it?

"Is that a common defense?" Dad asks.

"You'd think," Gail says. "We hear about it in the media. Crimes of passion and the like. But it's used a lot less often than you'd suspect. Has about a thirty-five percent success rate."

"You're hedging your bets on a thirty-five percent success rate? That's less than half!" Mom says.

Gail's unruffled. She lays her forearms on the table and leans forward. "It's about as good as we're going to get. I'd take thirty-five percent over zero if I were you."

"Well... well— Isn't Jada going to get in trouble too?" Mom says. "I mean, she's the one who discarded her child like a piece of trash."

"It wasn't like that," I say defensively, to my own surprise.

But Gail doesn't listen.

"Oh, undoubtedly. Don't worry, I'll throw a heavy hammer her way in court. I crush people for a living—that's what I do. She'll be looking at child endangerment charges. It's a misdemeanor but could still come with jail time. Some people just shouldn't have children. I doubt the judge will see her favorably."

My stomach roils. Child endangerment, just as I guessed. Even though I want to be victorious here, I'm queasy at the thought of Jada going to jail.

Mom, Dad, and I nod along even though this is the last conversation we'd ever anticipate having. I'm completely dazed. How did I go from snuggling my baby boy less than twenty-four hours ago to talking about charges and custody? If I had anything in my stomach to purge, it would surely come up.

I lay my head on the kitchen table. The tears don't even

come—I'm either in shock or don't have any left to cry. Maybe it's both.

"Don't worry," Gail says, pumping herself up. "You're in the best hands with me. Remember, I don't lose. We will win this. We'll get Henry back."

FORTY

We go to the police station as a unit: me, my parents, and the lawyer whose promises are keeping me afloat. After explaining everything to Becky on the phone yesterday, Dad told her to give me space.

"But I can have Shane pick up the boys," she'd said. "I can be there in fifteen minutes."

"Let us figure a few things out first, okay? I'll call you and fill you in later."

I was grateful not to have another set of judging eyes on me.

We're ushered to a small room with table and chairs in the center. A camera hangs in the corner near the ceiling, and I feel like I'm in an episode of a crime show. How did I get here?

Two uniformed officers take a seat across from us. The shorter, blockier of them speaks. He has a symmetrical face and tightly cropped hair. "I'm Officer Kane; this is Officer Reilly. I understand you want to file a court petition for custody of a minor?"

"Yes," Gail speaks for me.

"But these are unusual circumstances, no?"

"They are." She's stoic, secure in this argument we've

formed. "However, we feel that the means justified the ends here. Given the state of the birth mother—what she did—the baby's best interests are to remain with my client."

"You know birth-parent rights surpass just about everything."

"Including abandonment?"

Kane folds his hands on the table. "With all due respect, Gail, your client unlawfully kept a baby that wasn't hers."

"All my client did was love and protect a vulnerable child. It was no more wrong than someone caring for a baby while the parents are out of town. No one was hurt; no one was put out. This was never a missing persons case. Lying to the grocery store attendant isn't a crime."

Kane purses his lips. Gail is ferocious, and I'm glad she's on my side, not against me. Maybe we'll be able to win this after all.

"Have you contacted Ms. Morales?" Gail asks.

"We're in the process of locating her."

My heart leaps; I wonder where Henry has been for the last fourteen hours. Did he sleep? Was he fed?

"We'll be talking with her," Kane says. "But our office needs time to gather information. Social services is at your client's house now doing a welfare check."

Gail leans forward. "For what? The baby isn't there."

"This is a highly unusual case, Gail. We secured a warrant for both residences."

There's no rebuttal to that. *Go ahead*, I want to say. Search my house and all you'll find are neatly folded burp cloths, bottles drying by the sink, enough baby clothes to dress a daycare. This baby was nothing but *loved*.

Kane closes the folder in front of him. "For now, you're free to go and we'll be in touch."

"But Henry..." I speak for the first time, as though I expected them to go track down Jada and bring Henry back to me right now, this exact second.

Gail puts a firm hand on my leg. I bite my lip. I guess this won't be as fast a resolution as I thought.

Waiting at home is harrowing. We try for normalcy, but there's nothing normal about this situation. It's like we're waiting for a volcano to blow or a bomb to go off—all I know is that the pressure is almost too much to bear. This is either going to go in my favor or it's not. If I were to believe Gail, I'll soon have Henry back in my arms.

I think of the tiny human who changed my life, the bandage that closed a massive hole in my heart. He felt like mine. Henry and me, a duo ready to take on the world. He completed our family—him, along with his cousins and my parents and even Becky. I finally fit in with the rest of them. I was finally worthy. I finally realized my dream.

Mom is nervous baking in my kitchen (I'm surprised she found all the necessary ingredients), and Dad scrolls a news app. Six hours have passed, and nothing. Where are they? Why haven't they found Henry?

When there's a knock on the door, we all vault off our chairs. I rush to the door and fling it open, expecting them to thrust Henry into my arms. Instead, Kane and Reilly stand there, empty-handed, and my bubble of hope bursts.

"Did you find him?" I say.

Kane's face is firm. "There's been a new development."

I'm waiting for him to explain. Is it a good development or a bad development? But then Kane steps forward at the same time he unhooks handcuffs from his belt. My body seizes.

"Catherine Connally, you're under arrest for falsifying a government document with intent to commit fraud." Kane pulls my hands behind my back. Click. "You have the right to remain silent..."

The rest of his words are drowned out, as everything in the

room blurs. I thought he was about to tell me something to do with finding Henry. Instead, I'm getting arrested?

"Wait!" Mom yells, tugging on my arm. "What is this about? Cate didn't do anything wrong!"

But I have—I did. It comes into clear focus. I forgot all about it until just now. And for the first time, I understand the transgression.

The birth certificate.

I don't feel my feet moving, but I'm walking out the door toward the cruiser, Kane guiding me by the elbow with calculated steps. I can't breathe. This can't be happening.

I'm at the car, Kane opening the door and guiding me in the back. This is a hallucination. Wake up, Cate—you're dreaming! Only I'm not. I'm very much awake and wearing very real handcuffs. The cold metal bites my skin.

"I'm calling Gail!" Dad calls.

I look back. Mom is crying; Dad wraps an arm around her shoulder. This has gone downhill faster than an out-of-control skier, and with just as much possibility for catastrophe. All I'm waiting for is to hit a tree on the way through the chaos.

I can't believe I didn't consider the birth certificate. The thing I thought was going to protect me is now my downfall. Would we have called Gail if I'd remembered that I'd ordered a fake document online? Would we have gone to the police and pushed for this? I knew it was probably illegal, but I didn't realize it was *this* bad. I didn't think it would ever see the light of day. It was a backup, a safety net.

I curse myself, but there's no time for second-guessing. The car pulls away from my house, and all I can do is look forward and scramble for safety. The uncertainty feels like walking through a room of blackness.

PART 4

FORTY-ONE

JADA

Yesterday

WHEN I SPEED AWAY FROM CATE'S HOUSE, MY ADRENALINE is racing. I hadn't planned for tonight to be *the night*, but when Cate stepped out of the room, I knew I had to take my chance. My heart thundered in my chest as I grabbed the car seat Cate kept tucked in the corner of the room. I'd been waiting for just the right opportunity. Maybe it would never come, maybe Cate would never let Nicolas out of her sight. But she did, and I acted.

My hands trembled as I rushed to get him buckled. Cate could be back any second. I heard her muffled voice from the other room. How much more time did I have?

"Shhh, shhhh," I soothed Nicolas, swiped my coat from the arm of the couch, and slipped out the door. I didn't breathe again until we were down the street. Inhale, exhale. I'm glad it didn't have to be a tug-of-war—I didn't want to have to get in Cate's face, but my mind was made up: He was coming with me one way or another. I buried the seed of sadness I felt for Cate. She'll have another chance.

A few minutes from the house, I look back at the rear-facing car seat. I can't see him, but just knowing he's here with me is all the relief I need. Maybe saving all those things from the first week of his life was proof that I never wanted to give him up in the first place.

We get further away from Cate's cushy neighborhood and head back toward downtown where apartment buildings and condos replace the green grass of the suburbs. I'm not going to my place, that I know for sure. I'm going somewhere else. Because if this is my life now, there's someone I have to tell.

Mom's car is parked on the street, and for once I'm glad to know she's home. I find an empty spot not too far down, park, and lift Nicolas's car seat from the back. It feels so good to have him at my side, and I'm overcome with guilt for ever giving him up, ever thinking I could live without him, even if it was only for two months. He's mine and I'm his. We're going to figure this out.

I climb the steps and use my key to go in through the front. Mom's at the stove, stirring something in a shallow sauce pan. A box of rice lies on the counter, and I'm hit with the garlicy scent of sofrito. A catchy pop song comes from the Alexa, and Mom bumps her hip to the bass. I place Nicolas in his car seat behind the wall and out of eyesight. When I come around the corner, she jumps.

"Jada, don't scare me like that—good Lord! What are you doing here?"

I'm not one to just pop by for visits, and I'm sure her mind immediately went to how much money I'm going to ask for this time.

"We need to talk," I say through heavy breaths but with a slight smile on my lips. This is good news. She might be surprised at first, but then she'll be thrilled. A grandbaby! "I've been keeping something from you."

Her face drops. "Tell me you're not using again. Oh, Jada!

Please tell me you didn't relapse. You just finished treatment. I can't do this again..." Her shoulders round forward and she's all but ready to crumble to the linoleum under her slippered feet, but I stop her.

"No, no, it's not that. I'm clean. I promise. It's something else."

She searches my eyes, fears allayed but still concerned. With a past like mine, she never knows what's going to come out of my mouth. Something tells me she'll never expect what I'm about to say.

"I had a baby."

She stares, poker-faced, waiting for the punch line. *Ha! Gotcha!* When I don't budge, turmoil settles over her demeanor.

"You *what?*" She bristles.

"Two months ago. I didn't tell anyone."

"Is this some sort of joke? Because it's not funny, Jada."

And then, as if on cue, Nicolas makes a gurgling noise.

"I'm serious," I say, reaching from behind me to pull Nicolas's car seat around and onto the floor three feet in front of Mom. Her eyes are as big as an owl's, and she mouths, *Wha? Wha?*

"Whose baby is this?" she spits, all shook up. It must be equally as shocking for a baby to appear in her kitchen as it was for one to come out of my body in the bathroom.

"Mom, he's mine."

She looks between us. I see the recognition cross her face. There's no denying this is my child, with our matching irises and perfectly paired skin tone.

"Jada," she whispers. "How?"

And so I tell her. About not knowing I was pregnant, the horrific pain, his birth in my bathroom. She listens in a state of shock, continually looking back and forth between Nicolas and me. She hasn't budged, hasn't bent to touch him, and within a couple minutes we're met with the smell of burning pepper.

"Shit," she says, yanking the pan off the burner then returning to me.

"Why didn't you tell me?" she says, and this is when the tears come, as though her only child having a baby was one thing, but not knowing about it was the kick that thrust her over the edge.

"I was scared," I say, feeling a quick stab of guilt. This was never just about me. "It all happened so fast. I was literally at work, and then a few hours later he came flying out. I couldn't process."

"But I would have helped you, afterwards."

I look down. "I was ashamed."

"Ashamed? Of what?"

"Another thing to add to my list of fuck-ups. I can barely take care of myself—how was I supposed to take care of a baby? I thought it would be best if no one knew, not even you."

"But I don't understand. Where has he been? You were gone for weeks. I've seen your apartment lately—there was never a baby there. I'm so confused."

Here comes the worst part, admitting what I did. I can only hope that my reversing the situation will be enough to make up for doing it in the first place. I dig at the skin around my fingernails. "It was so hard. I couldn't handle it."

"What are you saying?"

"I gave him away."

Her tan skin turns pale, which is saying a lot. "Excuse me?"

"I left him with a woman. Someone I knew from work. She's never been able to have her own kids, and I knew she'd look after him. I just couldn't do it, Mom." I'm crying now, my whole body shaking from regret. "The drugs—they overtook everything. So I did what I thought was best for him."

"I can't believe what I'm hearing," she says, placing two tented hands on the sides of her head, long nails like stilts.

I try for redemption, talking fast, like my later actions will cancel out the early ones. "But I got clean again. I had time to process it all. And I realized I made a mistake. I wanted him back."

"After two months of being MIA? That's not how it works!"

"Well, I mean—"

"You should have called me. I would have helped you. How could you just give up your baby, Jada? Your flesh and blood. And it's not like it was an arranged adoption—you *left* him. You're lucky that woman took him in."

My arms hang heavy as regret engulfs me. When I think back to that day, my knees go weak. "I knew she would. He was never at any risk of harm."

"Ay, Dios mío," she says, slipping into Spanish.

I give it a moment to set in, knowing this has got to be one of the biggest shocks of her life. "It's okay, Mom. Everything's cool now. He's right where he's supposed to be—with me."

"But... but how? Why do you have him if you gave him up?"

It's a tricky question, but one so obvious to ask, and now I'm asking myself which is worse: Leaving Nicolas in the first place or stealing him back?

"He's mine," I say by way of explanation, though it does a shitty job of that. Then, "I was in such a bad place, but then I got clean and everything changed. I realized I'd made a mistake, and I wanted him back."

"So she agreed to return him?"

We're talking like Nicolas is a pair of shoes instead of a living, breathing human.

"Not exactly." A beat, and then, "I took him."

"Took him?" Her jaw goes slack, eyes wide. "Without her permission?"

"He's my son, Mom," I snap back. "I had every right."

It takes her a minute to process everything. First a baby, then the unheard-of events surrounding the last few months.

I step toward her, trying to soften what must feel like a

blow. The room is as still as the air before a tornado. I hold my breath. Will she accept us?

"This is all..."

"I know," I say. "I'm sorry. But he's here now. And everything is going to be okay."

She looks back and forth between Nicolas and me then kneels down in front of the car seat in awe.

"He has your eyes." She strokes his head, runs a finger around his cheek to his chin. He breaks out into a wide smile, making us both hum with joy. It's a reminder of his innocence in all of this. He didn't ask to be born, didn't ask to be abandoned, didn't ask to be shuffled between homes and mothers. I'm thankful he's too young to remember any of this. From here on, he'll never know a time without me.

"He's so beautiful," Mom says softly, and I can tell in her voice she's no longer mad. "What's his name?"

My pulse rests. "Nicolas."

FORTY-TWO

WE SPEND THE NIGHT IN MY OLD ROOM AT MOM'S HOUSE. It's weird being back in this space, the bleak, beige walls a reminder of a past life I'd like to forget. How many times did I get high in this room? There's where I kept my stash of weed behind a stack of books I never read. Here's where I hid the needles in the back shelf of the closet. It's triggering to surround myself with things from the past, but I have to get over it—I need Mom's help. I can't do this alone.

I go through the list of coping strategies Karen taught me:

I am strong and capable.

I choose to be sober today.

I seek progress not perfection.

Maybe if I repeat them enough, one will stick.

Mom pokes her head in when she hears Nicolas cry at one and four a.m. "Can I do anything?" she asks.

I rub tired eyes and shake my head no. There's no sense in both of us being awake. But she comes in anyway, sits on the edge of my bed while I change and feed Nicolas. We don't say much, but her presence is a life raft.

In the morning, Nicolas and I emerge in two very different states: one happy and rested, the other ragged as a scarecrow.

"Morning," Mom says. She's at the table, bending down to tie the laces on her black waitress shoes. The toes are scuffed, but she covers it up with black Sharpie like Julia Roberts in *Pretty Woman*.

"You're working?" I say.

Her eyebrows rise. "Yes?"

"Well, I mean... with Nicolas and I just getting here, I thought..."

"Bills don't pay themselves, Jada. You can't keep calling off either. You're going to have to find a daycare for him or something. See if Mrs. Telfrey can watch him."

It's a huge pill to swallow, the realization that life goes on even after a baby enters the picture. In a normal world, I'd have had weeks of maternity leave to adjust to it all. Even though Nicolas is no longer a newborn, it all feels fresh to me. How am I supposed to balance everything? I surely won't be relying on our eighty-year-old neighbor who can't even open a jar of tomato sauce on her own.

Mom stands, puts her hands on her hips. "You can stay here for a while if you want. I'll help when I can. But I have two jobs I can't afford to lose." She walks toward me and plants a kiss on Nicolas's head, leaving behind a ring of rosy lipstick. "I'll see you around four—at least today's not a double shift."

"Okay," I say, annoyed that she's leaving but glad she'll be home at four instead of ten. I'd hoped she'd watch him for a while so I could take a nap. I guess that's not happening.

When she goes, I lay Nicolas on a throw blanket in the front room. "Well, it's just you and me today," I say, and he smiles, ignorant to the struggles of adulthood. I scratch my head and twist my mouth into a question mark. What the hell do you do with a baby all day? What did Cate do with him all day?

· · ·

There's a knock on the door at three, just as I'm about to start another *Kardashians* rerun.

"Who could that be?" I say and then think maybe Mom lost her key. I go to the door in my plaid pajamas. I didn't bother showering today, didn't even put on a bra—what's the point? When I open the door, I wish I had.

Two police officers stand in the hallway, hard expressions written on their faces. "Are you Jada Morales?" one asks.

"Yes." I close the door to a sliver.

"Can we come in?"

"What's this about?" I've watched enough cop shows to know they can't just barge their way in without cause. And I haven't done anything wrong. Nicolas is my son, and I had every right to take him.

"You want to do this in the hallway?"

Ooooh, tough guy. Two can play that game. "If you're wondering whether there's a baby here, the answer is yes. He's my son. I gave birth to him, not that other woman, or whatever she's telling you."

"Ms. Morales, I'll ask you again, may we come in?"

"No, you may not."

They look between each other and give a sigh. "Fine. Jada Morales, you're under arrest for the abandonment of a minor."

He pushes the door open, and I don't resist because I'm too stunned. While he's reading me my rights, the other officer goes to where Nicolas is on the floor.

"Stop!" I yell. "Don't touch him!"

But he continues without a beat, swooping Nicolas up with rough hands. He places him in the car seat near the door.

"This is ridiculous—he's fine! You've got it all wrong."

While one officer leads me out of the apartment, the other carries Nicolas in the car seat to the two waiting cruisers on the street. They won't even let us ride together, and that's when it hits me: Where are they taking him?

Neither of them answers my questions as we pull away, and I'm left with nothing to do but hurl profanities from the hard, cold back seat.

FORTY-THREE

I'M BROUGHT TO A SMALL ROOM WITH A TABLE, TWO chairs, and a box of tissues. I wait, alone, for what seems like hours, before finally the door opens and a man in a suit enters.

"Who are you?" I say, quickly followed by, "Where is my son?"

"My name's Ed Blackwell, public defender."

Ed—what a dumb name. This is who they give me? He's got a rich-boy combover and perfect teeth. How will he be able to relate to my life?

"I want to call my mom," I say.

"She's on her way."

"Where's Nicolas? Where did they take him?"

"He's fine; he's safe."

"He's not fine—he's supposed to be with me, and now he's... who knows where."

"He's with child protective services until we get this sorted out. Don't worry—they're taking care of him."

I clench my fists into balls. I want to punch a hole through this table.

"I didn't abandon him," I say. "It's not like I left him in the middle of the woods or something. I took him to a house where I knew he'd be safe. I did the right thing."

He sighs. "May I call you Jada?"

"That's my name. What else would you call me?"

"Jada"—he clears his throat—"you left him on a doorstep in the freezing cold without making any arrangements or even knowing if the homeowner was home. There are Safe Haven laws for a reason—you could have taken him to a hospital or a fire station, but you didn't. It was dangerous, reckless. The outcome could have been very different."

I know what he's implying, and it makes my stomach churn.

"I want to see my son," I say.

"I'm afraid that's not possible right now. We need to focus on these charges. Child abandonment can be a felony. This is serious."

"A felony? Like, jail time?"

"It's possible. We'll have to see what the judge says."

At that, the door flies open and Mom comes in. "Jesus, Jada. I was so scared when I got home and you were gone. I thought you'd..." She trails off and I know what she must be thinking. "I went to your house but you weren't there either. And then a police officer came by and told me what happened, where they'd taken you."

"They won't tell me where Nicolas is," I say.

She shakes her head. "Don't worry about that. I'll figure it out and bring him home, okay?" She's still wearing her waitress uniform: red polo shirt, khaki pants, and those god-awful black shoes.

"Do I have to stay here?" I ask Ed.

"I'm working on securing bond," he says. "There will be a court date. You'll just have to sign an assurance that you'll appear. That you're not a flight risk."

"Where the hell would I go without my son?"

They both look to me and I realize the absurdity of the

statement. I've left him before. Instead of getting defensive, I nod. This is unbelievable. Arrest, court, a judge. I need air—this room is sucking everything out of me. "Where's the restroom?" I say.

Ed points. "Around the corner, couple doors down." Then, "Come right back."

I wonder if he's going to escort me, but he doesn't. There are enough officers around to prevent someone from escaping this place even if they wanted to.

My feet are heavy as I walk, my head trying to put all the pieces of this story together to understand how we got here. There are so many faces on me, judging eyes, smug expressions. Fuck you all, I want to say. You don't know anything about me. How about you try living a day in my shoes.

I turn the corner, ready to duck into the privacy of the bathroom, when I see her. Cate Connally exits another room, face swollen and red, a look of defeat in her slumped posture. Our eyes meet, stopping us in our tracks. She's the first to speak.

"How could you?" she says, chin quivering. "You knew what he meant to me."

"He's my son. I had every right," I say.

We take slow, deliberate steps toward each other. I'm tense, ready to pounce should she attack.

"You gave up those rights when you left him with me! I was the one who was up for the nighttime feedings. I was the one who treated his diaper rash, and who made sure he took his vitamin-D drops. I was the one who cuddled him, who kissed each of his little toes. Not you!"

I wilt with each word that comes from her mouth because I know they're true. I might not have been a good mother at the beginning, but I've turned it around. I'm ready to be the parent Nicolas deserves. Two months might not seem like a lot of time, but it's enough for me to see clearly. I want him. I'm ready to deal with the goods and the bads.

"I'm sorry for that," I say. "But it doesn't mean you can keep my son forever. I made a mistake, okay? It was temporary. Now my head's right. And I'm sorry about what you've been through —the adoption stuff—but that isn't my fault."

"Where is he?" she growls.

"I don't know."

She lunges then. "Where. Is. He?" Her nostrils flare. She grabs at my shirt, and I put a stiff arm out to keep her back.

An officer hurries toward us. "Hey! Break it up!" He pulls Cate back. Her teeth are exposed, like a snarling lion's.

"CPS took him," I say. "I don't know where he is."

It's a heartbreaking admission that crushes me as much as I assume it crushes Cate. Her face cracks into an awful jumble of emotions, making me feel even guiltier.

She looks at me like there's a storm brewing inside. Then, quietly and with curling lips, "You don't deserve him."

And at that, she turns away.

PART 5

FORTY-FOUR

CATE

Ryan and I park ourselves in the living room with the TV on low in the background. I pull the shearling blanket up to my neck, as if it could block out the outside world. This morning, a reporter knocked on my door and I stood there in shock, staring at the bulky white news van parked in front of my house, before quickly slamming the door shut in his face.

"It's gaining traction," Ryan says as he scrolls on his phone. "There's a front-page story on *The Observer*'s website."

I yank the blanket over my face, suffocate in the heat of my own breath. I whip it down again when I hear what comes from Ryan's phone.

"*Listen, there's lots of women out there who can't have babies. That doesn't give her the right to steal someone else's.*"

"What are you watching?" I ask, aghast.

Ryan quickly swipes and the voice stops. "Sorry. TikTok."

I groan and fling my head back against the cushion. "I can't believe this is happening."

"It'll blow over," he says unconvincingly. If he doesn't believe it, then I surely don't.

When the local news comes on, I flip the channel. I don't want to hear the things they're saying about me.

"It's not just you, you know," Ryan says. "Jada's getting crucified too."

"Please don't say her name."

"Sorry."

It doesn't make me feel any better. This is a lose-lose situation. If I get my way, there will still be people who will never understand. Am I ever going to be able to leave this house without my name being dragged through the mud?

Another knock at the door makes me startle. "Not again," I say.

Ryan gets up and peeks through a slit in the curtain. "No, it's your neighbor."

I'm washed with relief. Thank God it's not another reporter with a camera looking for a statement.

I open the door with the blanket still wrapped around me. It's Jill, the same woman who'd organized the meal train when Henry first arrived. She's in duck boots and a Patagonia fleece, arms crossed and hands tucked into her armpits.

"Jill, hi," I say, getting ready to invite her in. She must have heard the news. It's nice to see another friendly face here to console me. Only... her face doesn't read consolation. It's more rigid with tight lips and eyes that could rip someone to shreds.

"I just had to come by," she says with a curt shake of her head. "This isn't the type of street where crimes take place. We're a wholesome neighborhood. A safe neighborhood. A lot of us have been talking, and it just makes us wonder what type of person would do such a thing."

My mouth is agape. "Jill, I—"

"I thought I knew you, Cate. I mean, you come from a nice family, you have this nice house." She gestures up and down. "I just... I just don't want you to expect us all to be behind you in this."

I'm speechless. Jill stands there, waiting for a response, but nothing comes. But then Ryan's next to me.

"I think it's best you leave," he says to Jill.

"I have every right to my opinion, and—"

"You do." He takes a step forward. "But not here. This is Cate's property, and we're asking you to leave. You don't know the whole story."

Jill huffs, offended, then turns and recedes down the steps, taking a right on the sidewalk toward her house.

My heart races as I close the door. "Thanks," I manage.

"You don't need to take abuse from anyone. There's going to be some who will say things, but just remember who your people are."

"You."

"And your family. We know you."

A pang to my heart. Do I deserve this support? All I know is I'm glad I have it.

We return to the couch and try to watch a show but are both too distracted to focus. Ryan opens a bag of carrot sticks and chomps away, making me wonder how on earth he can choose something so healthy in a time like this. I have no appetite, but if I did, it would be for all the sugar in the pantry.

I grab my phone and type out a text to Darci.

I'm sure you've seen the news. Can we talk? Might need to take a few days.

The message goes from "delivered" to "read." I wait for her response, imagining her saying, *Of course!* That's what friends do. They understand. They're willing to be flexible.

No little dots appear. No response comes. My message sits there, unanswered. And after two hours with still no response, I'm beginning to feel like my neighbors aren't the only thing I'm losing. Piece by piece, my world is falling to dust around me.

. . .

Later that evening, after Ryan's left, the door opens without a knock, and I have a brief moment of panic thinking the reporters have crossed the line of decency and are now storming my house.

I sit up straight—then relax when Becky comes in through the garage. I let out a heavy breath. "I thought you were the news people again."

"Sorry," she says. She's in leggings and an athletic quarter-zip. Even her hair in a ponytail manages to look put-together.

"What are you doing here?" I ask, and I realize it sounds rude. I don't mean it like that—it's just Becky isn't the type to show up unannounced. She's not Ryan. We don't have that type of relationship.

"I figured you could use some company." She brandishes two pints of Häagen-Dazs from a grocery bag. "You still like Vanilla Bean?"

A tingling spreads through my chest. "Yes."

"Good. Cuz that's what I got." She pops the tops, grabs two spoons, and joins me at the table, where I'd been forcing myself to eat a plain Eggo waffle. I have to admit, ice cream sounds much better.

Becky doesn't speak, just takes small bites from her tub. I'm reminded of how as kids we sat outside in the dead of summer eating popsicles, the sticky liquid dripping down the sticks to our grubby hands.

I've been sitting in silence for hours, but now, my body itches to talk.

"Where's Shane?"

"At home. I bribed him to take bath duty tonight. Thought we could have some sister time."

"I think I might lose my job," I say, even though I don't have proof, only an ominous suspicion.

She nods. "You might."

I join her nod, like it's an inevitable acceptance.

"But it's not the end of your career."

"What do you mean?"

"I mean, you're wildly talented. More brains than I ever had. I've always been jealous of that—your career, your drive."

Becky, jealous of me? I let the rich dairy swirl around my mouth, and it all becomes clear. For as much as I've loathed my perfect sister all these years, here she is, front and center. Not once did she question me. Not once did I feel judged. It's taken this experience for me to finally get it: Becky was never the wicked sister I imagined. I created that image—my own insecurities projected onto her, blocking me from a closeness we could have enjoyed. My fault, not hers. And now to realize that she feels jealousy toward any aspect of my life? My limbs go heavy with the sudden need to repent.

"Listen, Becky. I want to apologize."

"Apologize? For what?"

"For... everything. For being a brat. For thinking you've been out to get me all our lives. I'm sorry we haven't been closer. But now I see that it was me, not you. It's my fault. And I wish I could do it all over again."

"Don't be silly."

"No, really. I'm serious." Is forgiveness offered that easily?

Our faces meet and our eyes lock for a brief moment.

"No one's perfect, Cate. I'm going to be here for you, you know," she says, and then she puts a hand on top of mine.

I don't flinch; I don't pull away. Her touch is light and familiar, like a twin to my own hand. It feels like comfort. We both smile and return to our ice cream.

"Did you hear Sarah Elliott's getting a divorce?" she says. "Lots of drama apparently."

We slip into casual conversation about old high-school classmates and the latest internet gossip. It's her way of trying to distract me, to prove that there are other people whose lives are falling apart too. And while it doesn't work completely, I appreciate the effort.

FORTY-FIVE

IT TAKES ONLY TWO WEEKS FOR US TO GET A COURT appearance. Gail explained that the nature of the case—and a baby hanging in limbo—sped up the process. "Most people would have had to wait months with charges like this," she'd said, and I'd looked at her like she was crazy—two weeks is forever when you're not with your child. We've had zero contact. The idea of Henry being with a foster family makes me sick, but there's nothing I can do except pray he's okay and that he'll be back with me as soon as the court hears our story.

I nervously squeeze my toes in my shoes. Courtrooms seem like they'd be cool—until you're the one in the hot seat. On TV, they look regal, with their shiny wooden witness stands and wide fronts where attorneys stride back and forth as they make their cases. Perhaps those are the courtrooms of major cities, not a small Ohio suburb. This courtroom is tight and cramped, so much so that only inches separate me and the front row of the gallery where my family sits on benches etched with nervous scratches. Their presence gives me an extra dose of strength. I have a support system, which is more than some people can say.

Becky is dressed to the nines in a crisp black blazer and

blouse with French cuffs and large gold buttons, as though this were some nationally televised case with a twelve-person jury instead of a closed-door deliberation with only a judge. On the other side of the room, a woman I assume to be Jada's mother sits alone behind her daughter's table. She looks as weary as my own mom. It says so much, the burdens parents carry for their children.

There are no cameras allowed in the courtroom, no audience permitted, but that doesn't mean there aren't a handful of reporters outside. The media caught wind of the case when the charges reached the paper, and they jumped on it. Two women, two crimes, a whole lot of crazy. I recall the TikTok video blaring from Ryan's phone. People are talking about who should "win." News flash: there are no winners here.

We all walked in together, Mom and Becky flanking me on either side, the roses to my thorn, Dad in front leading the way, Ryan behind us. Camera crews aimed their equipment at me, and reporters shoved mics in my face.

"Cate! Cate! What do you have to say for yourself?"

"Were you ever planning to give him back?"

"Why'd you do it, Cate?"

We kept our lips sealed but didn't put our heads down. Gail made that clear—keep your chin up. Don't wear your guilt on your sleeve. I hope they were equally harsh to Jada when she arrived. After all, if she hadn't left Henry in the first place, none of this would have happened.

Now, I sit up straight in this hard wooden chair next to my fierce attorney. She's poker-faced. Suit with shoulder pads, big hair held with so much hairspray it's like a raven helmet. Her jaw is set before anyone's even uttered a word. This woman's intense, and I can't help but think once more how glad I am to have her in my corner. My family can afford the best—still, it feels like an unworthy privilege. I don't like the idea of our money being the reason I prevail.

"We got this," Gail whispers to me. Her lips are even pinker up close, something I didn't think possible. "Stay strong—don't let them break you. Trust me. Okay?"

Trusting her is my only option.

I nod, trying to emulate her confidence, although I want to cry. Throw up and cry. Act like you're not guilty, she tells me. Pretend you haven't done anything wrong.

It's nearly impossible. There's a large part of me that just wants to give in and give up, accept the consequence of my action with any glimmer of pride I might still hold. But we're so wrapped up in this now. We have Gail on retainer. I had to take an unpaid leave from work because of the stress, submitting the request through our portal system without even a word from Darci.

The past two weeks have been a new circle of hell. Dante only talked about nine, but I'm certain there's a tenth. It's deeper than sorrow, more painful than grief. It's desperation. And I've been swimming in it.

Losing Henry took a piece of my soul. I hear his phantom cries at all hours of the day. I am bombarded by babies on TV, babies in my dreams, babies everywhere. Taunting and tormenting me. I still smell his scent on my shirts and pillow. Clean, fresh, and sweet—a delicious trifecta. Now, everything is bland and colorless. The nursery door is closed again, I hope just temporarily.

When I'm not crying over losing him, I sob over the very real guilt that quickly became clear. I made a horrible mistake. I should never have ordered that fake birth certificate. At the time, I didn't see it. That day, it didn't feel like a mistake. It was just a piece of paper, something that would sit in a drawer some-where to yellow and age. I'd been too blinded by longing to realize it was wrong, to see the deception. Now, I see how twisted it was, what I did.

Given the same choice today, I wouldn't do it. I'd have

found another way—I think. But that's not what happened. That's not what a fractured heart does. When faced with desperation, human beings become animals. And now I'm paying the price.

A hand from behind squeezes my shoulder, and I turn. Becky's face scrunches, eyes watery. *We're here*, she mouths. And they are. Mom, Dad, Becky, Ryan.

Any chatter in the room comes to a halt as the bailiff speaks. "All rise!"

We stand, and I wish I felt steadier on my feet. Not even flats help me feel grounded in this moment.

"Third circuit of the northern Ohio district is now in session. The honorable Judge Steele presiding. Please be seated."

Steele is a thin man with salt-and-pepper hair and a long nose. His back is ever so hunched at the top, making him seem like a vulture about to swoop down and pick at my carcass.

The judge takes the stand, fanning his black robes as he folds his hands. "Good morning, ladies and gentlemen. We've got quite the complex situation here, don't we? I understand that both women take claim to the child involved. Given the charges and delicate circumstances, I'd like to give each of you a chance to speak. Something tells me this isn't a clear-cut case. I need to hear both sides in full detail. When there's a minor involved, it's the court's duty to do what's best for the child, so I will be taking everything into account."

He looks to Jada's side of the room. "Mr. Blackwell, why don't you start?"

Her lawyer stands and buttons his jacket. "Your Honor, my client is one of the over eight million people in this country who suffer from illicit drug use disorder. It's something she doesn't deny, and something she has sought treatment for on more than one occasion."

I peek at Jada. She stares straight ahead, and I imagine her lawyer giving her the same *look confident* speech Gail gave me.

"On the afternoon of January twelfth, Ms. Morales was at work when she became ill and went home. Unbeknownst to her, she was nine months pregnant, and it was there, some hours later, when she delivered a baby alone in her bathroom. The shocking nature of this birth, along with the sudden arrival of an unprepared-for newborn, thrust Ms. Morales into relapse after being clean for nearly two years. Scared, and frankly traumatized, she did what she thought was right: She gave her baby away.

"Now, we know that she didn't follow the Safe Haven guidelines, but that's because she wasn't aware of that option. In her mind, it was all about finding a secure place for her son, and the first person that came to mind was Ms. Connally."

Butterflies tickle my belly. I'd felt so chosen—an elected official, approved for the job. Underneath the table, I press my hands together.

"In the time that Nicolas Morales was with Ms. Connally, my client received and completed treatment, returned to her job, and has stayed clean for over two months. Given the time to process what had happened, she came to realize it was a mistake to give her baby up and, since there were no formal agreements in place, it was within her rights to take him back. It's quite simple, Your Honor. Ms. Morales is the birth mother of this child, and he belongs with her."

Judge Steele listens intently, nodding along and taking notes.

When Mr. Blackwell sits, the judge turns in our direction. "Ms. McCafferty, would you like to respond?"

Next to me, Gail reaches out and gives my leg a little tap—her version of comforting. It's a *don't worry* reminder. A *watch this* warning. Gail stands and presses down her blazer. I suck in a giant breath. Here we go.

"Good morning, Your Honor," Gail says, putting on a face that's much softer than usual. The way she can turn it on and off amazes me. A true Jekyll and Hyde. "Under the law, a person is to be presumed innocent until proven guilty. However, that's not the exact case we find ourselves in today. My client admitted to falsifying the birth certificate. She has nothing to hide here. Rather, she has everything to lose.

"Ms. Connally is an ordinary woman who found herself in an extraordinary situation. In a moment of trauma, she made a choice that was wrong—we all agree on that—but this cannot be held against her, as she was not in the right frame of mind to know right from wrong. Desperate people do scary things. My client was in a state of unbearable shock and trauma to the psyche, after suffering an unimaginable, repeated setback in her personal life. It was enough to alter her way of thinking, completely affecting all rational thought."

Again, I'm struck with the same notion: Was I insane? I can't help my eyes from drifting to Jada's side. She's still stoic, but her mother occasionally shakes her head. Every time her arms move, the bangles on her wrist clink together.

Gail points an outstretched hand in my direction. "Your Honor, she's not the villain here. She's a kind, loving person, an upstanding citizen with good intentions. She took the child in, provided him food and shelter, not to mention unflinching love. He's come to know her and is thriving in her care. Ms. Morales admits to having an addiction that can interfere with her ability to parent. Who knows when something will trigger her enough for her to throw in the towel again? We all have problems, but that doesn't mean we can just give up our responsibilities. Parenthood is one of the greatest privileges in life, something that requires sacrifice and selflessness. I believe my client has proven she possesses far more of these things than Ms. Morales. And for that reason, we ask that the baby be returned to Cate Connally."

A small woman with veiny hands types away on a court transcriber. I can't read her. Is she looking at me with sorrow, the poor soul who just wanted a child? Or am I nothing more than a baby snatcher?

Gail's head is high. I scan the room. The judge hasn't made a peep. He's unreadable. Gail looks so sure, even gives me a wink as she sits, but she and I both know Mr. Blackwell's opening statement won. It's no secret that the court favors birth parents. I just pray this might be the exception.

The chair is hard against my back, making it impossible to get comfortable. Maybe that's the point.

FORTY-SIX

JADA

It's quiet, with only the occasional muffled chant coming from the crowd outside. Everyone's come to see the battle of the two moms. The privileged versus the poor. Which one will come out on top? We're like the mothers from the fable I remember learning as a kid—the one where Solomon has to decide which woman is the righteous mother—only neither of us will stoop to sawing Nicolas in half. What a fucked-up story to tell children.

When Mom and I entered the courthouse, there were reporters waiting, asking me things like *Did you really not know you were pregnant?* and *Why'd you do it?* and *Do you consider yourself a fit mother?*

"Like you've never made a mistake," I hurl back before being scolded by Ed, who told me to keep quiet.

"We have no comment," he said, shuffling me through the door.

Now, as I sit here in my best turtleneck sweater and H&M dress pants from the second-hand store, my son's fate rests in the hands of a white dude who looks like he's had a privileged existence. I'm a heroin addict with brown skin, so how could he see anything but guilty? Any hope I had was false. I never really expected him to have an open mind. That's all society thinks of addicts: weak, unproductive, a waste.

My lawyer stands again. "Your Honor, Ms. Connally lied and pretended to be the rightful mother of the child for over a month. She forged a government document. That alone calls her ethics into question. She deceived the public and paid no mind to the legal course of action. If my client weren't able to care for her son at that time, there could have been family to step in." Ed points to Mom in the front row. Her dark hair frames her face, and I can't remember the last time I saw it down. She's trying to advocate for me: *Look, we're normal people even if we don't have the money this other family does.*

"Your Honor, I ask that you not be swayed by her pleas of the heart. Ms. Connally's biological circumstances are unfortunate—no one argues that. But that's separate from the issue at hand. Nicolas Morales is not her child. Period."

I look across to Cate. Her head is down, and I see a tear drop to her lap. A part of me does feel sorry for her and what she's been through. But not enough to give her my son. Not anymore.

Ed's words hit the nail on the head. All we have to do is express remorse, explain that I'm clean, and prove I'm a changed person. The judge has to see it, right? What I did was far less bad than what Cate did. I hurt myself; she destroyed an entire family. Just because I'm a junkie doesn't mean I don't love my son.

Ed flips a page in his notebook then looks back to Judge Steele. "I'd like to address our charge of child abandonment. Please keep in mind, Your Honor, that my client put thought behind where she would leave her son. It wasn't in the middle of Edgewater Park. It wasn't at Tower City Center, where he could have been picked up by any old stranger. No, she cared enough to make sure he would be safe. She loved her son, and loves him to this day."

A chair slides on the floor, making me turn.

Cate's lawyer flies up. "Your Honor, forgive me but let's cut the crap. It was freezing and she left him outside. What more needs to be said here?"

There's nothing to argue on that point.

FORTY-SEVEN

CATE

I'm not this monster Mr. Blackwell claims, am I? It takes everything in my power not to stand up and defend myself. It feels like a massive character assassination. Then again, maybe the morals I thought I had aren't the ones that match my actions.

I can't help the tears from forming, despite Gail's strict warning not to show emotion. The memory comes with such pain, such fear. That moment, seeing Jada for the first time in the hallway of the hospital—I thought I was about to lose him, and I couldn't, I just couldn't let that happen. Not then. Maybe I knew it was inevitable, but I needed a bit more time. Just a couple hours, just enough for a few more cuddles and a bitter goodbye. I sniffle and quickly wipe a tear before it drops.

"Think of something else," Gail whispers to me.

But I can't. It's impossible. Gail's ready to drive our point home, and I'm glad because this is so all-consuming, so utterly crushing, I don't know how much more I can bear.

"I'd like to give a little backstory, if I may," she says. "Mr. Blackwell has expressed empathy for my client's 'medical condition,' but it's so much more than that. On January twentieth, Ms. Connally was getting ready to adopt a baby when she received a call that the adoption had fallen through—again. This was the second time such a rare occurrence happened within an eighteen-month time span. Very unusual."

The mention of the adoptions shoots through me, and I hang my head. Would any of this have happened if those birth moms had stuck to the plan? If I had been at the hospital that morning, and not crying on the couch, would Henry still have been left at my door? With a baby of my own, I can't imagine I would have felt the same urge to do what I did. But those are all what-ifs, scenarios that didn't play out. Here, in this courtroom, Gail continues.

"The fact that Ms. Connally cannot carry her own biological children is something that would be considered daunting to begin with. Something she would have had to cope with, an irreparable loss. Combined with not one but two failed attempts to secure the dream she couldn't achieve naturally, the trauma would have coupled and multiplied.

"Cate suffered from what we call acute stress disorder, wherein a person experiences psychological distress immediately following a traumatic event—in this case, the phone call from the adoption agency. This diagnosis has similar symptoms to PTSD, but it is temporary, typically resolving within a matter of days. And it's not uncommon. Estimates suggest up to nineteen percent of individuals will experience an episode of acute stress disorder following a traumatic event, such as the death of a loved one, motor vehicle accidents, and sexual assaults, for instance."

I search the judge's face to see if he's following along. He listens intently, making me hold out hope that our defense will be enough. Across the aisle, Jada sits with her arms crossed. I wonder what she thinks of all this—a very scientific justification versus a simple note written in black pen. I want to scream, *I was just following instructions!*

"The call from the adoption agency triggered Ms. Connally into this state. It was comparable to a death, in a way. The dramatic end of a life that was supposed to be hers. Again, we're not just talking about this happening once. The effects are more severe for repeat instances."

Gail paces the front of the room like she owns it. "There are a range of symptoms one can experience from this disorder. The most common would be disassociation, flashbacks, intrusive or irrational thoughts... temporary insanity. You see, her irrational thoughts were so strong, it took an otherwise mentally competent woman and made her do something she normally never would have. Keeping the baby, ordering the birth certificate—it was all in an effort to do what she thought was right for the child. Her intentions were always positive. She's a good mother."

A good mother. What does that even mean? Two things I know for sure: A good mother doesn't abandon her child. And a good mother doesn't take a baby that's not hers. I'm not perfect, but then again, no one is.

Judge Steele removes his glasses and rubs his eyes. "This case is very complex," he says. "I'd like to take a brief recess to go over my notes and talk with the attorneys. Ms. Connally, Ms. Morales, please wait in one of the adjacent rooms. I'll call you back shortly."

I exhale, but it fails to calm me. I can't completely rest —not yet.

"Now what?" I say quietly to Gail.

"Now we wait. Don't worry—I'm confident." She nods assuredly.

We gather in a small room down the hall. Someone hands me a granola bar. I couldn't say who; I'm in a trance.

"Eat," Becky says, but I have no appetite, and only pick little pieces off and let them fall to the ground.

She scoots in closer to me and wraps an arm around my shoulders. I can't remember the last time we were this close.

"It's going to be all right, whatever happens. You know you always have us."

Slice my heart open, why don't you?

And then it's quiet again. There's little to say. Either I'm getting a baby or I'm not. Either I'm facing jail time or I'm not.

One thing's for sure: Gail will be furious if we lose.

We watch the clock. Try for small talk and fail miserably. And then there's a beep from my phone, a new email in my work inbox. It's from Cal Douglass, CEO of my ad firm, and instantly I know I'm about to lose something else.

The email's swift and detached, not the way I'd expect to be addressed after a decade of employment, but somehow just as I predicted the other night with Becky. There are words like "regretfully" and "misconduct" and "terminated." And as much as the brevity stings, I'm not at all surprised. I nod along as I read, wondering if this means I'm also losing Darci's friendship. She hasn't reached out since my arrest.

I tuck my phone back into my purse without a word to anyone. I'm learning to respect my debts.

Twenty minutes later, a head pops into the room. "The judge is ready," the woman says.

My body breaks into a cold sweat. No one says a word, only shifts their eyes back and forth among each other. We don't speak —we don't want to jinx anything. But I know what everyone's thinking because my brain's there too: Will I be leaving here today? And more importantly, will Henry be coming with me?

Dad's the first to get up. His voice is heavy. "C'mon, Birdie. We have to go."

No, Daddy, please, I want to cry into his big, safe arms. *Save me. Protect me.* Instead, I stand on wobbly legs and fight a swirling stomach.

I take a step to go, but Mom grabs my elbow and pulls me to her. I'm enveloped by the smell of orange blossoms and jasmine. It's the scent of my childhood—the mother who I never quite understood and who never fully understood me. But here in this moment, it's the best thing I've ever smelled, a comfort I will take with me no matter what happens next. It's a short hug, nowhere near the one she gave me after the first adoption fell through. Then, I was small and helpless. Now, she wants to make it very clear I'm responsible for my actions. And while they'll always support me, my decision-making goes against the way they raised me.

Becky's eyes are wet. Someone whimpers. It might have been me.

"No tears," I say. "I'm ready."

I've cried all I can cry, I have nothing left to release. The outcome is sealed; now I just have to go find out what it is. It's terrifying. There are three things you can't control in life: The past, the future, and other people.

FORTY-EIGHT

THE COURTROOM IS STUFFY DESPITE THE AIR conditioning. Maybe it's just my own body temperature that's raised. My hands are clammy like I've been in a sauna.

"Thank you for your patience," Judge Steele says as we take our seats. "Does either side have any final words?"

Gail stands. "We do, Your Honor."

Gail, my own personal gladiator, stands wide-legged in front of the man who will decide my future. There's not an ounce of hesitation with this woman—only the backbone of someone who's good at getting her way. And if one thing's for sure, she's not going down without a fight.

"Ms. Connally saved a life that day. If it weren't for her quick thinking, that baby would surely have frozen to death. What we have instead is a child who is alive, who was given a second chance at life. Ms. Connally is a respected member of the community. She has no prior criminal record of any kind. What she suffered on that morning—the crumbling of yet another adoption—sent her into a state of disillusion. Post-traumatic trauma is real, and it can make people do things out of character. There was never an intent to hurt the baby. On the contrary, there was only love. She's a better, safer parent for this child."

A hush falls over the courtroom. That was good. Even I believed her. She might have just pulled it off. Something lifts off my chest, and I can breathe a bit easier. Maybe, just maybe...

The room is as silent as a coffin. The judge folds his hands, and I make a silent plea through eye contact. Please don't be harsh on me.

My heart pounds in my ears like a bass drum, so loud I imagine everyone must be able to hear it too. This is it. I don't have much to go home to—no job, barely any friends—but I'd sling burgers if it meant keeping Henry and not going to jail.

I glance over at Jada in her turtleneck and dress pants. She looks like she could vomit. One of us is about to get custody of this baby. Judge Steele shuffles papers on his desk. *Please, please, please,* I think.

"This is a sad story," he says. "A case of trauma on both sides, with an innocent life in the middle. You've both been charged with crimes, having knowingly broken the law and put a child at risk. These are not small things. Endangering the welfare of a child is a serious offense, Ms. Morales, with penalties of up to eight years in jail."

Jada's face blanches. Her mother dabs her eyes with a tissue. If we both go to jail, what happens to Henry?

"However," the judge continues, "much of this case rests on intent and the set of very unusual circumstances that surround it. I do not believe you acted out of malice, Ms. Morales, nor that you had any ill intentions for your son. For those reasons, I'm treating this crime as a misdemeanor instead of a felony, and hereby sentence you to twelve months' probation."

Jada's sentence is like a gut punch to me. That's all the punishment she gets? I break out in heat at the thought that I could soon be getting the brunt of the penalty. Whose crime is worse?

Judge Steele addresses me next. "Now, Ms. Connally, your offense is of a completely different nature: obtaining a forged government-issued document with the intent to defraud. While it might seem insignificant in the grand scheme of this case— one crime involving a life, the other a single piece of paper— forgery is not taken lightly by the court. The charge is second-degree forgery, which is classified as a felony and faces a maximum sentence of five years and a one-hundred-thousand-dollar fine."

My soul leaves my body. Five years in prison? All because I was trying to do what was best? I hold my breath waiting for the *but*. There has to be a *but*. Jada got a *but*.

"Again," Judge Steele says, "it's tricky because of the intent behind the crime. I believe you were doing what you thought was right, however it doesn't excuse you from knowingly procuring and using a birth certificate you knew to be false. I'm afraid I have no choice but to sentence you to three years."

There's a gasp behind me, and I can't tell if it was Mom or Becky. I hear muffled voices saying, *No, no, no.* Gail gives the table a little pound, twists her jaw.

That's it—I'm officially a criminal. A felon. My breathing becomes restricted, something blocking my airway. This has to be an error. Jada deserts her baby and gets probation, while I order one little thing online—*for his benefit*—and get jail time? It seems completely backwards and wildly unfair. Surely the judge misspoke. I wait, but he doesn't amend.

Judge Steele raises his voice to quiet the room. "Sadly, we're not finished yet. There's the matter of custody."

My stomach clenches. I'm still trying to process the fact that I'm going to jail, so it's hard for my brain to switch gears. I don't belong here. I've never even had a speeding ticket. Still, I try to focus. This is what matters more. If I get custody, Henry can be with my family until I get out. There are still filaments of hope here, and I lean forward as though I can reach out and grab them.

"The court must act in the best interests of the child. We take into account the ability to meet the child's physical and emotional needs, mental stability of the parent, home environment, as well as the overall safety of the child. These are varying factors, some of which have room for improvement." He lets out a long breath. "The court puts great emphasis on keeping birth families together..."

My heart drops. No, don't say it.

"... and it is my opinion that Ms. Morales has shown not only remorse but also that she's able to provide for her son in a safe and loving manner with the support of family..."

This can't be happening. Everything is collapsing around me. Behind me, Mom whimpers.

"... Therefore, the court grants full legal and physical custody to Jada Morales."

I'm not sure who sobs louder, Jada or her mother. The elder of the two leans forward so far I fear she might fold in half. I'm too stunned to cry, but when I turn around to meet my family's faces, their eyes are wet. Dad bites his lip.

Everything drowns out after that. I barely hear the judge give his final remarks—all I know is I'm being handcuffed again and led away.

FORTY-NINE

JADA

IT'S BEEN A MONTH SINCE MY SENTENCING. UNDER THE terms of my probation, I have to live at Mom's house so she can help care for Nicolas. I'm also forbidden to use any substances—not even a sip of beer. Break these conditions and they'll throw me behind bars.

I wish I could say it's been easy, but it hasn't. Life's not a fairy tale, and even though I got off easier than Cate, it's not like the happy ending of a movie where Mom, Nicolas, and me ride off into the sunset never to face another burden.

No, the baby phase is hard. Nicolas cries a lot. I don't get much sleep. I'm working full-time and taking care of an almost-four-month-old. Despite all that, I wouldn't trade it. I still often wake up in a sweat that he's been snatched from me. That the judge rescinded his decision and decided to put me away after all.

But then I look over and see Nicolas asleep in his crib on the other side of my room and remember being reunited after those long two weeks when he was in foster care. How I left the court-room, flew to the station, surprised that camera crews had already managed to show up, and burst through the door. The social worker handed him to me, and the pieces of my heart magically mended.

"Nicolas! Oh my god, Nicolas. I'll never leave you again!" I repeated it over and over like he would understand. Like he would forgive me. And we fell to the floor in a puddle of tears and regret and complete gratitude.

Now, it's the weekend, and while most people my age are sleeping in, grabbing brunch with friends, or going shopping, I'm trying desperately to get my son to nap. He fights sleep like a champion, like he doesn't want to miss a minute of the day, which frustrates me to no end. "Please," I beg. "You're killing me. Just go to sleep."

My phone buzzes and a text pops up on the screen. It's from Hugo, and my fingers immediately tingle.

Aunt Hazel's here. You in?

There are so many code words for heroin, but it doesn't matter what anyone calls it—all you have to do is imagine the brown liquid to feel the rush. My mouth goes wet with saliva. I haven't heard from him since the day I left rehab and deleted his texts. In this moment, I wish I would have blocked his number completely. But I didn't. And his offer is like a familiar friend offering to make everything better. A piece of candy when you're having a bad day.

Nicolas screams in my ear, and I give a loud, repetitive shush, bouncing up and down and willing him to sleep. I promised I wouldn't use again. I swore to Mom and to the court. Why does it have to be so hard? Is this temptation going to follow me around forever? There are a dozen places within walking distance I could go score drugs. It would be so easy.

But then what?

Something hitches in my throat. I angrily swipe to delete the text and then do what I should have done long ago: Block his number. But it only makes me feel somewhat better. I'm too stifled here. My past is everywhere, popping up when I least expect it.

Nicolas calms for a brief second, allowing me to think. I shouldn't be alone. At rehab, Karen talked about the importance of a support person. Well, Mom's at work, and an infant can't talk.

I pick up the phone again and click a name I didn't think I'd ever call. I pray she answers.

"Hello?" she says in that friendly voice I haven't heard for months.

"Frankie? Hey, it's Jada." There's a tremble in my tone.

"Jada! Hey! Wow, it's been a while. How are you?"

I give a weak laugh. "Actually, not so good."

"What's wrong?"

And then I tell her everything, starting all the way back on the day I thought I'd eaten bad Chipotle that turned out to be a baby (still wild to accept) and ending with the present moment —the never-ending crying and the text that's making me want to use.

"A baby in your bathroom?" she says. "Holy shit."

"Mmm-hmm. I'm just feeling so..."

"I get it. It's okay. I'm so glad you called me. Are you at home? Is the baby— Is he safe?"

"Yeah, we're here. I haven't done anything." Yet.

"I'll stay on with you until it passes."

"That's the thing—I don't think it's ever going to pass. Not here. Not in this house. Not in Cleveland. There are too many memories."

Frankie's calm and level. "Okay, well, what are you thinking?"

"Remember when you were leaving treatment, you said maybe someday I could come visit you in North Carolina? Does the offer still stand?"

"Of course. You're welcome here whenever. You *and* your son. It's not perfect, but no place is."

I sniff. "I think I need a change. A fresh start."

"I get that." Then, with uncertainty, "But your probation..."

"After that. As soon as I can. Think there's room for another recovering addict in your town?"

Frankie gives a chuckle. "There's always room."

FIFTY

On days when I work and Mom doesn't, she stays home with Nicolas, which helps keep my daycare payments *slightly* lower. Today, when I get home, Mom's playing on the floor with him, teaching him to roll over. She has him in a firetruck onesie and little red shorts. They cut into his chunky thighs—my boy's a good eater. He's going to grow into a strong man.

"Hello, mi amor," I say to him. His bare feet are like chubby little blocks that I just want to squeeze. Coming home to him is a light at the end of a long day.

But tonight I'm more jittery than normal. Tonight I have to break even more news to Mom. After talking with Frankie, it became so clear: I need to get out of here if I have any chance of staying clean and keeping my son.

Are there times I envision being a decent human being? Yes. But more often than not, I fantasize about the high and the escape from reality it gives me. It's a bitter pill to dissolve, knowing that regardless of how well you're doing, the pull never completely dies. You're not defined by your past, they say. Well, what if your past is just too awful to get over?

That's why I need a fresh start, a chance to leave my demons behind.

I drop my purse and join them on the floor.

My face must give away my thoughts because Mom gives me a look of concern. "Things will get better, mija. We're still adjusting. Be patient. You'll see—we're all in this together."

Together. The three of us. Isn't she sick of me?

My throat tightens. I dig at a hole in the bottom of my pocket. "Why do you keep rescuing me?"

Mom's smile drops. "What do you mean?"

"You. You're a good person, and you had your whole life ahead of you until I came along. And I've been nothing but a problem from day one. You could have given up on me a long time ago, but you keep showing up."

"Jada, you're my child. I'll never give up on you."

My voice hitches then. "But why? You didn't want me in the first place. I've ruined your life."

She gapes. "That couldn't be further from the truth. You made my life."

"But... him." She knows who I'm referring to, and it's not the little boy in front of us.

Her face goes firm. "*He's* not part of this conversation. He wasn't then and he isn't now. Yes, what happened to me was one of the most painful moments of my life, and I'd be lying if I said it doesn't cross my mind more often than I'd like. But guess what? I wouldn't go back and change it. I wouldn't stop that man, that evil predator, from doing what he did. Because it gave me you."

I'm ugly crying now. This is a river I'm not stopping—probably couldn't even if I tried. The dam has broken. "How can you even look at me?"

"Oh, Jada." Mom extends a hand, runs it along my forehead, down my cheek and cups my chin. "When I look at you I see the same big brown eyes that met me from inside the crib each morning. I see the little girl who put on plays in the living room. You acted out all the parts, you know. I see the smile that reminds me of my own mama—the way your right side tips up more than your left; it was just like hers. And now I see Nicolas, my grandbaby, and the features he inherited from you." She holds Nicolas up so he stands on her lap. He flaps his arms, gives a squeal. Mom smiles, her eyes misty. "Don't you understand, Jada? I don't see *him* at all."

I hiccup, wipe my cheek with the back of my hand. "So you don't—you don't resent me?"

"Resent you? Mija, how could I? You're my daughter. It hasn't always been easy for us—you've put me through a lot—but a mother's love is unconditional. I loved you then, and I love you now."

"But what I did..."

She strokes Nicolas's hair. "In a way, we're all just small desperate things. I'm not here to judge. Please believe me."

Can I? Can I believe these words she says so surely? It's like a foreign language, so opposite to what I've believed for over twenty years. If Mom doesn't wish I were never born, maybe that means I do have a purpose here.

I look to Nicolas. There, that boy. The one whose eyes match my own. He's my purpose.

But can I leave her behind?

"You don't have to keep living with the pain, Jada," Mom says.

I nod. It's a hard concept to even consider. I've known nothing but self-inflicted torture, a punishment for existing. Will I be able to let it all go and actually live?

All I can do is try. For her. For him. For me.

"I have to tell you something," I say.

I relay my call to Frankie. About how I want to leave this place, try somewhere new. That Frankie will be a good support for me. That staying here is certain failure.

Mom cries too, choked with sadness and fear, but mostly because she knows I'm right. We'll always have each other, and who knows, maybe there will be a time when we're together again. Perhaps a day will come when she too will leave, searching for a blank canvas to paint her next chapter.

We hug and hold each other, passing forgiveness and understanding between our pressed-together hearts. There's a lightness in the air, and for the first time I feel hopeful.

PART 6

EPILOGUE
CATE

Twenty years later

THE AUDITORIUM WILL BE PACKED THIS AFTERNOON, AND the thought of being smack dab in the middle of all those people makes me break into hives. Fear of tight spaces—it's something I never had before. I guess a year and a half in jail will do that to a person. I now think of my life in two phases: Before prison and after prison.

Sometimes I dream I'm still back there, wearing that stiff beige uniform, sleeping on the thin mattress. Locked away, paying for my crime. Eighteen months was long enough, and not a day goes by I'm not thankful to have been let out early, thanks to good behavior and overcrowding. That was eighteen years ago. I can still smell the stale air and body odor. Mashed potatoes now make me gag.

Across the table, Ryan folds down the newspaper he's been reading with his morning coffee. He removes his cheaters. He hates that he needs them to read, but like I keep reminding him, we're in our sixties now. Things are sagging; things are failing.

"Should I get dressed up?" he asks, flustered. "Are you

getting dressed up? I mean, I don't know what I'm supposed to wear to a high school graduation, I've never done this before."

"Never graduated high school?" I joke.

"You know what I mean. As a parent. I want to fit in with the other dads. I want Emmy to be as proud of me as I am of her."

"Eighteen-year-olds aren't typically proud of their parents, Ry." His face falls, so I add, "Emmy adores you—you know that."

As if speaking her name conjured her from her bedroom, Emmy comes around the corner. She's beautiful—I'm biased, I know—with her long chestnut hair and toned limbs from playing three varsity sports. She looks nothing like me of course, because she's not mine—not genetically at least.

"Mom," she says, "can I take the car? Jess and Morgan are going to Bluebells."

I put a finger to my lips. "Let me guess—Morgan changed her mind about the lace dress."

"She said it's too wedding-y. And you know she can't pick out anything without input."

"That's what friends are for." I smile. "Be back in time to change. You have to be at the school at two."

"'Kay."

She takes the keys from my purse on the counter and circles behind the table, giving Ryan a kiss on the forehead. My breath catches.

"Wait," she says, looking dramatically concerned. "Dad, you're not wearing that, are you?"

"See?" he says to me, and I chuckle.

Emmy gives us a look—parents!—and is quickly at the door.

"Drive careful," we both say at the same time.

"I told you," Ryan mumbles now. "Fashion matters to these kids." He returns to the paper—cheaters replaced on the bridge of his nose—but I watch Emmy go. Her existence is the greatest blessing of my life, and the unique recipe of our family is never far from my mind. For as much as I pined for a child, I never expected this would be the way I got one.

The day Ryan sat opposite me eighteen years ago and said he was adopting a baby girl, my heart exploded in more ways than one. I'd been out for only a matter of months, trying to readjust to the free world, looking for a new job.

"You're *what*?" I'd said, hands to my cheeks, pools of water springing in my eyes. He'd beamed, and at that moment I felt two conflicting emotions: Pure happiness for my best friend fulfilling a life-long dream—but also sadness for myself. He was getting what I'd always wanted, what I'd tried, and failed, and then ruined. There'd be no third chance for me. Surely a convicted felon would never be allowed to adopt. Every hope I'd had crashed the minute I'd bought that fake birth certificate and taken everything to a new level.

"I tried to bring it up—remember that day at the Italian restaurant?" Ryan said. "You were distracted. And then, I didn't want to tell you when you were away. It felt cruel somehow. I started the process shortly after Henry—er, I mean, Nicolas—was in the picture. You inspired me. But then... well, everything happened, and..."

Neither of us needed to relive that horrible time.

"And?" I probed, trying to keep my emotions at bay. I wanted to be happy for him. I *was* happy for him.

"I just got the call today. It's a baby girl. I'm getting a daughter."

I'd never have dampened his joy with what I truly felt in that moment: Be careful, Ryan—adoptions can fall through just when you think they won't. He had to have been thinking it too, but neither of us said it aloud. Instead, I reached out and clasped his face then pulled him into the tightest hug. We jumped up and down the way we did when I got my own adoption news, and cried a cocktail of happy and knowing tears for the future laid out in front of us both.

It wasn't a month later, Emmy brand new in his life, when Ryan approached me with his idea over a twenty-dollar bottle of California red.

"Let's raise her together," he'd said. "You're my best friend. And you'll be a great mother. What'dya say, Cate? We're forty-three. We're not getting any younger."

I moved in with them the next week.

Ryan pushes from the breakfast nook and stands, stretching his arms above his head. He's still in great shape, never getting that old-man belly like so many of our friends. There've been part-ners over the years—one for half a decade even—but nothing quite stuck. And no matter how many times I offered to move out, to get my own place so he could have a shot at a "normal" relationship, he refused. The small freelance design jobs I was able to secure couldn't compare to the director-of-digital-content position I'd held so briefly, but it allowed me to contribute to our life. The three of us were—are—a family, and in the end, it's all any of us need.

"I can't believe she's graduating," he says, mouth turning down. "We're about to be empty nesters."

"Don't start that, or I'll cry too."

"But really—can you believe eighteen years have gone by?"

I can't. It feels like a whole separate life: the years before *that awful time*, and the years after. Before Emmy and after Emmy. Ask me at the start of my sentence if I'd have ever dreamed my future could be so sweet, I would have told you it was impossible. Those were dark, dark days.

Ryan reaches out and gives my hand a squeeze. His skin is wrinkled, and a sun spot hugs his knuckle. "C'mon, this is a happy day. I'm going to shower." He holds the paper out to me. "Want this? I'm done."

I shrug. "Sure."

We have hours before we need to head to the school, and as much as I would have loved to tag along to Bluebells with the girls, I've learned I have to give Emmy space. She'll be leaving for college in mere months, and then... Oh god, Cate, don't go there. I fan my eyes to stop from sniveling.

I open the newspaper and flip through the pages, reading and skimming, until the last page where there's a list of obituaries. My old hobby, finding fascination in the morbid. I used to wonder how mine would read, whether there'd be anyone to list as survivors, or whether I was destined to die alone. Now, I take comfort knowing Emmy will be there, in black and white, forever linked to me.

There are quite a few listings today, and my eyes jump first from picture to picture. Mostly ladies with white perms or skinny old men whose eyebrows rest like caterpillars on their faces. These people look like my parents. At eighty-five and eighty-eight, Mom and Dad could be there any day. I'm fortunate to still have them.

Each picture is someone who's seen a long stretch of life— until one. My eyes stop on a picture of a woman with a bright smile and wavy brown hair. A tiny stud in her nose. She's young, too young for an obituary. It's these ones that I read first, the ones with the most heartbreak.

Mary Francis "Frankie" Berrington, 46, died unexpectedly at home on Friday, June 6. Frankie was born in Cleveland, Ohio on September 21, 1997, the beloved daughter of Margaret and Tom Berrington. She graduated from Chagrin Falls High School in 2015, after which she was employed at Debbie's Styling and Classic Cuts for a number of years before moving to North Carolina. It was there that Frankie graduated from the College of Wilmington with an associate's degree in Cosmetology. She soon opened her own salon, which she ran successfully for fifteen years. In addition to her passion for hair styling, Frankie enjoyed taking long hikes with her golden retriever, Max, and hosting game nights for friends. But her greatest joy came from her daughter, Violet, who survives. Frankie was a generous soul and will be remembered for her infectious laugh and kind heart. In addition to her daughter, she is survived by her parents; a brother, Andrew Berrington; and a dear friend who was like a sister, Jada Morales, and her son Nicolas Morales.

A sharp gasp escapes my lips, and time slows down. I frantically finish reading.

Per the family's request, there will be no services. In lieu of flowers, donations in Frankie's name may be made to the Substance Abuse and Mental Health Services Administration, or to a treatment facility of your choice.

I bring a hand to my mouth as vivid memories swarm my brain. My Nicolas? My Henry? For a long time, there wasn't a day I didn't think of him, when I wouldn't scour the internet for any traces of him. Then, over the last decade, I'd occasionally make it through a week and think, *Huh.* The little baby and our time together—and the aftermath—hadn't crossed my mind. But now it all doubles back in rich, blinding color.

I reread the section with the obituary from start to finish. Could this be the same people, all these years later? The last line comes with a somberness, making my arms go heavy. It seems addiction won this battle. I wonder about the connection between Frankie and Jada. It's been so long, but I can still hear Gail's commanding voice in the courtroom, talking about drugs and dependency and how it all impacted parenthood.

Is Jada clean now? Or will it be her obituary that runs next? There's nothing else I can take from these two paragraphs, but it sets my brain in motion. Just seeing their names brings up feelings and memories I thought I'd long overcome. I blink as tears fall in rivers down my cheeks. I didn't know this boy—now a man—longer than two months, when he was so tiny I could wear him on my chest. But that doesn't mean I haven't pictured him growing up in my mind. That I didn't pass the mundane hours of solitude in jail imagining him drawing hopscotch in chalk on his sidewalk, singing in the school concert, hitting a home run at the final game of the season. Did he do any of these things? I'll never know, but I hope he did.

What I do know is that Jada Morales got her son back that day when she left the courtroom. After that, it was all a mystery I was only too happy not to investigate.

I don't realize I'm audibly crying until Ryan's next to me, eyes wide, hair wet.

"What is it?" he says with an edge of panic. Emmy—he's thinking of Emmy.

I can't speak, so I just pass him the newspaper, folded so that the obituary is front and center. He looks to the paper and back to me several times before I finally press a finger to the spot where their names appear.

He sucks in a little breath. "Oh, Cate."

"Even after all these years," I whimper. "It's just hard to forget."

As expected, the school's gymnasium is packed. Red, fold-out bleachers line the long sides, and a temporary stage has been erected before two dozen neatly arranged rows of chairs. Ryan and I pass the small orchestra playing "Ode to Joy." I try hard not to be a basket case. This I promised my daughter.

"Emmy said she's closer to the right, middle of the pack," Ryan says.

The seniors did a trial run yesterday, and Emmy came home with specific instructions of where to sit so we would be able to best see her. She wants pictures—lots of them—for social media.

We take aisle seats in the second row. I fan myself with the program and scan the rows of empty chairs that will soon be filled with a sea of black caps and gowns. It's not the best view—higher would be better—but it's not just about us today.

"There they are," Ryan says, pointing to the door, and I look. Becky comes in first. Mom waves with her free arm, the other one gripping a cane. Dad's behind her, back hunched in old age—he's lost at least four inches—followed by Shane. Despite arthritis (for her) and what we think are early signs of dementia (for him), my parents still manage to live unassisted in the big house on Oakridge Lane. Well, except for the fluffy Maltese named King William naturally. Mom calls him Wills for short and insists we curtsy to him. The kids think she's cuckoo. The royals have had their fair share of scandal, but the Connallys take the cake.

Becky cups Mom's elbow, leading her into the gym and to where we've saved room on the bleacher. My sister has aged like fine wine, still glowing and as stylish as ever, hair naturally salted with gray in the way that makes her sparkle. They finally make it to the bleachers, every step an inch.

"Hi, Mom," I say, giving her a gentle hug.

"Oh my, it's so loud!" She turns down the volume on her hearing aids then gives Ryan a pat on the knee. Becky and I grin. He always was her favorite of our friends. Now, an honorary son-in-law.

Moments later, the ceremonial notes of "Pomp and Circumstance" begin and I sit up at attention.

"This song always gets me," Becky says, clutching her heart. "I remember the boys' graduations like it was yesterday."

We don't see Landon and Owen as often now that they're grown—off starting careers and lives. But Emmy rounded out the Connally grandkids, and today we celebrate a new chapter of life for her, the final one of this generation.

"Here they come," Ryan says, making a quiet clap with his hands.

A line of graduates files into the room two by two. Their eyes search the audience, then hands rise, faces light up in smiles as they spot their families.

"Where's Emmy?" Dad asks. The students all look the same to him. He reads large-print books and has one of those phones with the giant buttons.

"She should be coming," I say. Then, "There she is!" My heart balloons behind my ribs and I'm drenched in a swell of warmth. She has that way of upending the floodgates inside me.

She finds us seconds later and beams. Our beautiful girl, a graduate.

Becky grabs my hand. "Oh, Catie, aren't you so proud?"

There are hardly any words, so I nod. I'm prouder than I've ever been. I didn't think I'd ever see this day. Didn't think I'd have the honor of holding the title of "Mom." Today is one of the biggest blessings, and my head swirls with a gambit of thoughts.

But it's not just Emmy. I'm thinking of a boy. A little boy who altered my emotional landscape, and who I once called mine even when I had no right to. A boy who grew into a man alongside his rightful family. He'll always hold a place in my heart, and I suspect it will take a while for the sting to go away.

Maybe it never will.

The students are all to their seats now, the ceremony underway. We listen to speaker after speaker. A curly-haired valedictorian with a wild zest for life, oblivious to the cruelty of the real world. Oh, to be young again. To restart your path, to make different choices.

That is but a dream.

"Here comes the degree part," Becky whispers, as though she's the only person who's ever attended a graduation ceremony.

I could shoot back with sarcasm but instead opt for a quiet "Okay, great" and a smile.

Here's the thing about Becky: The things I've always found intolerable were only my own projections. Sure, she still has the good hair, but damnit, who cares? The truth is, she's never been anything but a loving, supportive sister. Raising Emmy brought us closer, and I couldn't be happier for my daughter to share a close relationship with her aunt.

The principal calls names. The As, the Bs, and finally we make it to S. I get my phone ready to video. Six more kids, then:

"Emmy Jeanne Stadler," he booms through the microphone. The crowd claps, as they've done for each student. Ryan stands to snap what I know will be at least thirty pictures.

"Yay, Em!" we cheer. It's impossible for any of us to smile harder.

Emmy crosses the stage in her platform sandals, long hair cascading down her back from under the black cap. She shakes hands with the principal and superintendent, then turns toward us, diploma clasped between both hands. Ryan whistles, pumps the air with a fist.

And then she's done. Walking back to her seat, high-school diploma in hand. One major milestone checked off her young life's list. Where will she go in this world? What will she choose to do? Those things don't matter to me now. What I want is for her to be a good person. A person who knows her worth and who feels nothing but love and acceptance from her parents.

I let out a sigh. High school? Check. A relief and a moment of joy.

I look to Mom; there are tears in her aged eyes. She leans in close to my ear. "My granddaughter. My only granddaughter. She's the true princess of this family."

She lays her head on my shoulder like a child—like I used to do to her half a century ago—and I gently stroke her hair.

"I'm proud of you, Cate. You know that, right? You're a wonderful mother. I couldn't love you and Emmy more. None of that... that other stuff... matters anymore. You two—you and Becky—you've always been my greatest source of happiness. Both unique, but both perfect."

"Not quite perfect."

She gives my leg a pat. "Life is ten percent what happens, and ninety percent how you respond to it."

I swallow hard, wrap my arm around Mom's bony body. She's so frail now, another version of the woman I tried to live up to. Maybe I didn't need to try so hard. They say forgiveness doesn't change the past, but it sure does open up the future.

We stay like this, our bodies curved together, for several minutes. All around us, people applaud the remaining graduates. But to me, the rest of the room disappears. It's just Mom and me. When she sits back up, Mom's eyes are misty.

The grief of past mistakes and time lost threatens to descend on this happy moment, but I push it away. You've got to travel a lot of wrong roads to find the right one. That time will always be a part of me, and it's something that I own. People make choices that don't always come with second chances. I'm holding tight to mine.

My gaze lands on Emmy, my girl. My present and my future. A beautiful symbol of what's possible in life, if only you stay open to the unexpected. We stand and clap as bright young faces look up into a rainfall of tossed caps.

. . .

Later that evening, long after the family has gone home and Emmy's friends have finally dispersed from the house, I find myself tucked into my reading corner, computer on my lap. Something's still nagging at me from earlier—the obituary, the mention of Jada and Nicolas. My curiosity is piqued. I have a sudden need to know what happened to them.

I start with a Google search using Jada's name and "Cleveland." The top results bring up headlines from twenty years ago—our simultaneous cases, the aftermath. I quickly type in another search to make those memories go away. I try "Jada Morales, North Carolina," as that's where the obituary said her friend lived. I scroll, finally landing on something near the bottom of the page.

LOCAL ARTIST DEBUTS CHARITY COLLECTION FOR SUBSTANCE ABUSE SUPPORT

I click on the link. A new page opens with the same headline, only now it's accompanied with a photograph of a woman with smooth, deep skin and liquid dark eyes. Her brown hair cascades over her shoulder in a thick French braid. I know this face well.

I read the caption under the photo.

Local artist, Jada Morales, poses with premier piece from her Sparrow Collection, a charcoal on paper titled "Moment to Moment."

The artwork features two dark birds on a branch, one firmly rooted, the other with its wings spread, looking back toward the other as if deciding whether or not to take flight.

I scroll further down the page, skimming the article, my eyes drawn more to the pictures themselves.

In another, Jada points to a framed portrait of a small child reaching up to the watercolor sky while sparrows engulf him. And then, I make it to the last image on the page and my breath stops. There he is, all grown up. It's Nicolas, in a shirt and tie, huge smile on his face and arm wrapped tightly around his mother's shoulder. The pride on his face is undeniable—it radiates from the screen with a force that makes me retract my hands.

A cool shiver overtakes my body, and I spend far too long staring at them, the happy mother and son in an image I might never have come across. He's so handsome. She looks so healthy. Life, it appears, has been okay to them.

I study the image, searching for anything I remember from that time. But they're different people now, with stories separate from my own. When I close the laptop, it's with a profound sense of fulfillment. It feels something like peace.

"Mom?" Emmy says, coming into the room. She's changed into leggings and a T-shirt from one of her college visits. "Want to watch a show? I made popcorn."

I let the corners of my mouth draw up into a smile. "Be there in a second." Everything's as it should be.

I replace the computer onto the desk then gaze out the window at the hues of blue layering into twilight. There's just enough clarity left in the sky to see the outline of flying creatures, soaring into the night. One gets closer, swooping in and landing on the flower box outside the window.

It's a sparrow.

A LETTER FROM JEN

Dear reader,

Thank you so much for reading *The Baby Left Behind*. I hope you enjoyed it! If so, and if you want to keep up to date with all my latest releases, just sign up at the following link.

https://www.bookouture.com/jen-craven

Your email address will never be shared, and you can unsubscribe at any time. I would also be very grateful if you could leave a brief review of your thoughts—reviews are so helpful for increasing a book's visibility and also make a difference in helping new readers discover one of my books. Hearing from readers makes my job all the more enjoyable—you can get in touch with me on Instagram, Facebook, or through my website. Again, thank you for your support. You had endless book choices, and I'm very appreciative you chose to read mine.

Jen Craven

https://www.jencraven.com

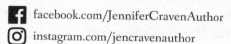

facebook.com/JenniferCravenAuthor

instagram.com/jencravenauthor

BOOK CLUB DISCUSSION QUESTIONS

The Baby Left Behind, as with Jen Craven's other novels, lends itself well to book clubs as it's rife with meaty discussion points, juicy plot twists, and plenty of room for insightful conversation. If you're interested in selecting Jen's books for your book club, please reach out at www.jencraven.com. Jen regularly meets with book club groups and would love to join yours!

Here are some discussion questions to consider:

1. Cate justifies taking in the baby because of the note that essentially tells her to do so. Do you think it was enough? What would you have done in that situation?

2. Cate and her mother, Marcia, have a complicated relationship in which Cate feels unworthy or less than because she doesn't live up to Marcia's standards. Do you think this perception is true, or is it all in Cate's head? Why or why not?

3. Jada feels defined by her past and the circumstances of her birth. As a reader, did you feel sorry for her? Or were her actions unforgiveable?

4. Both Cate and Jada make mistakes, yet receive different verdicts. In your opinion, which crime was worse? Were the rulings fair?

5. The sparrow is an important piece of symbolism throughout the story. Was the sparrow a positive or

negative image? What did the sparrow symbolize
to you?

6. The story could be interpreted as a modern take on
the biblical Judgment of Solomon. Do you think the
baby ended up with the right mother? Why?

ACKNOWLEDGMENTS

The idea for this story began with Cate, a woman so desperate to experience motherhood she was willing to risk everything. That desire, and the choices that follow, explore a slice of what I'll call the maternal experience. And for that reason, I must start by acknowledging the three individuals who allowed me to tap into the minds of such deeply flawed yet inherently good characters. To my own children—Josephine, Elizabeth, and Michael—I don't think I could have written such a story with all its highs and lows if not for being a mother first. Thank you for being my littlest cheerleaders, for helping me organize chapter notecards, and for incessantly asking questions about my books (all of which are a bit too old for you yet).

I'm eternally grateful to the Bookouture team and my brilliant editor, Harriet Wade, for taking on this project and championing it to its fullest. Having such a skilled support system behind me has made the writing process that much more exciting, and I can't wait to see where future books take us.

The book readers see is never the same as the first draft, and for that I'm thankful for my loyal beta readers and critique partners: Kerry Chaput, Caitlin Weaver, Maggie Giles, and Carmen Lewis. Your feedback was invaluable, and I don't think this novel would be what it is today without your insight. Likewise, I'm indebted to the Women's Fiction Writers Association, the connections I've made there, and the takeaways I've applied to my writing.

Thank you to my incredibly supportive family and friends,

and to my husband, DJ, who is a fantastic brainstorming partner and all-round pillar in my life. Writing is very much an isolating profession, but having people around me who are genuinely excited to be part of the journey makes it all that much better.

And finally, to you, dear reader, thank you for choosing this book from a sea of books. It means the world.

Made in United States
North Haven, CT
22 April 2024

51656638R00189